INFALLIBLE

VOL 3

TJ SPENCER JACQUES

NOVELS BY
TJ SPENCER JACQUES

NINE NOTCHES

BURGUNDY DOUBLOONS SERIES

INFALLIBLE SERIES

This is a work of fiction created by author TJ Spencer Jacques. All the characters, organizations, and events portrayed in this novel are either products of the author's imagination or used fictitiously.

Printed in the United States of America.

For more information visit tjnovels.com

ISBN 978-0-9903732-7-8 Paperback

First Edition: August 2018

INFALLIBLE

VOL 3

TJ SPENCER JACQUES

CHAPTER 1

Madden Thursday
June 15, 2017
5:55 a.m.

RASTA

Someone is trying to kill me with a chainsaw, and I'm strapped to the bed. Each time he attempts to cut me in half, the saw stalls inches from my skin. He's standing over me. His face is covered by a black hood, but I can smell him—he's decayed. I try with all of my might to free myself from the leather restraints, but resistance is futile. This is how it ends. Not in the hood where drive-bys are common, not in my bed after swallowing twenty-two Tylenol PMs, and not from the hot bullet of a drug thief who heard about my weed cabinet—not even close. The end of my life will come here in the West Jeff Behavior Medicine Center at the blade of an active sawer.

On his tenth pull of the starter line, the chainsaw roared back to life with the determination of one thousand serial killers. A cloud filled the room, but it wasn't the cloud I relished at Uncle

Glenn's—this was a cloud of exhaust and heat bellowing out of the chainsaw as the black-faced man returned to my bedside. I watched him raise the saw high in the air as I screamed for the hospital staff, but no one came to save me. *This staff ain't worth shit.* Or maybe I'm last—who knows?

But just as the chainsaw hovered right over my belly, my brain sent a signal to my bladder that it was time to piss.

But I can't move, I'm strapped to the bed.

But I'm not strapped.

But I was awakened by a loud noise that I thought was a *mutha-fuckin'* chainsaw . . . but it wasn't.

But, but, I want to drift off again. I tried to hold it.

When I opened my eyes, I felt like I had to apologize to the staff for accusing them of leaving me to die at the hands of serial killers. That wall-trembling roar didn't come from a chainsaw— it's coming from a walrus over in Levi's bed, snoring his ass off. At least that's what I assume it is—I'm fully awake now, staring at a mass of blubber in the dim light of morning. It's definitely a big, black walrus, and it sounds like he's playing the trombone while eating a piece of fried chicken.

Huuuuuuuuuuuuuuun, huuuuuuuuuuuuuuun, smack, smack, huuuuuuuuuuuuuuun, smack, smack.

Fuck it.

I'm up.

With my back against the wall, I sat up and gazed in astonishment at the trombone-blowing, chicken-eating walrus as he sucked air deep into his lungs, then exhaled with enough force to inflate a flat tire with his lips. His blanket is on the floor next to a pile of his clothes, and his face is turned to the wall. If not for a pair of black satin tighties, he would be butt-ass naked. Across the back of his drawls is a sentence written in pink, but my eyes are still a blur. Next to his bed there's some equipment recording him while he blows the trombone, and from the equipment, a plastic air tube connects with his breathing mask. Periodically, the snoring stops for about fifteen seconds, but right at the door of death, the machine clicks into action. Then the cycle repeats. Breathing stops.

.

.

.

Huuuuuuuuuuuuuuuuuuuuuuuuuuuuuuuuuuuuuuuun!

That last one was the final straw.

Immediately after washing my face and brushing my teeth, I made a straight line for the nurses' station to bitch someone out about the walrus. From down the hall, I recognized DeShonta at the nurses' station updating her logs. Her eyes blinked in slow motion. She's too cute to cuss out.

"DeShonta. DeShonta."

She lifted her head with a smirk. She was expecting me.

"Is there something I can help you with, Mr. Ross?"

"Don't Mr. Ross me, who in the fuck is that in my room?" I whispered loudly.

"I'm not sure, let me see who was admitted overnight."

"DeShonta, you don't have to look it up—the walrus in the stripper drawls, who is that?"

She giggled. "That's just Marcel."

"Who?"

"Marcel, he's another one of our regulars. You haven't met him yet?"

"No I haven't, but I had a dream someone was trying to chop me up with a chainsaw and when I woke up, there was this dude in Levi's bed. Why is that dude in Levi's bed?"

"Because this is his second home." Her weary eyes returned to her logs. "You will see Marcel at least twice a month; he lives in a group home facility for special needs men. We're monitoring his sleep apnea over a two or three-night stay. Then you get Levi back on Sunday."

"DeShonta, I'm not trying to be difficult or anything. I can stomach sleeping in a room with Levi because he's like a child, but I can't sleep in a room with another grown-ass man. You have to find Marcel another room," I lobbied.

"*Misterrrrrrrrrrr Ross.*" Her face was partly cordial and partly annoyed. "I apologize for any inconvenience, but we don't have any more rooms for adult men. As you may have noticed, we've had a spike in teenage girls, and unfortunately, we're left with no other choice than to house them in rooms normally reserved for male patients."

"So there's no more available rooms for Marcel?"

"You can chalk it up to Louisiana budget cuts. Whenever it's time to save money, the vampires in Baton Rouge suck the life out of mental health services at sunset."

Over the last several days, I have noticed increase in teenage girl patients of all demographics. Some cry along the walls, while the ones who cried for attention at home no longer want any attention—they want to go home. Crying doesn't shorten your stay here. If anything, it extends your stay.

DeShonta referrs to them as *the typicals*.

Some were admitted for cutting themselves, some were admitted for something they wrote, some tried to overdose, and one of them tried to commit *suicide by cop*—you overhear a lot when you've got nothing but time on your hands. And then there's me and the walrus. Only one adult room reserved for men is straight bullshit.

"DeShonta, I have a suggestion . . . how about they discharge me, and that would free up a bed?"

"Mr. Ross, I hate to bust your bubble, but every patient in here is going to go home before you. I can say that for certain because I just printed out six student badges."

"Student badges?"

"Yes sir, for med students from Tulane. Whenever Dr. Morton has a unique patient, he invites the students to sit in on a session. You're our latest Hannibal Lecter . . . hehe."

"That's not funny, DeShonta, I have to get out of here."

"*Can't help you with that.*"

"Can you put walrus on the sofa?"

"Can't help you with that."

"Can't I sleep on the sofa?"

"Can't help you with that, either. You've been here three weeks, you know the rule." She pointed to a laminated page over her left shoulder.

PATIENTS MUST REMAIN IN THEIR ROOMS UNTIL AFTER SHIFT CHANGE.

"DeShonta, I'm going to lose my mind if you don't get me out of this room with Marcel." *Fuck, why did I say that?*

She reached for a binder that had my name printed boldly on the spine and started to enter a note.

"Hey, hey, what are you doing?"

"You cannot make comments about losing your mind, dying, killing yourself, or freaking out. I have to document that."

"I didn't mean it literally . . ."

"Says the guy who's in a mental institution."

I sighed and watched her write. She's left handed. I'm left handed. Her perfume smells like freedom.

After making her entry, DeShonta closed the binder and placed it back on the shelf. There isn't another bed, I can't sleep on the sofa, I'm caged in with the walrus, and I have a new entry in my log to explain during my morning session with Dr. Morton. A single self-deprecating gaff could make the difference between getting out today or Christmas Eve! *I hate this fucking place.*

"I understand you have to do your job," I told DeShonta. "Hopefully I can clear up everything with Dr. Morton. Speaking of which, do you know what time my session is scheduled for?

"It appears you're first right after breakfast."

"I'm first? Hey, that's the best news of the morning."

"In this place, being first isn't a good thing. You're first because you're the worst," she chuckled as she moved around the nurses' station like her shoes were roller skates.

Defeated and demoralized, I sulked my way back to my room. The walrus wasn't in his bed. He was in the bathroom. *My bathroom.* The thought of sharing a toilet with him grossed me the fuck out. I'd rather he was wearing a diaper like Levi—that would be better than taking turns shitting on that toilet with a walrus. I just heard him end a ten-flusher, then I heard the water running in the sink. After a moment, the walrus opened the bathroom door, and the funk marched in front of him like a drum major.

"What's up?" he said in groggy voice.

"I'm maintaining, what's up with you?" I replied

"Nothing, just chilling." Once out the bathroom door, he made a hard right toward my bed. The next thing I knew, the walrus was standing on the side of my bed in his black, satin drawls. I was cornered. He extended his damp hand to shake. "I'm Marcel."

Our hands connected and locked. His grip was damp and painful. He didn't release my hand within the acceptable timeframe, but I held my composure even though deep down I was freaking out enough to earn sixty log entries. I started hallucinating about shit particles slithering up my arm toward my mouth. Once they arrived somewhere near my elbow, I'd had enough of the unwanted touch and finally managed to free my hand.

"Nice to meet you, Marcel. I'm Roderick."

He nodded in approval. "Roderick, that's cool name—very easy to remember."

Oh no, not another name expert.

"The band will dig you."

I didn't invest one brain cell trying to figure out what he meant.

Before I knew it, Marcel crawled his big ass back into bed like a three-year-old, leaving the bathroom door wide open. Judging from the horrific stench, his spirit was still on the toilet shitting. Once he was comfortably positioned, in the bed I got up to close that bathroom door, and that's when I heard the second annoying sound of the morning.

"*Doom, doom,* now that you're, *doom, doom,* here with me, *doom, doom,* I want tooooo . . . keep you free, *doom, doom,* to do the things that you want to do, *doom, doom,* the joy in life is loving you, *doom, doom,* but now the day has come, *doom, doom,* to let you know where I'm coming from, yeah, *doom doom.*"

I have to get the fuck out of here.

"You got your part?" Marcel asked as he stiffly pointed at me.

"Excuse me?"

"I just gave you your part. You weren't paying attention?"

"What part?"

"If you're going to be a member of this band, you have to pay attention. Your part is *doom, doom.* Need me to sing it again?"

The loud *doom, doom* sound was his fist pounding his chest.

"Marcel, I'm sorry brother, but I'm not interested in singing, and besides, I need to collect my thoughts before session this morning."

No sooner had I spoken than Marcel rumbled to his feet. In the space between our beds, he stood in those black satin drawls—huffed and tensed.

"*Fool, you don't like Al Green?*"

"Cool it, man, I didn't say that, but I don't feel like singing."

"*You wanna get something off your chest?*"

Did I mention that Marcel is about thirty-five years old, stands about six-foot-six, weighs 320 pounds at least, and has a nappy afro in the center of his chest, a matching beard, and a nine-months-pregnant stomach hanging over his black satin drawls? For three minutes, he stared down at me with bloodshot eyes and a nose that had doubled in width. Then I noticed his right hand compressing into a fist as his left index finger aimed between my eyes.

"You mean to tell me I put my neck out for you, added you into this band because I like your name, and this is how you pay me back?"

"Marcel, I think you need to back up and relax—you have me

confused with someone else. I'm not in a band."

"Didn't I give you the part to play?"

"Huh?"

"If I gave you a part, then you're in the band. In my band, everybody has to know their part or it will be hell to pay."

"Marcel, I don't know what the fuck you're talking about, or who you think you are, but—"

"I'll tell you who I am—I'm the lead singer of this band. The concert is a few days away and you will not have me on stage looking like a damn fool." I could see beads of sweat forming along his Mr. T hairline.

He took another step closer to my bed and placed his knee on my mattress.

"Marcel, I don't know anything about a band. I'm just waiting to go home, okay?"

"You trying to go home?"

"Yes, I'm trying to get out of here. This morning I hope to get discharged and haul ass out of here."

"Oh, oh, oh, I see how you're trying to fuck me over. You're trying to leave me hanging without a bass player? The concert is Sunday. That ain't enough time to find another bass player." His head reared in frustration. "I know what *imma* do . . . *imma* fuck you up."

It was then that I realized DeShonta had placed me in a room with a schizophrenic walrus who had a concert this upcoming Sunday. Suddenly, his left hand transformed into a precisely-measured claw that slowly traveled toward my neck. I'm thinking, *on the count of three imma punch this nutty nigga twice on the jaw and scream like a bitch for DeShonta.*

In Ike Turner's voice, Marcel said, "If I can't have you, then nobody will."

I started counting down.

3 . . . 2 . . .

"*Get your musty nuts out of Roderick's face.*" It was Philip. "Put on those clothes and sit your ass down."

"No, Mr. Lee, this fool has violated me."

"Marcel, I will have a talk with Roderick about the band, but if you don't have a seat and get dressed, I will call the promoter and cancel the gig." Marcel didn't move. "Marcel, do you want to lose your snacks for the day?"

Only then did Marcel make eye contact with Phillip. "No, sir, I need my snacks."

"Then put on your clothes and have a seat, it's almost time for breakfast."

And that's when another mystery of the morning was solved. As he turned around, I saw that *I'm A Star* was written in hot pink letters across the back of Marcel's drawls. Phillip looked on from the doorway as Marcel squeezed his big ass into a pair of skinny jeans and a hot pink T-shirt with glitter wording across the chest: *Baby Cakes*.

In his hand, Phillip held the shift change clipboard. After roll call, we're free to sit in the dinner hall or stay in bed. With Marcel looking pacified, Phillip turned to me.

"Good morning, Mr. Ross."

"I can't say it was a good morning, but I'm happy to see you."

"My apologies for not giving you the heads-up about Marcel," Philip said in a quiet voice. On his clipboard, he marked us both present.

"I would've appreciated that heads-up." I shot him a look.

"Don't concern yourself with Marcel, he's a big old baby, but the sooner you learn Al Green's "Look What You Done for Me," the better things are going to get in here. Just a piece of advice."

Not only am I imprisoned in this mental hospital but I have to sing, too? Fuck this place.

Once Marcel was fully dressed and seated, Philip tossed him a pack of graham crackers. He also offered me a pack.

"Yes please, thank you."

It wasn't that I was hungry, but graham crackers are golden in here. They're how you keep the crazies fifty feet away. Graham crackers are a method of currency for the patients who are really violently psychotic, like the singing walrus. For this reason, I am convinced that there's a medicinal ingredient in graham crackers, a type of sedative that calms these crazy motherfuckers.

Finally, I have my own pack.

Breakfast this morning is pancakes, eggs, and sausage, or I have the choice of cereal. I always pick the cereal because the individual containers are sealed, and I don't trust the prepared food. I noticed that after the patients eat the prepared food, they always fall asleep within five minutes. Fuck that, cereal it is.

Normally I sit by myself, but this morning I have a guest at my table.

"Good morning," I said.

"Hello, darling, I can't believe it's pancakes again," she said.

"I'm Roderick, nice to meet you."

"I'm Mary."

"Nice to meet you, Mary."

"Same here, darling."

Mary appeared to be in her seventies, and despite the fact that she was overdressed in a ruby-red, sequined ballgown with elbow-length white gloves, she was a breath of fresh air. On every finger was a ring, including her thumb. Around her neck hung a rope of pearls, and she wore dangling pearl earrings to match. At a glance, one could mistake her for actress Betty White, even in the tone of her voice. This morning, the fact that she was way overdressed didn't matter, because I was just happy to have a normal conversation.

"I haven't seen you around, you just checked in?" I asked.

"We arrived last night. We are exhausted."

"So you were admitted with family members?"

"My husband and son. They will join us shortly. How long have you been here?"

"Tomorrow will make three weeks. I'm hoping to go home

today."

"So you need a miracle?"

"Yes, a huge miracle."

"You should share your need with my son, he has a streak going with miracles."

"Oh really? I can't wait to meet him."

Mrs. Mary cooled the top of her coffee when she spotted her husband and son. She looked over my shoulder and waved them to our table.

"Roderick, meet my husband Joseph and my son Jesus."

There was no one there, but she waited for me to acknowledge Joseph and Jesus.

"Nice to meet both of you." I greeted them in a bewildered tone.

"Jesus, my dear son, Roderick needs a miracle. I hope you don't mind that I shared with him the success you've had lately in delivering miracles. I was hoping you would grant him a miracle this morning. That is, if it's in your will, of course."

With her deep blue eyes locked on me, Mary nodded her head twice in the direction of where Jesus sat. I had no choice but to tell Jesus about my upcoming session and how badly I wanted to go home.

"Jesus said he'll get back to you after his walk in the garden," Mary said.

"Please tell him I said thank you."

"For God's sake, why don't you tell him? He's sitting right there . . ."

"Jesus, thank you in advance for all your help." Hey, I know it was wacky, but when in Rome.

"Jesus says you're welcome."

I quickly gulped my little bowl of cornflakes and sprinted as fast as I could away from Coo-Coo Mary and Kitchen Jesus—only to find Marcel waiting for me.

"Let's go again from the top. Here's your part again, and if you don't pay attention this time I will break your nose." On his face was the type of seriousness more commonly found on the face of an FBI hostage negotiator; the threat was real even if the band was make-believe.

"*Doom, doom,* sometimes I want to leave, *doom, doom,* but then I say, *doom, doom,* it wouldn't make sense at all, *doom, doom,* anyway, forgive me baby, *doom, doom,* if I do wrong, *doom, doom,* I haven't been a true man for so long, *doom, doom,* but let me say before I forget, *doom, doom,* lovin' you baby, it's where it's at, yeah."

"Mr. Ross, it's time for your session. I'll walk you over," Phillip announced. For the second time this morning, his perfect timing has saved me from a for-sure ass-whipping.

Marcel was perturbed. As I turned to walk away, he whispered, "You better know your part when you come back or *imma* fuck you up . . . you heard me?"

Kitchen Jesus, please help me.

CHAPTER 2

Madden Thursday
4:28 p.m.

BIYELL

The funk hit my nose when the door cracked halfway. It was horrible. It made my eyes water. It never fails; the customers who are the most trifling are also the most generous with their food. For real, this house I just finished had thirteen cats and not one litter box. The lady had the nerve to offer me some tuna casserole, in a house that smells like hooker coochie. Not that I have any firsthand knowledge about hooker coochie, but that's how I imagine it would smell at the end of a night shift.

"Ma'am, my wife has been slaving over the stove all day—if she knows I had a pre-dinner I would never hear the end of it," I lied.

The cats were surrogate children for an elderly couple who appeared too frail and ill-stricken to care for each other, let alone thirteen cats. While it's on my mind, I have to ask, why do some people feel the need to have dogs and cats in the house when they have a big, beautiful backyard?

In the cable business, I've been in and under my share of nasty homes, but those homes were what I call *normal nasty*, this house was *call the police nasty*. I kid you not, in one of the rooms, the piss smell was so thick I didn't want to open my mouth for fear of ingesting the piss. And of all the rooms to not have an existing cable wire, this would be the one I have to drill through the floor, then crawl under the house to run the wire. What I thought was carpet padding was actually a half inch of cat piss. The reason I didn't see a litter box was because this room was the litter box.

I don't see any occupants in this room, therefore the cable install has to be for the cats.

That's when I wanted to kick my dispatcher's ass for sending me to Cat House. The house was a good eighty degrees inside, with paneled walls and no ventilation. This created a piss-sauna in that one particular room, but I got the house installed, and that's all that matters. I am an independent contractor who works for Direct TV and Cox Cable; I'm the one they call when an install appointment was missed the previous day. I know why the appointment was missed—in the notes, it read:

An elderly customer with cats, unsanitary, Health Department contacted.

But they still placed this job in my queue. This is the reason I was counting on winning that challenge—I'm tired of getting jobs like Cat House. I had a dream of flipping real estate; buying low and selling high and eventually building several apartment complexes, but here I am on the side of the funkiest house ever washing my face and arms with a garden hose. I need a real bath.

This house is also going to force me to skip Madden Night. I have to get home immediately and brush my teeth. I think I swallowed some hepatitis A in a mist of cat urine. I shot Uncle Glenn a text.

Uncle, I have to miss tonight because of this funky-ass house;

headed home to scrub in a tub of bleach.

This morning, I routed my last job nearest to my house, which was two blocks over. The only problem is, I no longer live in that house. Tamera lives there, and I'm not allowed to come within five hundred feet. Our court date is in six weeks. Then this marriage is over, and those six weeks can't go by fast enough.

I'm tired of being married to no one; married in title only, with no woman to show for it.

And I'm still hot in the collar with Tamera. I never got over her conspiring against me with some bitch she didn't know the day before. It was that easy—I will never get over it. That's not karma, that's proof you were out to get me the whole time.

Fuck Tamera.

I want to see my baby. I haven't seen my child in over two months. How is it legal to lock me out of my child's life? But my confidence is in Telly, and he's confident that he can land me a joint custody deal without supervised visitation, because there isn't a history of domestic violence, nor was there a history of bullshit until Tamera invited GiGi for dinner.

Yeah, I did my dirt, I admit it, but GiGi—Tyra—is the only woman who ever knocked on our door, and as I said, Tamera was the one who invited her.

"Fuck Tamera," I said aloud after taking a quick hoe bath on the side of the house. Then I tossed my uniform shirt in the back of the truck.

"All right, horsey, you put in a good day's work and didn't cost me too much gas—it's time to take it home." I drove away from Cat House. Then I crossed Tupelo Street, and that's when I saw a truck.

Hold up. Hold the fuck up.

A red Chevy Avalanche truck in my driveway?

Lil Glenn: It's not your driveway or your house anymore.

Me: My name is still on the utilities and insurance; the house is still in my name. Until she changes that, this is my house.

Pimp B: Looks like Tamera has moved some dude into your house. You're not even divorced yet, and she has moved some dude into your house? Around your daughter?

Lil Glenn: It's not your house, Biyell. Just keep driving and remember the protective order.

Pimp B: Check that out . . . the nigga has a customized license plate that says *BIG MIKE*—oh hell no! Back this truck up and go kick the door in.

Lil Glenn: You will do no such thing—you don't live there anymore. You have to respect her boundaries; this is your life now, there will be other men around your daughter. This is the consequence of FUP (Fucking Unauthorized Pussy).

Pimp B: Fuck that restraining order, she should have never brought a stranger around your daughter. She still has your last name, and your house, and your child. The nerve of that bitch.

Lil Glenn: Biyell, don't go knock on the door, don't go anywhere around that house. Your court date is in six weeks and if you knock on the door, you will justify that restraining order and will have supervised visits. Let her live her life, and you go live your life. Focus on developing a *peaceful and productive parenting partnership* for your daughter—be the bigger person, Biyell.

Pimp B: Press mute on Glenn with that Dr. Phil bullshit—nigga, this real life out here. She got the restraining order because she's been fucking with Big Mike. I say we go introduce him to Big B!

Me: I'm a dawg, and a dawg can smell another dawg. So dude had to know this is my house because my shit is all around here. He must think I'm a hoe?

Pimp B: And your mama wasn't a hoe, and your daddy wasn't a hoe—don't let this nigga play you *like a hoe.*

In the back of my mind, I started to hear Mystikal's song, "The Man Right Chea."

Lil Glenn was muted.

I hid my wallet under the driver's seat and changed my work boots to a pair of red and black vintage Jordan's. It was time.

I didn't bother knocking; I kicked in the door. When I entered the house, a dude was on my sofa—the sofa I paid off after 104 weekly payments to Rent-A-Center. Tamera was in the kitchen. I didn't see my daughter. She was probably at the babysitter's, and this was a romantic evening they had planned. To my left Tamera, was frying fish. To my right, her dude was seated on my 104 weekly payments. I decided to deal with him first.

Big Mike could have been Timothy's twin; there wasn't shit big about Big Mike. He leaped to his feet with fear on his face.

"Hey, hey, cool it, brother."

"Nigga, you're not my brother."

"Biyell! Biyell, stop!" Tamera screamed from the kitchen. "I have a restraining order against you!"

Mike backed against the wall. "I don't want any trouble; there's no need for hostility. She told me y'all were separated. She said it was over. Y'all, y'all going through a divorce," he tried to explain as I continued in a straight line towards him like a black Hulk.

"She didn't tell you I would fuck you up if I caught you in this house?"

"Now, wait a minute—"

WHACK! An overhand left landed in his face. He fell to his knees first, then flat on his back. On the floor, he started snoring with one arm extended upward.

"*He need some milk,*" I said to Tamera.

Every bit of rage I had in me was contained in that one lick. It had been building from the night GiGi hit me in the face with the brick all the way to the night of that dinner. And it wasn't jealousy that brought out the beast—not at all. It was the boldness of Mike to step foot in my house with no fear—that's what conjured the beast.

In the kitchen, Tamera gripped the handle of the frying pan. Frantically, she looked around for her cell phone, but it was on the kitchen table right in front of me. I retrieved it first. It was un-locked. I scrolled through her pictures, then enlarged the screen.

"That ain't my dick, that's his dick." Apparently, she loved his dick. In the next picture in her gallery, she was sucking that same dick. "When you start sucking dick? I thought *saved and sanctified bitches* didn't suck dick?" That was the bullshit she'd laid on me, so if I wanted my dick sucked, I had to keep a mis-tress who could do it all.

Pimp B: They always give the next man everything. And look, she has even lost weight—but she wouldn't lose a pound for you. Ain't that some shit?

"You're sucking a lil' dick these days and you've lost a lil' weight? Hmmm, and you were with me for how long? And didn't do either?"

"Biyell, I'm not fucking around. Take one more step," Tam-era threatened.

I took a step.

"I will throw this grease in your face if you come anywhere near me."

I took two more steps. "You brought this nigga in my house? You fucking him on the same mattress? The same sheets? This nigga using my shower? My towels? Bitch, are you crazy? Have you lost your fucking mind?" I was disgusted.

"It's not your house, and you don't live here. Get the fuck out of *MY* house before I call the police."

I slid her phone down the counter where it stopped short of the gas burner. "Call the police and tell them to bring the Crime Lab when they come."

I've heard it described, but I never thought I would experi-ence it—that pivotal moment when you don't give a piece of a fuck about anyone or anything. I wanted to kill her. No, I'm lying. I wanted to kill both of them.

Lil Glenn: Biyell, don't throw your life away—you have so much to live for and do. You can't tell Tamera what to do with her pussy. You had your turn; it's Mike's turn now. Even if you two were to reunite, Mike has nutted in her; you will never see her the same way.

"He nutted in you?" I had to ask.

"Biyell, get out of my house."

"You let that pussy-ass nigga fuck you bare dick?"

"We're in a relationship; you didn't want me . . . *remember?* I've gone on with my life."

"So you let him nut in you?"

"Biyell, he proposed to me. We're engaged."

Pimp B: *Kill that bitch.* It hasn't even been three months, and she's engaged? My nigga, she played you. Tamera's been fucking this dude in your house.

"You been fucking this dude, huh?"

"I don't owe you an explanation."

Pimp B: That's a fucking lie.

"That's a fucking lie."

"Biyell, I don't want to hurt you, but I will."

"You have already hurt me when you brought that nigga in this house."

"Biyell, it's over between us. I am going on with my life. You left with Tyra. You picked her over me. I'm not cheating on you. We are not together. It's over."

"It ain't over until I say it's over . . ."

Pimp B: Kick her arm, and that grease will splash in her direction. Then choke the tongue out that bitch for disrespecting us. This is our house . . .

CHAPTER 3

Madden Night
9:05 p.m.

T here's an automatic voice no one likes to hear when they answer the phone—a voice that's always the bearer of horrible news.

This is a call from the Orleans Parish Jail. To accept this call, press one.

"Uncle Glenn, this Biyell. Press one, this Biyell—"

To decline this call, please press two or hang up.

Of course, I pressed one.

Thank you for using Global Telcom.

"Biyell, what did you do?"

CHAPTER 4

Monday, June 19, 2017
8:03 a.m.

BIYELL

Yesterday was Father's Day—I wonder if my daughters asked for me? I wonder if they missed me? My son doesn't know me, but I still miss my kids. I miss the life I had a life before this challenge with Uncle Glenn. I miss the control I had over everything in my life. I've lost that control; I've lost everything trying to be something I'm not. That's how I landed here, in a torture room, sitting on a cement a bench of regrets.

Hoe is me.
Hoe is me.
Hoe is free?

It's called a holding tank—the area in booking where they process you in or out depending on your charge—and in this room, every charge you can imagine is represented. We're not in separate holding tanks according to our charges, not at all—the traffic ticket guys are in here with the domestic violence guys who are stuffed in with the murderers. We're all packed into a vile fourteen-by-eighteen-foot cell with concrete benches on each side, a toilet that's working overtime because of the junkies, and two large flat-screen windows to watch cops roll in more assholes—assholes like me.

I haven't had a bath since I arrived here Thursday night. I still reek of Cat House. The deputy offered me a shower yesterday, but I don't shower with men. I'm ready to go home.

A pot-bellied sheriff's officer who resembles Martin Lawrence just unlocked the door.

"All right, listen up! When I call your name, holla back at me. If you want to know your bond, holla back at me when I call your name. Other than that, don't ask me shit because I don't know. If you don't have a bond when I call your name, step out into the hall for Magistrate Court," the officer demanded in a hostile voice.

For the first time since they booked me on Thursday, I'm outside of the holding tank. I'm also shackled for court with six other men.

Monday morning Magister Court, and if everything goes my way, I can still make it to work. Thank God Uncle Glenn and Diana picked up my truck and drove it to his apartment. I knew I was going to jail when I made that hard right on Tupelo Street and spotted his truck in my driveway—that's why I hid my wallet under the driver's seat. I've been here before, but never for anything serious—mainly failure to appear on traffic tickets. This is my first felony charge, and it's a good thing I still have twenty-thousand dollars remaining from the money Uncle Glenn fronted us. My bail shouldn't be any more than a thousand to get out of here.

Chained by hand and foot, they marched our musty asses down a long corridor to a room that had pews like a church. About fifteen minutes later, a judge appeared from a side entrance, and we were ordered to stand. That's when fear entered in for the first time.

"All rise, the Honorable Judge Rant presiding. You are ordered to remain silent until your name is called. Once you return to your seat after you've seen the judge, you are to remain silent. If any of you disrupt this court this morning, it will result in additional charges. You may be seated."

I was hoping for a male judge, but the person in the black robe was an older, stiff-faced woman who reminded me of Roseanne Barr, only bigger. She didn't waste any time setting the tone for the morning—the first guy up for bond was refused. He would have to sit until his lawyer filed a motion for a bond hearing.

After his case, there was a pause as the judge shuffled through the docket. Judge Rant has to give me a bond; I've slept on the floor since Thursday night and eaten cold bologna sandwiches and something that looked like red beans. I'm not cut out for jail, but I've earned my stay.

I would have killed both of them if it hadn't been for the voice that called out to me. The voice was the only thing that kept me from killing them. It was the voice that calmed the beast. Just as I was about to kick that skillet out of Tamera's hand, I heard that voice coming from down the hall.

"Daddy . . ."

"Daddy?"

"Daddy!"

The fight had woken Bylisha . . . she had been in her room napping. I've never raised my voice in front of my child. From down the hall, she ran into the kitchen and wrapped her arms around my leg.

"Daddy, pick me up."

I looked down into a face of my first-born child, and I had to pick her up. Picking her up became more important than fighting with her mother or that Sweet & Low nigga on the living room floor. We settled down in her room. We sat down on the floor and played with her toy cars. That was the first time I held my daughter in over two months, and that's where the police found me.

"Mr. Baltimore, you're not supposed to be here," the officer told me as he approached my daughter's bedroom.

The arresting officer was my first cousin, and he was able to get the other officers to relax. "Cuz, let's go take a ride."

"Coming right now, Booker."

I turned to my daughter. "Daddy's going to take a ride with the police officer, but when I come back, I'll bring you to Chuck-E-Cheese, okay?"

"Chuck-E-Cheese?" Bylisha repeated with a wowed expression.

"Yes, next time I will bring you to Chuck-E-Cheese. Be a good girl for Mommy, okay?"

She nodded.

I handed my daughter to that bitch who fucked her new nigga in our bed bare dick. Afterward, I placed my hands behind my back while trying to strangle Tamera with my eyes. At that moment in time, she was the worst mother in the city.

When Officer Booker walked me to the front of the house, an EMS worker was attending to Mike. He was still stretched out on the floor as if I'd shot him with a sawed-off shotgun.

"Boy . . . you a hoe! Every time I see you, I'm fucking you up," I threatened him.

As they escorted me out to a waiting patrol car, I heard Tamera, a woman who still has my last name, crying sorrowfully over Big Mike. Hearing her cry over him dried up everything I felt for her. As usual, Lil Glenn was right. In that moment, Gi-Gi's value shot up like a rocket while Tamera's value as a woman was flushed down a jailhouse urinal. I watched the EMS guys roll Big Mike out on a gurney, with one of the techs holding his head between his palms to keep it stabilized.

Look at his bitch ass. "Boy, you-a-lil'-bitch . . . I barely touched you!" I yelled through the crack at the top of the window.

The final insult came when I watched the EMS truck speed away from the house with Tamera and my daughter trailing in a car that was in my name.

"Pimp B was right, I should have kicked that skillet of fish grease in her face," I grumbled in the backseat as my cousin entered the vehicle.

"Cuz, cuz, cuz! What the fuck is wrong with you?" He half-turned to face me. "No woman is worth your freedom. She told my supervisor you had a look in your eye she's never seen before; you were going to kill her."

"Bitch played me, cuz."

"I know, but all domestics are escalated to my supervisor— her sister was murdered by her ex-husband, and she hates men who violate restraining orders. Tamera will be with him while you're still in jail—this is a holiday weekend. Biyell, it's never worth it." Booker was the oldest of all the grandkids and dreaded seeing me in his rearview.

When we arrived at the station, Booker turned to me and sighed. "I hate to do it, cuz, but I have to." He locked me in the holding tank.

My cousin did his best to minimize the situation, but he was right—I was under a protective order and I came within five-hundred feet. Protocol mandated that all domestic violence arrests were escalated to a supervisor. It was the supervisor who wrote out the charges; she was also in court this morning.

1 Count: Violation of Protective Order
1 Count: Breaking and Entering
1 Count: Aggravated Assault
1 Count: Terroristic Threats
1 Count: Aggravated Stalking
1 Count: Destruction of Private Property
1 Count: Trespassing
1 Count: Pending

That's eight charges from kicking in my own door and punching one pussy-ass nigga in the face.

Pimp B: She never sucked your dick, that's all I'm saying.

"Your Honor, our next case is Biyell Baltimore."

I was disconnected from the chain gain and instructed to stand in front of a podium. The judge read off all eight of my charges, but the last one didn't make any sense.

"Mr. Baltimore, it seems you have a lack of respect for the orders of this court. That was a protective order I issued, and you still kicked in her door."

"Your Honor, I apologize for that, but I hadn't seen my baby in over two months, and she had no right to keep my child away from me."

"And you had no right to kick in her door and attack her fiancé. The only reason I'm not locking you up until your court date is because of your record. I will issue a bond in accordance with your charge, and I'm placing you under house arrest with an ankle monitor. Bail set at fifty thousand . . . next."

"Excuse me, Your Honor; it says the eighth charge is pending?"

The judge called over the NOPD supervisor. The supervisor looked over the notes on her clipboard, and she provided Judge Rant with additional information on the pending charge.

"Mr. Baltimore, your eighth charge is from another county. It says here that you are a fugitive out of Baker, Louisiana."

"That can't be, I have never been arrested in Baker. This has to be a mistake."

"I'm sure they will explain it all when they get here."

"But can I still make bond today and get released?"

"Yes, *but* . . ." I knew there was going to be a *but* somewhere in that bullshit. "After you post bail in Orleans Parish, then we will notify Baker police. They have thirty days to come pick you up. Until then, you're my guest. Make yourself comfortable in our luxurious accommodations. Next case . . . Calvin Brown."

GiGi lives in Baker.

CHAPTER 5

2:30 p.m.

When you come from a family that consist of mainly boys, you keep the number to a bail bondsman saved on your phone. In my mother's case, she would always keep that number at eye level on her refrigerator, right next to the calendar from Rhodes Funeral Home. I just hung up with Jerry of Free at Last Bail Bonds, who provided me with the latest update on Biyell. Even he couldn't believe how high the bond was.

"Your buddy must have called the magistrate judge a bitch to get a bail this high. I have a negligent homicide in the same holding tank whose bail is only twenty thousand," Jerry told me.

While I'm working the bond from home, Telly is beating the pavement at the courthouse. Telly knows Judge Rant; he donated to her campaign. He's trying to get Biyell's bail lowered, but it's very difficult to accomplish because of past cases in which the husband received a generous bail reduction and later killed his wife. Judges are not lining up to have their names attached to another murder-suicide. What a jam Biyell has gotten himself into, but thank God we're in a position to help.

It is a strange phenomenon how many men are comfortable confiding the truth to their buddies but would lie to their wives in the time it takes to open a can of beer. When Biyell was going through that juggling act with Tamera and GiGi, I knew the status of those relationships up to the minute.

Like the time Tamera informed him that they could no longer practice oral sex because of a sermon her pastor had preached. Biyell had to settle for a hand job; dude didn't want a hand job, and he couldn't wait for Madden Night to voice his *pisstivity.*

"How in the fuck can a pastor tell us what we can't do in our bedroom?"

"I'm not trying to get in your business or anything with your wife, but was oral sex a major part of your marriage?" I asked.

"Not really, but sometimes after dinner and my shower, I want her to take care of me. She's my wife. How can a pastor tell her she can't suck her husband's dick?"

"That's why I don't deal with church women," Rasta piped in. "They all belong to the pastor. He defines what holiness is or isn't. He tells them what to wear, how to treat a man, when to come to church, when to stand up and praise, when to kick a man out, and how much to give. And the bitch better have his money. If the man protests the control of the pastor, then she's programmed to slap his lips off with the word *yoked. How are we going to function in the Kingdom if we're unequally yoked?* The next thing I knew, my wife was filing for divorce."

"Exactly, that's exactly what I'm talking about. The pastor will be the end of us. If his words have that much power and authority, then she should marry him," Biyell agreed.

That conversation about church pastors and church women went well into the night, and interestingly, that very same pastor who preached the sermon to Tamera was later exposed for being on the down low. A hotel room video was posted on Facebook of him humping the choir director.

Biyell resented the control that pastor had over his wife, and the fallout was an immediate hunt for women who would do everything Tamera wasn't doing at home. I'm not making excuses for him because he's like a brother to me, but I can put my finger on the day he started to spiral, and it was the Sunday Tamera heard that sermon.

From jail, he's called at least twice a day, sometimes to get a status, and other times to complain about the conditions and how badly he has to shit. He says, *I can't shit in front of people.*

"But they're shitting in front of you. Go handle your business and send it to the river," I advised. That boy is still holding it.

His other calls are to complain about the men who are booked with more serious offenses but are being granted permission to go home. And then there was the conversation after court this morning - Biyell was close to popping a blood vessel.

"Uncle Glenn, I have to get out of here! The judge said Baker Police have thirty days from today to come get me. How is that legal when I haven't been charged? You have to get me out of here."

"Biyell, if we could have gotten you out on that bond, we would've had you out of there this morning," I tried to get him to relax. "What the fuck happened in Baker that has you as a fugitive?"

"Unc, I don't know!"

"When you broke it off with GiGI, was there a physical altercation?"

"Just the brick she pitched at my head—that was the only altercation."

"So you never laid a hand on GiGi?"

"Never!"

"Telly's taking you at your word and trying to nail down a meeting with the judge in her chambers to reduce your bail, but that still doesn't negate the fugitive charge in Baker. Are you sure you didn't slap her?"

"Why would I lie? Now see that Tamera? That bitch?! I'm not gonna lie; she was going to get it for having that nigga in my house. GiGi would never bring another dude who she just met around my daughter. Yes, I lost my temper, but he was in my house."

"Biyell, it's not your fuckin' house, bruh! Why is that so hard to get through? You don't live there, and you don't own Tamera."

"Whatever, but GiGi and Tamera are different."

"But you're the same."

"There are certain things I don't do, and beating women is at the top of that list!"

"Biyell, do you understand how this looks? It looks like you're on some *OJ shit* right now. You have a stalking charge; from where I'm sitting it is what you do. You put yourself in that funky holding tank. I'm sure a voice in your head told you *to drive away*, but you ignored the voice and kicked in her door."

"Unc, please call GiGi—Tyra—for me and ask her if she pressed charges that night." I could tell he was emotional. "That's the only thing it could be; in the heat of the argument she pressed charges and forgot to drop them. On my mother and my children, I did not hit her. Please call Tyra," he sobbed.

"I'll call her when we hang up," I assured him.

Relieved, he gave me her number.

"I'm not OJ, but I get your point," he sniffed. "I saw him in my house, and I saw those pictures of her kissing on his dick, and that did it. I married her, and she gave him more than she gave me. That shit hurt. I can't deny it, she stung me."

"Biyell, pull yourself together," I ordered. "Call me later today, and I will have an update. I advise you to take this opportunity alone to think about the mistakes you've made and the improvements you can make once you get out. The good news is, you didn't kill them, which means you're getting out . . . eventually."

Once the call ended, I needed a few minutes to compose my thoughts before I called GiGi—or shall I say, Tyra. Today was the first time we addressed her as Tyra; it's always been the code name exclusively. There were so many of them—those mistresses—the code names were the only way I could remember them all. The wives, on the other hand, were simply the wives. The wife wasn't hot, she wasn't described as *my sexy bitch*, or *my bad bitch*, and she wasn't mentioned as alluring. She was simply . . . the wife.

The wife was never bragged about in the same highlight video with the mistress. I knew every inch of the mistress's body in detail, from the way her ass jiggled during doggy style to the blowjob on the way back from Gulfport; the guys and I knew it all. And I'm not sure if we avoided sexual conversation involving our wives out of respect or a lack of interest, but the only time a wife was discussed was in the context of a complaint. That's the way we functioned, and that is why I'm about to call a woman who was a mistress to ask her information about Tamera's husband. This is fucking nuts.

She answered on the first ring.

"Hi Gi . . . *Tyra*, this is Glenn, I'm a friend of Biyell."

"I know who you are."

"Did I catch you at a good time?"

"Give me a second to hand the baby to my mother, hold on."

I almost forgot about the baby; I believe he's about three weeks old. I almost forgot that children are caught in the middle of all this—like victims of a drive-by shooting, the kids are always the ones in the line of fire. I almost forgot that Tyra's little girl Braylyn and Tamera's daughter Bylisha are the same age. I almost forgot how I sat back and cheered Biyell on as he drove out there to sleep with Tyra. I was instantly reminded that I had been an accessory to his man-hoe lifestyle.

"Hi, I'm back. How can I help you?" Her apathetic tone was deafening.

"For starters, I wanted to apologize to you."

"What for?"

"Because I knew, and I have known for a while, what Biyell was doing, and I didn't intervene until it was out of control. I own up to my role and ask for your forgiveness."

"Biyell is a grown man and made his own decisions." I braced myself for her to unleash on me. "While I appreciate your apology, it's not necessary. I've gone on with my life. What's the real reason for this call?"

"Biyell is in jail."

"I know."

"He called you?"

"She did."

"Tamera?"

"Unless there's a third side chick."

"Sorry, I was caught off guard that you and Tamera are still interacting."

"Not really, but she did call to warn me about him. She made it sound like she was calling out of concern, to inform me of how deranged he was, but the whole thing sounded more like she was bragging. She is pleased as punch that Biyell is sitting in jail; it sounded like he may well deserve it, but she kept going on about how she had to hold back her boyfriend from beating him up."

"Of course you know that part isn't true."

"I'm like, *you had to hold back your boyfriend,* but you're the one with a *protective order?* If you have a real man, then he's all the protective order you need. After she called me, I started hearing about her telling coworkers that Biyell is dangerous and jealous—putting her business all over the office. It's like she's proud to have a stalker."

"Of course you know there is more to it than that."

"Of course there is—but I listened to her *blah blah* until she ran out of gas. It was way too enthusiastic to be a warning. The thing is, I don't doubt that Biyell did some fucked-up shit, but I think she wanted some fucked-up shit to happen. The thing about Tamera's office is that people there gossip a lot—word got back to me last month that it hadn't been three weeks before that Mike guy was picking her up from work, and spending time with her daughter. It looked bad. I mean, Biyell fucked over both of us—that's all out in the open now—but he's always been a good father. Why block him from seeing his daughter but allow a stranger around her right away? Tamera knew that would set him off faster than anything else. Despite everything that's happened, that's some foul shit—she's getting him back every hour he sits in jail."

It was starting to make sense; Tamera knew exactly what to do to trigger Biyell's rage, and her boyfriend was in the wrong living room at the wrong time.

Tyra sighed. "I'm not saying Biyell doesn't deserve to be where he is, especially if he was about to raise a hand to her. I'm just saying she didn't see much like a victim when she called. You don't block a good father from seeing his child while letting your new boyfriend spend time with your child from day one."

"Wow, that's news to me, but it leads me to the reason I called. We're trying to get Biyell bailed out, but he's listed as a fugitive out of Baker. Do you have any information that could assist us in getting this sorted out?"

"Shit! Can I call you back at this number?"

"Yes. I'll wait for your call."

"Shit, shit, shit!" Tyra yelled.

The call ended.

CHAPTER 6

7:55 p.m.

TYRA

I cornered her so she would have little to no room to deny her actions. I know my mother—she hates Biyell. This is her mischievous signature.

"Momma, what did you do?" My mother refused to look me in the eyes, but I demanded. "Why does Biyell have an open charge here in Baker when he never laid a hand on me?"

She refused to answer, which confirmed her guilt.

I didn't ask her to intervene. I didn't need her help, but my mother has a bad habit of inserting herself into my life how she sees fit. Like a drone, she hovers and waits for the slightest opportunity to dive into my business. I'm not sure if called him that night or the following morning, but the chaotic events of that night presented the open window she longed for to get him involved. By him, I mean the man she handpicked for me with the help of her best friend Gail, his mother. His name is Julian, or should I say Sergeant Julian Freeman of the Baker Police Department. We dated from high school through his first few years on the force, but I never wanted to be the wife of a police officer, because my mother was the wife of a police officer.

My father was killed in the line of duty.

Like so many fallen officers, he died during a random traffic stop on a beautiful, sunny day—in a flash, he was gone. When we buried him, we also buried my mother alive, because she left us emotionally. It was both awe-inspiring and sad to watch and experience a woman raising us four girls with no father. She conducted our affairs with a stoic grace and never gave one thought to another man. My mother became Mrs. Coretta King, and spent the rest of her life dedicated to my father's honor. Even the thought of another man moving into our home was blasphemous. While I've always loved her for her dedication to him, my heart ached for her. I missed my father too, and so did my sisters, but my mother became trapped—she just could not move on.

I didn't want Julian to become a police officer. I begged him not to join the force, but he joined.

After his first officer-involved shoot-out, I knew I couldn't do it—I refused to become my mother. I was torn, because Julian was my best friend; we grew up together, and he was my first love. His nickname around town was Denzel because he was the spitting image of the famous actor in the movie *Training Day*. I gave him that nick name, and it stuck. He would even do the Denzel walk for me, and the more I laughed, the more he performed. He even impersonated Denzel Washington's vernacular. I adored him, but not his career path.

When I received the news that Julian was involved in a shooting, the day my father was killed reloaded in my mind like morbid video on YouTube—one of those clips you watch but can never un-see. I relived every minute that ticked closer to the evening my father was killed in the line of duty. The G-force of grief that swooped through my every memory, through every day of my childhood, through every birthday and graduation . . .

I experienced it all again when I ran through the hospital parking lot the day Julian was shot.

Twice in the arm and thigh, all non-life threatening, but all life altering. It happened on his one-year anniversary on the force, and I was one month pregnant. That was the day I texted my best friend Code 0627.

My mother never knew about the pregnancy, but Julian knew, and he wanted the baby and a family. I also wanted the family and Julian, without the daily fear of wondering if that day would be the last day he'd return to me. My mother, on the other hand, loved Julian—maybe more than I did—and she handpicked him for me.

In high school, Julian was the only boy allowed to call or visit the house, and the moment he entered, she would greet him, then vanish. When he joined the police department, my mother became obsessed with the possibility of us getting married. I think it was her chance to get a do-over; to watch the continuation of her marriage through me and Julian. Then I ended it, and she never got over it.

It wasn't until three years later that I came face to face with my decision to end our relationship, and my decision to use Code 0627.

Three years after I dialed that code, I was involved in a fender bender with a texting teen who rear-ended my new car. I was so cute that day in my floral-printed chiffon dress, which waved in the wind like a purple scarf. My hair was freshly styled and set from the salon . . . but my good mood quickly turned to pain when I saw the officer who arrived to take the report: Officer Julian Freeman. I will never forget the brokenness in his face when he saw me standing there, obviously pregnant, when he obviously wasn't the father. Julian didn't have to say it, because his eyes spoke clearly and painfully.

You never gave our child a chance.

I watched him struggle as he confirmed whether I needed medical attention for the baby. Even with his best efforts to remain an absolute professional, when it was time to hand back our insurance papers, I saw a single tear forming in his eye. I never saw him again after that intersection, but I knew then beyond all doubt that Julian still loved me—even though I was carrying Braylyn, he still loved me.

Julian Freeman is the man my mother called the night Biyell told me he was married. What she reported to him is unclear, but I just checked, and there was an incident report filed with her address attached.

"Momma, did you file a report with Baker Police?" I demanded an answer. "Answer me, did you make a report against Biyell? Momma, I just ended a call with one of his friends who said he's in jail waiting for transport to Baker. I'd rather hear it from you—what did you report to the Baker Police?"

"*I never liked him, that no good bastard.*"

"I know that. Biyell knows that. This entire family knows that, but what did you do?"

"I told you he was married the first day you brought him around here. Deep down you knew he was married, and you still continued seeing him."

"Momma, I mean no disrespect, but I am a grown woman, and I have to live with my decisions—not you."

"That's foolishness; we're all living with your decisions. Where is your husband? Do you have one? You don't think that affects me as a mother and grandmother that my grandkids have a father like that lowlife Biyell man?"

"If babysitting his children is too much to handle, then I'll ask Aunt Sabrina to watch them."

"You will not do a *got-damn thing;* this isn't about my grandkids, this is about you getting pregnant twice for a married man." My mother rocked my son in her lap. "I didn't see this in the plan for your life. This wasn't in the plan."

"Momma, first of all, I make the plan for my life. Second of all, when I discovered Biyell was married, you found out ten minutes after I did. It was too late at that point."

"You had a good man and flushed it all down the toilet."

I felt a pang, and a swell of rage. "And I aborted his child."

"You did what?" My mother rose with anger. "You aborted Julian's baby?"

"Yes, I had an abortion."

"Lord Jesus, I turn her over to you," she spoke to the ceiling. "I didn't raise you like that, I don't believe in abortion."

"Would it have been better to do that to these two because of who their father is?"

"No, it would have been better to marry the man who wanted you!"

"Well it's too late now, Momma, so what would you have me do now?" I moved to the arm of the sofa. "Look my son in the face and tell me if it would have been best that I aborted him!" I stormed into the kitchen where Braylyn toyed under the table and returned to my mother with my daughter extended in my arms.

"Me-maw, me-maw!" Braylyn giggled as she hugged my mother's neck.

"Would you rather I had aborted this one, too?" I saw her eyes tear up. "Momma, I know you hate Biyell, but I sat on that table once, and I wasn't doing it again. I love my children, and I loved their father. I didn't have these kids after a one-night stand; I was in a loving relationship with a man who drove 170 miles round trip, three to four nights a week, just to see me. You may not like Biyell, and yes he lied to me about his marital status—I've dealt with that—but he never lied to my children."

It's all true. My cousin and her husband live right next door; his lazy ass don't lift a finger to help her, while Biyell proved his love for me every day we were together. I get that he was caught up; yes, I feel like a fool, and I know my family gossips about me like a dog, but despite how much he hurt me, I have to admit and focus on the fact that Biyell takes care of his children. My children are my priority.

"Biyell is being held in jail for something he didn't do. I need to know what you reported so I can get him released."

"I reported that he tried to run your cousin over with his truck."

"But Momma, that's not true. If anything, he was threatened. What else did you report?"

"That was it." She's lying.

"Momma, what else did you report?" I asked in a low, determined voice.

"And that he . . ."

"He what, Momma?"

"He was choking you."

"Momma, you know that's a lie. Why did you do that?"

"Because I wanted him to stay far away from here—because I didn't want you to take him back."

"So you lied?"

"I did what I had to do to keep my daughter away from a married man."

"Momma you lied, and now Biyell has to get transported on a warrant back to Baker to answer charges on something that never happened." I hurried to my cell phone.

"They will never believe he didn't hit you."

"Because you knew exactly what to say to get these charges to stick. You made those officers think I'm a battered woman. They also know that I'm the daughter of a fallen officer, therefore that entire precinct is going to do everything to protect me—but it's all a lie, and you will tell them it was a lie."

I leaned into her ear. "Momma, I promise on my father's grave, if you don't drop these charges, tonight will be the last night you'll see my kids." I lifted my son out of her clutch, grabbed Braylyn by the arm, and stormed next door.

Once inside, I placed my son in his bed, where he continued his nap, and dimmed the lights on a very hyper Braylyn. She fought a good fight to avoid sleep, but after about fifteen minutes, both kids were out for the night. I then returned the call from Uncle Glenn.

"Hi, Uncle Glenn, this is Tyra, did I catch you at a good time?"

"This is a perfect time. Were you able to get to the bottom of that charge?"

"Yes, my mother made a false police report—she told the cops he beat me that night I threw that brick. She lied. I was the one who attacked him; I'm the one who should have the warrant. My mother filed those charges, but I will get her to drop them in the morning, so help me God. She will drop those charges."

Uncle Glenn asked me to hold while he explained to the room what I had revealed about the charges. In the background, I heard snippets of the conversation. *That has to be his friend Telly, the one they call Crowd Noise.*

"That's bad news on many levels," Telly explained in the background.

"How so, if her mother drops the charges?" Uncle Glenn asked.

Moments later, Uncle Glenn returned to the phone. "If the charges are as you described, then it's not up to your mother. Telly just informed me that the state will more than likely review the case before it's dropped."

"Meaning the state will pick up the charges regardless?"

"Yes, unless you know—"

"Unless I know someone with influence in the prosecutor's office?"

"That's correct—unless you know someone who would listen to your explanation of how this unfolded, we're confident those charges will stick, at least for a while."

"I know someone who might help me out, can I call you in the morning?"

"Please do, and when this is all over, we can't wait to meet Braylyn and Fat Boy."

"You can count on it."

When the call with Uncle Glenn ended, I knew there was only one person I could call to help me—but would he? Would he believe me or write me off as just another battered woman trying to get her wife-beater out of jail? I know it's late, but there's only one way to find out.

I scrolled through my contacts, and there he was: Julian Freeman. I pressed *Call*, and he answered in the space between the first and second ring tone.

"Hi, Ju-Ju," I said fearfully.

"Hi, Tyra . . . I was expecting this call."

"I need to speak to you about something very important."

"I know, but it will not happen."

I had to be out of my mind to think he would help me after the way I broke his heart. Julian has every right to be angry with me; I deserve it.

"Well, thank you for at least answering the phone."

"We can speak about whatever you like, but it will not happen over the phone. Whenever you're ready to speak with me face to face, only then will we talk."

"I'm ready now."

"Where?"

"My house."

"I'm on my way."

CHAPTER 7

8:30 p.m.

TYRA

When Julian entered my front door it happened; my heart skipped. There's something about his powerful, deeply masculine presence that makes me weak. There's no cure for it—he still has that effect on me. The only difference tonight is that his uniform shirt is white: the color of the supervisors. It was the color of shirt my dad dreamed of wearing . . . but two days before his promotion ceremony, he stopped the wrong driver for speeding.

In the span of time it took him to walk from my front door to the middle of my living room, I regretted everything but my children. *How could I be so stupid to let him go? Is he here to rub it in my face?*

"Julian, thank you for coming, I wouldn't have asked if it wasn't important."

I invited him to have a seat across from me.

Then came the silence.

I rewound back to the eleventh grade, to our first prom—to how in awe he was when I stepped off my front porch to pin a single red rose on his tux. Then we turned for the picture. Correction, I turned. When the photo was developed, it captured me looking forward and Julian's eyes glued to the side of my face. Tonight I'm looking into the same eyes. He still loves me.

"Hi Tyra," he broke the silence.

"Hi Ju-Ju."

His head shook from left to right, his lips wore a tight smile. "Your mother called me twenty minutes ago; she explained her side of the ordeal, and I have already spoken to my partner at the DA's office."

"You have?"

"Yes, and it's done."

"What's done?"

"Charges in Baker have been dropped, and my warrant department removed the hold."

My head fell into my chest. "Thank you so much, and I'm sorry my mother involved you."

"I know your mother—next to my mom she is my number one supporter. I totally understand what happened here. Within a day or so, he'll be free to go."

"I don't know how I will ever repay you for your kindness."

"I can think of one way."

"What is it?"

Julian walked over to a picture on my wall of Biyell and Braylyn. He removed it and returned to his seat.

"You can give me an explanation." He slid the picture across the coffee table to me. "That's all you owe me."

What a heavy price to pay for the freedom of a married man, I thought. I wanted to give him the truth, but which version of the truth? The one where I was afraid of becoming my mother, or the truth that he was my first sexual experience and I was curious what else was out there? The truth that he loved Baker more than I did? I didn't want to be born here, raised here, married here, pregnant here, and die here. I wanted to see if the world was truly round; I wanted to know that I was with him because he was the greatest, and not because he was the only man I'd ever known or was allowed to know.

I know arranged marriages are largely frowned upon, but that's what we would have had. We would have been paired by our mothers the same way their husbands were handpicked for them.

Technically, it wouldn't have been an arranged marriage, but my mother controlled my options by disqualifying every young man in town, leaving only one worthy. Julian Freeman was worthy, and my mother made sure our paths always crossed. Then I broke his heart, which broke her heart. While he was recovering from his gunshot injuries, I ended our relationship and never gave him a real explanation why. He was here to collect.

"I'm sorry for the way I walked out of your life."

"Tyra, why did you end our relationship so swiftly?"

"Because things were moving so fast, and I heard through a little birdie that you were in a jewelry store. I knew a proposal was next."

"Did you love me?"

"Yes, with all of my heart—you were the only love I'd known."

"Then why?"

"I was scared."

"Scared? Tyra, everything happened according to your timing and your comfort level. We made love the first time when you were ready. I bought that double wide because you thought it was cute. I don't understand how a person who was in control of everything was afraid of the pace. You set the pace."

"Julian, you're right, and you were very patient with me—"

"Then why did you leave me the hospital? You came to visit one time and never returned."

"Because the room smelled like my daddy's room! When I opened the door and saw the tubes everywhere, and heard the beeping of the machines, and the weeping in the hall, it was my daddy all over again. I couldn't relive the worst day of my life all over again."

"So you ran?"

"Yes, I ran."

"And you never looked back until your true love got arrested."

"He's not my true love . . ." I tried to look away, but his eyes illuminated the room a burnt orange hue, like flaming coal. I thought the side of my face would blister. I couldn't escape this hour of reckoning. The twisting of the knife came when he slid the photo to the edge of the coffee table; I caught it before it hit the floor.

"He's your true love."

"Julian, he's not. I know you find that hard to believe, but he's not—it was you."

"Tyra, how could you say it was me when you gave him everything?"

"That's not true—"

"Then what happened to my baby?"

At that point I wished there was a Scotty to beam me up. I couldn't lie to him; he deserved the truth. He already knew, of course, but he was here for closure, and I was the only person who could provide answers to every question. If Julian didn't hate me before, I'm sure he will hate me after I tell him about Code 0627.

"I went to the clinic." His hand formed a veil—only the lids of his eyes were visible. "Three weeks after the pregnancy test, I went to the clinic."

"Who drove you home?"

"It's not important—"

"Who drove you home?"

"Julian . . ."

"I need to know why I wasn't even allowed to be there for the drive home. How you made this decision for the three of us?

Tyra, who drove you home?"

"Your sister."

"Brittany?"

"Yes, Brittany. She is the only one I trust unconditionally."

"While I was still recovering, Brittany drove you to have an abortion?"

"Julian, please don't be angry with her—I had no one else to call. Brittany protected me during that painful chapter of my life, and she kept it private."

He folded forward and cried into the sleeves of his shirt; I had broken him again.

"I never wanted to hurt you, Julian; I even prayed you would find someone you loved more than you loved me. I prayed for your happiness."

"I never found happiness." He slowly inflated upright. "I looked for you in every woman I met but could never find you. Then I saw you that day—in the purple dress, standing at the rear of your car, carrying his child. What was it about him?"

"Julian, I can't answer that . . ."

"Yes, you can, what was it? What made you love him more than me? I have to know."

"Julian, I didn't . . . you have to believe me."

"Tyra, we started this conversation honestly, and it will end as it started. You carried his baby full term. My child never saw daylight. So what was it?"

"Julian, I don't know how to convince you, but it wasn't Biyell, it was me. I couldn't go through that experience again; I still haven't recovered from the coldness of that table. Ours was the right child, but the wrong me. I wasn't ready when we conceived—"

"But you got ready for him?"

"Not true."

"Tyra, losing you raked me out, and I came here for closure . . . but there is no such thing as closure. There was something about Biyell that made you want his child."

"I WAS REPENTING FOR YOUR CHILD. I NEVER GOT OVER IT!" I yelled at the curtains. I couldn't look him in the eye. "I carried his children full term because I . . . I . . . *felt so bad.* I was tired of feeling like a horrible person. I couldn't put myself through that again. I wanted the nightmares to end. So many nights I had a dream I dropped your son off at daycare, but when I returned to pick up my child, they stared at me like a deranged crazy person: *you never dropped a baby off.* I wanted the dreams to end." Wiping tears at this point was a waste of good tissue. "Allowing my second child to live was my way of apologizing to the first. That is God's honest truth. I have never loved any man as much as I loved you."

"I hear he's married?" Julian asked.

"That's true, but I didn't know he was married."

"Are you still involved with him?"

"No, but I do allow Biyell to see his children."

"So, it's over . . . after two kids it's over?"

"Yes, the relationship was a mistake, but I love my kids, and he's a great father. It's over."

"So what happens when he's released?"

"I just said it's over . . ."

"You know as well as I do that dude is coming back for you. Is it really over?"

"I could never trust Biyell again. If I can't trust you then it doesn't matter how many kids we have together—it's over."

"Tyra, I'm only asking because I never got over you. I never stopped loving you. I never wanted any other woman, but losing you the way I lost you damaged me. Tyra, you are still the only woman I love because I have never allowed any other woman to get close to me. The part you don't know is I have called your mom at least once a week to check on you and the kids. When Biyell crushed you, I knew about it the night it happened, and I wanted to come here—not as an ex-boyfriend, but as your friend. You were my best friend, and when you left me five years ago, I lost that friend."

Julian inflated himself and adjusted his uniform. He then walked around the table and held out his hand for the picture. He hung it back in its place and gazed at it for a moment. I felt so stupid—for thinking there was someone else out there who could love me more than this man.

The way you walk, the way you talk
The way you say my name and smile
The way you move me, the way you soothe me
The way you speak softly through the night.

He started to sing my favorite song over by the photo wall.

That song was playing the night of our senior prom; that song was playing the night we made love for the first time. That song was like a key entering a rusted lock, and it unlocked feelings that I'd kept hidden, even from Biyell. With Biyell the attraction was sexual, but the bond between Julian and I had been sealed over two decades.

The name of that song is simply "You." I'm convinced Jesse Powell wrote it for me so that Julian could sing it at the right moment. Like right now, when I needed to feel real love, and I needed to feel forgiveness.

Every morning you rise and open your eyes
I just wanna be there with you baby
I just wanna be yours, from this day forth.

He didn't sing all of it; he didn't have too. I was broken over, crying into my arms. His voice was so beautiful, and he knew it. Julian came from a family of dynamic singers, but none in the family had a voice that could match his. If he quit the police department today, he could release a YouTube video of himself singing and it would go viral—but he only serenades me. Suddenly, I heard him place something on the table.

"Thank you for the truth. Before I go, there's one more thing I want you to know." Julian kneeled on the side of the sofa where I sat crying into my lap.

"I was in the jewelry store that day—saved an entire month's salary plus one week. I know he's going to make another try to win you back, but here's what I guarantee. He will never love you as much as I do, because it's impossible. He will never wait for you as long as I've waited, because it's impossible—the last time I made love was with you. I'm leaving this box with you because it's time for me to go on with my life, but in the meantime, if you decide you want me, then text me a picture of this black box and I will come to you, slide this ring on your finger, ask you to be my wife, and welcome these beautiful children into my life with open arms. That's all I ask of you."

Julian opened the box to reveal a beautiful diamond ring. Then, he kissed me on the side of my wet face and left out the door singing.

I just wanna be yours, from this day forth . . .

CHAPTER 8

Monday, April 10, 2017
8:30 a.m.

TELLY

It's late, and Uncle Glenn is worried about Biyell, which means we're discussing the same fucking topic on loop—getting Biyell out of jail. We have gone through every scenario three times of what to do if the state picks up the charges, but hopefully we can get it resolved without me making a trip to Baker. I have to say I feel sorry for my buddy; even though he put himself in a really bad situation, to have GiGi's mom file a false report is a perfect example of when it rains it pours.

Seated at the kitchen table are Diana and Rasta's mother, who has this long look on her face. Every time I ask where Rasta is, I can never get a straight answer. I may not be the best lawyer, but I know when a witness is deliberately avoiding my questions. Megyn is waiting for me at our love nest, but I am not leaving until they tell me where in the fuck my dawg is.

"If we can get that woman to drop those charges in the morning, then more than likely Judge Rant will—"

I cut Uncle Glenn off. "Where is Rasta?"

The question created a hush that blew around the room like a desert wind.

Uncle Glenn was quiet for the first time this evening; a look of dread replaced a look of grave concern. Something was wrong with Rasta, and it was obviously a secret, but not anymore. I needed to know what was up.

"Where is Rasta? I've been calling for him for three weeks. Rasta usually calls me an average of twice a week; it's not like him not to check in. He's not on a recruiting visit with his oldest son, and he's not in jail. Where is Rasta?"

Diana moved from the table over to the sink in search of something to wash. Rasta's mother suddenly became interested in a newspaper ad for a local meat market. That left Uncle Glenn, the person I talk to more than anyone else, and I had him cornered. He looked over at his sister-in-law, Rasta's mom Ms. Debra, and she approved with a nod.

"Telly, our Madden Brother tried to check out."

"Check out? Of a hotel?"

"No, life."

The pin was pulled out of my back. The weight of disbelief caused me to slouch on the sofa.

"Rasta is in the West Jeff Behavioral Medicine Center for attempted suicide. In my opinion, it was a successful suicide. If we hadn't kicked in the door when we did . . ." Uncle Glenn's eyes drifted back to the urgency of that day.

"Over LaDeisha?"

"Over a lot of things, not just LaDeisha."

"Can I visit him?"

"Yes, but not right now."

"Man, I wish I would have known."

"I know, but we wanted to keep it private because of the sensitive nature of the situation. We also wanted to him to tell his friends himself when he's ready."

"I understand, but I wish I would have known."

"Telly, I know, and I wanted to call a huddle and tell you guys, but I needed to respect the wishes of his mother to keep this private. I hope you understand."

I understood, which is why I walked over to Rasta's mother. As I approached Ms. Debra, I opened my arm, and she met me halfway with a full-wrap hug.

"Ms. Debra, you know in the past I have worked for your son for free because I love him like a brother. If you need anything for him, please let me know. Thank you for trusting me with the truth."

She wiped her tears on my suit as I walked her back to the kitchen table. "Thank you, Telly. I promise, as soon as the doctor gives us more information, I will make sure you get an update."

After hugging Diana goodnight, I turned to leave. Uncle Glenn asked to walk out with me. It was just starting to drizzle. Glenn closed the front door, then hopped to a patio chair just a few feet away.

"Unc, I had a feeling something was wrong—that's why I didn't press the issue of tracking Rasta down. I felt all of this."

"I was the one who found the note. Telly, he was gone. It was nothing but the grace of God that kept him alive."

"You do know I plan to fuck him up?"

"Rasta?"

"No, Timothy."

"I feel the same way, but we have to beat him with our minds."

"Just one right hook to the face to knock his fucking teeth out would make me feel better."

"No, that's what he's expecting. We're planning on resolving this by taking the high road. My attorney plans to drag it out and wear them down, and with a jury of all women, he feels there is no way Timothy would win in the end."

"I was thinking the same thing, but I still want to knock his front teeth out."

"Me too, but the last thing I need is to have you and Biyell locked up on bullshit."

"Speaking of bullshit, I didn't want to say it while you were on the phone with GiGi, but that District Attorney in Baker is a real asshole. I don't see those charges getting dropped. They will pick him up. You could be in Dallas; they're coming pick you up for a hundred-dollar speeding ticket."

"I've heard about the Baker DA, that's why I'm hoping GiGi can get this resolved. If Biyell has to sit another week in Orleans waiting for Baker to transport him, he will lose his job."

"That's my fear as well, but I will deal with it in the morning. I have some hot cat waiting."

"Erica?"

"No, Megyn."

"Megyn failed the cake test."

"But the pussy is on the honor roll, *ya heard me?*" I pulled Uncle Glenn up from the chair and dapped him off. I needed to get to Megyn.

"Erica won the cake test. She gets the man."

"And she will, Uncle Glenn, I just need a little bit more of Megyn and she will."

"Bad move. Just remember, I warned you. Erica won, and the cake test is never wrong."

I ran through the rain to my car. With Maxwell's "Fortunate" blasting on my radio, I threw up a fist to Uncle Glenn as I zoomed out of the parking lot. I was thirty minutes late, so I shot Megyn a text that I was en route. I arrived at my apartment ten minutes later, and from the side of the building, I could see the flickering of candlelight through my bedroom window. Through a bolt of lightning and a torrential downpour, I ran as fast as I could, but still managed to get soaking wet. When I opened the door, Megyn was leaning against the bedroom wall in a pair of black knee-high boots and no panties. She wore two little black bows covering her nipples.

"A tub of hot water is waiting for you," she pointed.

I wasn't interested in the bath; I wanted her right where she stood, up against that wall. I leaned in to kiss her, but a finger blocked my lips.

"I said, a tub of water is waiting for you—don't make me repeat myself."

Tonight I was meeting this Megyn for the first time, and I liked her.

"Okay, I will head straight to the tub."

Her lips were painted the color of blackberries; the shadow on her eyes was endless. Around her neck she wore a black leather choker; a spiked dog collar with a long chain that hung down the middle of her breasts.

In seconds, I was out of my clothes and in the tub. I heard her boots tapping across the tile floor to the kitchen area, then slowly back to me. Then, she kneeled on the side of the tub with a silver covered platter and a bottle of wine. When she removed the top of the platter, I found myself looking at strips of grilled steak, well done and seasoned. On the side of the steak strips was a serving of jambalaya and a sauce bowl of sweet marinade. She placed the tray on the edge of the tub and popped the cork off the wine. "So how was your day?"

I sipped the wine. "It was long and hard." I opened my mouth for the first fork of steak.

Fuck, that was delicious. She can cook.

"Well, long and hard is not a bad thing if it ends short and soft." Her hand snorkeled beneath the suds and found my dick, who was sound asleep. Another forkful of the steak ignited the buds in my mouth, but my dick snored through it all.

"I missed you today," she said in a desperate voice.

"I missed you too, and I thought about you all day."

"Is that so? What about?" she asked.

"I thought about us, and this, and forever."

"So you were reading my mind." She fed me another forkful.

"I think my thoughts about you were a little heavier than your thoughts about me."

"Think so? Then you go first."

I savored another sip. "While sitting in court today, I saw the fulfillment of all our dreams. Everything that we're building together, I saw it in a vision. It was amazing. We were extremely successful. Your turn."

Megyn dipped another fork of steak in the sauce and fed it to me. She followed it up with a bite of the jambalaya. "How can I sum this up for you?"

"Don't sum it up; please take your time."

"In my vision, the minister said, *you may now kiss the bride.* You kissed me."

"Wow, you won," I smiled. She smiled back. "Here I am thinking you're allergic to marriage."

"I'm not; I'm only allergic to the man I was married to, but I enjoyed being a wife."

"I learn something new about you every time. Here I am thinking marriage was the furthest thing from your mind because of the NFL pension."

"Only for a man like you would I do it again." Megyn closed the platter and gripped the neck of the wine bottle between her fingers. After taking a few paces away from the tub, she stopped and looked over her shoulder, allowing me a few seconds to appreciate her moon-shaped ass and those boots.

"Meet me in the bedroom—don't make me wait."

I sat the wine glass down and commenced scrubbing myself everywhere, because I know how much she loves to suck all over me. It was ten minutes later when I entered the bedroom to find her lying on her side, masturbating with one hand and pointing to where she wanted me with the other. She wanted me on my side with my back to her breast. When I was in position, she started biting my neck, stroking my dick, and whispering in my ear.

"I'm only giving you a little bit tonight. When I say stop, it's over. Do you understand?"

"Yes . . ."

"If you disobey me, then you will not feel this pussy for two months. Do you understand?"

"Yes."

Megyn slid across my body to the other side, and with her fingers, she held open her lips.

"Come fuck me."

I did as I was told. I entered her deep and slow, then shifted to deep and hard, then shifted into cruise control at that pace. She held on for dear life and loved every stroke.

"That's it, Telly, give it to me—that's it, baby."

Just as I lifted myself above her and she saw the look in my eyes and felt the pulsating veins in my dick, she spoke.

"And stop."

I ignored her.

"Telly, if I were you, I would stop."

"I can't."

"Telly."

"One more hump."

"No."

"Okay." I stopped.

"Now, back on your side."

I returned to the original position. Megyn slid back across my body and pressed her warm breasts against my back. Then she started beating my dick at the same pace I'd fucked her with, using long and smooth strokes.

"Ciara, I'm about to nut."

"Really?"

"Yes, it's right there."

"Cum for me, baby."

"Here it comes, Ciara . . ."

"I want it, Telly. Give it to me," she demanded. She started to jerk me even faster.

Seconds before I started to cum, she pretzeled between my

legs and continued to beat my dick in her mouth.

Then she did it again.

That finger thingy.

But this time, she tapped down on my prostate like she was clicking the mouse on her laptop. Then she held her finger down hard, like holding down the lever on a toaster. Her finger remained in my ass, milking me as cum dumped into her mouth forever.

When it was over, I couldn't feel my legs. Megyn pulled the covers over me, slid into a black skirt and a glittery black blouse, and left me there in the bed, empty. About an hour later, my cell phone buzzed with a text.

I own your body; I own your mind. Next I will own your heart, then I will own you.

After reading that, I started thinking.

I have to quit Erica.

I've been turnt out.

And I like it.

CHAPTER 9

Wednesday, June 21, 2017
9:27 a.m.

*T*his is a call from the Orleans Parish Jail. To accept this call, press one. "Uncle Glenn, this Biyell." *To decline this call, please press two or hang up.*
I pressed one.
Thank you for using Global TelCom.
"Uncle Glenn, please come get me. They just released me. I'm free."

CHAPTER 10

Madden Thursday
June 22, 2017
6:46 a.m.

RASTA

I reached out to her and she ran to me. It felt as if we'd never parted, not even for a minute. Then I asked for a kiss. It was the softest kiss, followed by the most genuine words. "Roderick, I love you, and if you want to try again, then let's try again."

"It's all I've ever wanted."

"And you're all I ever wanted."

"But what about your campaign and my background?"

"I don't care about that if I can't have you."

"Are you sure?"

"As sure as the sun."

I pulled her back into my chest and squeezed her around the middle of her back, nearly lifting her off her feet. He face was ageless and innocent, like the face of Kelly Rowland from Destiny's Child but after Beyoncé went solo. Everything I want in a woman is encapsulated in her. I love everything about her. I love her short hair and her milk chocolate skin, and I love the gleam in her eyes.

In LaDeisha I found the sum total of my ideal woman. If she were a stranger in a grocery store, standing over by the celery, I would still walk up to her and introduce myself. I would still ask for her name, give her my phone number, and pray she called. Deep down I don't blame Timothy. To meet her is to want her. I understand the effect she had on him. She had the same effect on me. It's the eyes. It was those eyes that caused me to forget every woman I'd ever known, and it was those same eyes that convinced Timothy to divorce his wife. Her lips would never utter something so scandalous—it was those eyes. He looked into those same eyes and felt the same thing I felt—those eyes that said *yes*.

Whenever.

Wherever.

Whatever.

The answer was always *yes*.

LaDeisha is the perfect blend of femininity and feminism topped with an unquenchable ambition, but in the bed her only ambition was to ride me until she collapsed. At the end of the day, she was just a girl who loved her guy—a girl who wanted to be held and protected.

That's how I knew she would come back to me—Timothy's arms are too short to lift a woman who's loaded with so much substance. Her love is too heavy for him; that's how I know we are forever.

"Roderick, what are we doing?"

"I don't understand."

"As a couple, where are we?"

"We're reunited after a quick time-out."

"I get that, but where am I with you?"

"LaDeisha, you're with me."

"I have to know."

"You're in my arms."

"But where is here? Please tell me!"

"Are you okay?"

"Yes, just feeling pressure."

"I understand. You have experienced a lot changes in a short period of time, but I rescued you. So relax—you're in my arms, we're in your bed."

LaDeisha placed her hands gently on the sides of my face. I looked up at her, and saw the intensity mounting in her face. "Roderick! Roderick! Where in the fuck am I?" Then she shook me.

When my eyes opened, LaDeisha was gone. She had been replaced with a woman who looked like Rachael Ray from the Food Network. I was in denial. My heart was panicked. I scanned the room for LaDeisha, but she was gone. I was alone with this Rachael Ray chick.

"That is your name, right? Roderick?"

She was close enough to kiss, and that's when I backed as far away as the wall would allow. "Yes, that's my name, but who are you? What are you doing in my room?"

"That's what I'm trying to figure out. Where in the fuck am I?"

"You're in a behavioral medicine clinic."

"Repeat that, please."

"You're in the hospital for mental health issues. The West Jefferson Behavioral Medicine Center."

"Like . . . a mental institution?"

"Yes, you've been committed to a mental institution. How did you get in my room?"

"I don't know . . ."

"Let's start from the top. What is your name?"

"It's Amanda." She extended her hand.

We shook. "Hi Amanda, it's nice to meet you."

"Nice to meet you, too . . ."

"So how much do you actually remember?"

"About what?"

"About your episode—your nervous breakdown or your suicide attempt—how much of it do you actually remember?"

"I thought this was a dream; I was rolling in a medical bed and I overheard a nurse say, *We're out of beds. The safest place I can put her is in the room with Mr. Ross. He's a really good guy.* Now what was the name of that nurse? Hmm . . . hmm . . ." Her eyes drifted to the upper left as she tried to recall.

"DeShonta?"

"Yes, that's it. Were you in my dream? How did you know that?"

"She intakes all incoming suicide patients."

"*You are sooooo* freaking me out right now—how did you know about my suicide attempt? What else have they told you about me?"

"Check this out—when I dozed off last night that bed over there was empty. This morning, you . . . were in my face. They haven't told me anything about you, but everybody in here is a threat to themselves or someone else. You are one of us," I explained.

"You too? But you look so . . . so . . ."

"Normal?"

"Yes, and I meant no offense, I'm just really freaking out," she said breathlessly.

"Rule number one: don't ever say things like *freaking out*, *losing your mind*, or *I'm going crazy* around any staff member. If you do, you'll never get out of here."

"Are they going to discharge me after today?"

"It depends."

"On what?"

"How did you try to kill yourself?"

"In the garage, with a garden hose and exhaust."

"Damn . . . I can pretty much guarantee you're not going home anytime soon."

"What makes you so sure?"

"Let's see . . . it's been nearly a month for me, and I see no signs that I'm going home."

That's when she really started to freak out. In the space between our beds, she paced from the door to the wall and back. I'm sure there's a story here—we all have stories—but I'm not interested. This Amanda chick has ruined the best dream I've had since I was admitted. I can still taste LaDeisha's kiss—and Rachael Ray chased her away.

"This can't be real!" Amanda dove back into her own bed, which made me very happy. "I have to get out of here. And my job? OMG! And my dog?! Who's going to let my dog out? And my online classes? I have exams coming up."

"No you don't."

"What do you mean, *no I don't*? I have a life. I have to get out of—"

"You don't have a life out there, and you're not going anywhere."

"Roderick, why are you saying these things?" Her face was flustered.

"Because you're dead."

"What?! So you're a ghost? Fuck . . . you're a ghost?" She leaned forward in the bed and extended her hand toward me, trying to touch my face.

"No, I'm not, but life as you know is over, at least while you're in this hellhole. What I'm trying to say, Amanda, is you had a life out there before you tried to kill yourself. Your family has committed you and you're now under physicians orders."

"They can hold me against my will?"

My entire morning was spent trying to explain to Amanda why she's not going home. Right after breakfast, it was time for my session with Dr. Morton. Phillip escorted me to his office.

After three soft knocks, a voice invited us in.

"Mr. Ross, have a seat. How are you this morning?"

"I woke up this morning and Amanda scared the shit out of me, but everything else is just fine."

"Mr. Ross, please accept my apology—we're experiencing a major crisis with available beds."

"It's no bother, I'm getting used to waking up and seeing a stranger on the other side of the room."

"Speaking of strangers, I'm bringing in some lobbyists and colleagues in a few weeks to observe our facility. They will help me stress to the powers that be the need for more funding and support for mental health services. I would appreciate if you could share this crisis with them from your perspective, from someone who is a first-time visitor."

"And a last-time visitor."

Dr. Morton chuckled.

"I wouldn't mind at all." I'm thinking, *that's the fastest way to get out of here—I do you a favor and you discharge me.* "I'm honored you considered me."

"That's great, we need all the help we can get to preserve our budget. Let's say we begin, shall we?"

"Fire away."

"What was the reason you cut your hair?"

"LaDeisha."

"Why is it you would cut your hair for LaDeisha but not for your ex-wife?"

My file contains my last three ID photos and a copy of my divorce. DeShonta wasn't lying—he's been studying me like a lab rat.

"Because my ex-wife demanded that I cut my hair or it was over. LaDeisha loved my hair. My ex hated me."

"What makes you so sure she hated you?"

"I felt it—she turned cold."

"When your ex-wife rejected you, did thoughts of suicide enter your mind?"

"Not at all . . ."

"When was the first time you thought about killing yourself?"

"The first night LaDeisha broke up with me."

"Have you had any of those thoughts recently?"

If I lie, he will know. If I tell the truth, then I am never getting out of here. Fuck it. "I thought about killing myself last night. I was missing her a lot. The pain was too much."

"Did you have a dream about LaDeisha?"

This dude is psychic! I'm never getting out of here.

CHAPTER 11

Tuesday, July 4, 2017
2:30 p.m.

Throughout the house, Luther Vandross's "Bad Boy" blared into every corner and crack, through every door and window—the same went for each apartment in my complex. On the patio, I tamed the grill and rearranged the meat; it's what I do better than anything, it's what I love to do. We're partying today, all day—nothing but *Madden* on the television and spades on the kitchen table. Diana and her company love spades, but I don't like playing spades with them—I don't like people talking that much shit in my house.

Speaking of which . . .

I know Rasta's mother is coming, and I think three of her six brothers. Don't get me wrong, I love my brothers-in-law—that is, until they get drunk. I know my crew is loud, especially Crowd Noise Telly and Biyell, but we're altar boys compared to Diana's family. You can be two feet from them and they'll still scream like you're two blocks away. And it doesn't matter if they're sober or drunk—they greet you with the most loving, the most heartfelt, insult you've ever heard in your life.

Take, for instance, Diana's oldest brother Calvin, who's no taller than the stove—a big mouth-ass munchkin:

"Glenn, you old JIVE ASS TURKEY . . . I ain't think you were gonna amount to shit when my sister brought you home back in the day. I asked Diana, when you started fuckin' with El De-Barge? HA-HA-HAW-HAW (cough, cough). Didn't he use to look like El Debarge? Y'all remember that?"

Once it was my turn to get it, Calvin always got a buy-in from the entire room: at my expense.

"Diana, remember Glenn had that long-ass jheri curl that ran down the middle of his back? The nigga wallet used to be soaked with activator juice."

Who didn't have a curl in 1985? Huh?

But anyway . . . after five minutes of laughing at my curl:

"But look you now, ole high-yellow-ass-nigga, you made out all right. Hand me a beer."

Calvin and 'em will be here within an hour—loud and hungry.

We also expected Telly to be here by now, but the first part of his day was spent by Erica's family. Dude sounded frustrated as hell when I spoke with him on the phone a few minutes ago. Even though I've given Telly the Three C's lecture many times before, my words have always entered into one ear then left out the other—but not today. I actually felt as if I made a breakthrough this afternoon. He was still annoyed at having to hang out with Erica's mom, but at least he was receptive.

"Telly, at this level of life you have to be willing to *commit* to Erica, *care* about the things that are sensitive to Erica, and be willing to *compromise*." Today marks the two-hundredth time we've had this conversation.

"Yeah, yeah, yeah, I hear all that Dr. Phil bullshit, but I'm with her on a holiday that I would prefer to play *Madden* until my fingers swell up. This is the *compromise,* Uncle Glenn."

"Lose the attitude and stop acting like a puss . . . boy, I almost called you a pussy, but I like pussy. Stop acting as if you're doing Erica a favor by spending time with her on a holiday—that's what families do."

"But I don't." I could tell he was covering his mouth as he spoke into the phone. "I hate holidays; I've always have. Not Erica—she goes overboard on every holiday. The Christmas spirit for her kicks in the day after Halloween. I don't do Christmas. The fact that I'm here today is proof that I am *compromising.* I promise, as soon as I drop them off at home, I'm headed there to get a game in before my meeting with Megyn in my Honeycomb Hideout."

"Telly, you haven't given up that apartment yet?"

"Fuuuuuuck no."

"Bye Telly." I hung up. I don't have time for his shit today. He gon' learn the hard way.

I don't get him—how he can be so hardheaded and take so many risks. Telly loves fucking up, and he loves slinging dick. That's what he is: a habitual dickslinger.

"Who dat slinging dick?" Biyell asked.

"Who do you think?"

"Crowd Noise still fucking over Erica, huh?"

"Fucking her over something awful." I seasoned a second pan of leg quarters and handed it off to Biyell to carry to the back patio. "I've never met her but from everything he has described, I don't understand why he wouldn't take this ripe time to settle his ass down. Erica sounds like the perfect woman to marry. How much extra pussy does one man need?"

"I plead the fifth."

"Jailbird, you better plead the fifth after that brick to the face!" Jarvis laughed as he arrived and hung his laptop bag across the back of a kitchen chair. "By the way, how many of those punks you fucked in jail for a pack of Camels?"

"Nigga, fuck you, I was only in jail for a week, but I wouldn't fuck a dude if were in the bitch for life."

"I hear you, but the word on the street is—"

"Ain't no word on no motherfucking street about me!" Biyell dragged his hoof like a bull that just saw red. "My love of pussy is ninety-four percent of my problems in life. You think I would be dressed like this if I were gay? Gay dudes have something I don't have, because of pussy."

"And what's that?" we asked.

"EXTRA MONEY! Nice rides and shit, while the pussy-loving niggas like us ducking child support, broke as fuck, looking like those Feed the Children videos that always seem to come on once you sit down with a plate of red beans and chicken. The video with the African fanning flies, hungry as hell, but still fucking. Flies hanging around the pussy like a liquor store, but still fucking, with dirty children in the commercial, but still fucking." Biyell powered up the PlayStation. "That's all I'm saying."

"Dude said flies hanging around the pussy like a liquor store . . ." Jarvis folded over in laughter.

"That's all I'm saying—if I were gay, I wouldn't have to wear cable clothes on my off day. Look at me."

Yep, he wears COX Cable or Direct TV shirts every day. Now that I think about it, in five years, I don't remember ever seeing Biyell in anything else but cable clothes. I'm just happy he's out of jail and coming back to life. I was worried about him. The first few days out of jail, he only requested one job each day, and after that job, he would ring my phone. Ten minutes later, he would be on my sofa. Biyell gets paid by the job and has always bitched about not getting a 'good route,' whatever in the fuck that means, but lately he's been in a purple haze. It's a bit better now than it was, but he's still here a lot.

Diana thinks he doesn't know what to do with himself since GiGi and Tamera have stepped off. His life was centered around juggling two women. All the balls have dropped. He's lost.

Your friend is here every day because he has a fear of being alone, Diana concluded.

"What time's Telly coming through?" Jarvis asked. "And where the fuck has Rasta been? I haven't seen that dude in forever."

"Yeah, now that you mention it, where is Rasta?" Biyell piped in.

I thought fast. "Rasta is taking some time this summer to hang out with his kids. He was on a recruiting visit with his oldest, and then he decided to take the younger boys on a road trip. He just needs some time away after all the bullshit."

"Understandable," Jarvis said. "I hope he gets back soon, though. *Madden* isn't the same without him."

Biyell nodded his agreement.

"As far as Telly," I continued, relieved I didn't have to explain further about Rasta, "he said he'll be here after he drops off Erica and the girls. He's all whiny and shit because he has to hang out with her on a holiday. I explained to him that holidays are for family—those special days when you leave all cares behind and enjoy each other—but not that knucklehead. He's still pissed they spent Christmas together," I told them.

"*Shiddddd*, I'm with him on that Christmas bullshit." Biyell paused the game just as he kicked the ball off.

"WHAT THE FUCK, BIYELL?!" Jarvis hates when the game is paused when he's about to get the ball. "PRESS THE FUCKIN' BUTTON!"

"Nigga, hold up one second, I have to testify to what *Unc talking bout.*"

"Jailbird-ass niggas always trying to run shit . . ." Jarvis continued to roast.

"Fuck you, Jarvis . . . nigga teeth big like Steve Harvey. But anyway, I'm with Telly on hating Christmas—that entire month stresses me the fuck out every year."

"That's because you were lying to Tamera about working in Jackson, Mississippi while sleeping with GiGi the Seventh Ward by your sister. You should have been stressed the fuck out." I wrapped a pan of moist honey barbecue ribs in foil. "Having bitches and Christmas don't go together. Christmas is mandatory attendance—and a player can't be everywhere."

As I spoke, I watched Jarvis step four paces away from the television; it appeared he was checking his voicemail. Afterward, he cuffed a text in the palm of his hand, as if we could read it from across the room. But that's how drama always kicks off—one minute we're having a good time, then comes a text, then that distracted look, then bewilderment, and finally anger. But not this time—the final stage today was something I'd never witnessed before in my living room. Out of my stereo, Frankie Beverly wished us "Happy Feelings," but I had to cut the song short. We had a man down.

Literally.

Something on Jarvis's phone caused his knees to give out, and he went down like a toilet seat. Worried, Biyell immediately went down with him as I hopped toward the window. His face was like a smashed tomato—tragic and emotional, but silent. His mouth wore that silent cry, the cry you made when you were a kid and Momma landed that leather belt precisely on the tender area of your thigh—silent like someone pressed a mute button on his throat. Jarvis balled in a fetal position against the wall with Biyell in a full panic, as if someone had shot our buddy in the chest. Biyell repeatedly asked, *what's wrong, bruh?* But received no reply.

When I finally made it over to Jarvis, his phone was face-down on the carpet behind him. When I opened it, I nearly fell next to him.

It was a text and a picture from Briana. That was it.

Today I threw a baby shower for myself. I understand why you didn't come. Just wanted you to know.

The picture that was attached ripped through me for the same reasons it ripped through my Madden Brother.

A selfie of Briana at a table alone holding a copy of Jarvis's book.

A glittery blue sash across her chest read *Future Mommy.*

A framed picture of her and Jarvis stood on the right.

A box of Pampers and a jar of baby powder.

A Build-a-Bear in a red shirt.

An embroidered name: *Jarvis Napoleon, Jr.*

An empty smile.

A vacant face.

Jarvis finally managed to locate that mute button on his throat, and the sound that reverberated was foreign and distorted, but we were able to decipher. It was then that I fully understood what had just sliced into him: the aftermath of infidelity. An innocent child. An abandoned mother he never intended to marry. A lie that refused to remain a lie. An ideal husband no more. A demotion to baby daddy status. A coat of shame every time someone would ask, *how many kids you have?* capped under a houndstooth fedora of humiliation with each explanation. He finally spoke, and I was sorry he did.

"When our game was starting, I missed a call from my mother." Biyell sat Jarvis upright, and his voice sniffled between each word. "When I listened to the message, it was so hard to hear, but I played it over and over, because I deserve every word. She said . . . she said, *Jarvis, I still love you because you're my only child. I raised you by myself and did the best I could, but I didn't raise you to become who you are. Before God calls me home, you owe it to all the women involved to make this right. You've hurt all of us . . . and I'm so disappointed in you, Jarvis.*"

That was the first time Jarvis's mother had spoken to him since she heard about that day in Dallas.

CHAPTER 12

Monday, July 24, 2017
8:36 a.m.

RASTA

It's been four days since I had a roommate and the peace has been wonderful. Having a room to myself still doesn't pacify my anxiety to get out of here, especially considering this week will make two months and my discharge is nowhere in sight, but it's a small consolation. My mom, Uncle Glenn, and Aunt Diana have been visiting at least once a week since I got here, and Telly's been visiting recently when he gets a break in the afternoons. It's great to see them when they're here, but no one has any information for me on when I can get back out there. Apparently the doctor has been telling them the same thing he's been telling me: I'm just not ready yet.

Last Sunday, Amanda's farting ass was moved next door. She would fart all night then wake up in the morning like no crime was committed. I never mentioned it to her because it occurred during the night, but my God I'm happy she's next door. But that's my girl. For the first time, I've developed a friendship with a woman without trying to separate her from her panties. Of course, this would've been difficult with Amanda because she doesn't sleep in panties . . . that's all I'm saying about that—keep it moving.

Amanda has a new roommate name Ashanti, who walks around all day and night like a hitchhiker. Since seven-thirty, she's passed my door eight times. She paces back and forth, searching for signs of life in my room; if she detects the slightest movement, then she floats in here. She's about twenty-five years old. Amanda says Ashanti has a mad crush on me and believes she can make me forget all about LaDeisha because she has "that *good-good*." I don't need her *good-good*, I need *out-out* of this hospital prison.

There she goes past my door again.

Ashanti reminds me of the singer Brandy Norwood during the *Moesha* years. She even wears her hair in braids like Brandy, but she's no singer, she's a lover. Watching her dreamy eyes every time I say hello makes me think of the way Jarvis described Briana, but where I differ from Jarvis is I never allow myself to think a single thought about Ashanti. To add to that, I'm attracted to grown women, who look grown—not teen-pop girls like Ashanti.

For fifteen minutes, I watched her tick-tock in front of my door as I pretended to be sound asleep. Since I'm still considered a Category Five suicide patient, I'm not allowed to lock my door. Yesterday, I didn't even get a chance to brush my teeth before Ashanti walked into my room wearing nothing but a onesie like Beyoncé. I can hear Biyell's voice right now:

"*Nigga, we don't want to hear all that—how was the pussy?*"

"I never touched her."

"*Bitch walking around in a onesie, bitch in the bunk bed next to you butt-ass naked with no drawls and you didn't fuck one of them? Not one? Boy, LaDeisha put the voodoo pussy on you as sure as I's black.*"

Amanda thinks Ashanti's crush on me is cute.

She told me they've developed a real sisterhood in a very short period of time. I hear them over there, late at night, giggling and gossiping about who's fucking who on this floor.

Apparently, there's a lot of patient-on-patient sex, but that's none of my business. And don't get me wrong, having Ashanti and Amanda to converse with has helped numb the pain of this place, but remember what I said about this facility: the people in here are here for valid reasons. I discovered Ashanti's yesterday; I'd just entered the dining hall for breakfast, hungry for a bowl of cereal, anxious to watch the NFL Network and scout my *Madden* team for the August release.

I wasn't at my table a minute when Ashanti materialized across from me, directly in my line of sight. Her T-shirt was extra tight and her yoga pants were painted on her body—she has a body like the singer Pink, that fact is too obvious to ignore. In her lips, I saw my reflection. In her eyes, I saw her mission.

"Hi, Roderick." She held my name for a whole note.

"Good morning, Ashanti."

"*Guessss whhhhat?*" she sang the question.

"What is it, Ashanti?" my eyes looked above her.

"*You have to guesssss . . .*" She peeled a banana, then formed her lips around the tip.

"You're going home today?"

"Nope, guess again."

"That's all I got . . ."

"Try again, it'll be worth it."

I had to play along—she wasn't leaving—so I leaned back in my chair with my fingers interlocked behind my bald scalp.

"Let's see, you and Amanda finally got the dance moves correct for Janet Jackson's 'Pleasure Principle'?"

Ashanti blushed. "You heard us?"

"All night," I revealed. "So tell me—what is it?"

"I had a dream about you last night."

"Really? I didn't know you slept like the rest of us humans."

"I do, and I have dreams, and last night my dream was about you."

"Ashanti, I'm flattered."

How dare she disturb me this morning? After all, I was the one who found the remote buried deep in the sofa and saved us from *Petticoat Junction.* That morning, the NFL Network was featuring my New Orleans rookie draft preview—this was my alone time to connect with the outside world, until Ashanti decided to interrupt. Directly over the peak of her braids, commentator Deion Sanders was explaining the Saints rookies to watch, but Ashanti blocked my line of sight like cataracts.

"Aren't you wondering what the dream was about?"

I conceded. "Please tell me." The dream was always the same.

"We were walking in the park, and you were holding my hand. You kissed me." She shared this same dream twice last week.

"Ashanti, that sounds like a really nice dream, but I'm old enough to be your daddy."

"What are you?" Her cat eyes squinted as she studied my face. "About thirty-two?"

"Thanks for the compliment, but I'll be forty in a few weeks, and I'm hoping to celebrate my birthday far away from here."

"Or we can celebrate it together before you leave? Every night?"

"Ashanti, how old are you?"

"Old enough."

"For real, how old are you?"

"I'm twenty-eight."

"Not eighteen?"

"I wish, but seriously, I'm twenty-eight and single. And a little birdie told me you're single?"

"I am, but only if you were a little older, like those two ladies who visited you—"

"My older sisters?"

"Yes, now they appear more my age."

"Even though I can do this?" In went the banana, all the way to her fingertips. Then she slowly pulled it out of her mouth.

"Not happening, Ashanti, but thank you for the compliment."

It was then that Ashanti appeared to take a ten-second nap. I wrote it off as sleep deprivation finally catching up to her and Amanda. But she wasn't sleepy; she was Ashanti, a regular patient of the West Jeff Behavioral Medicine Center. When she snapped out of her nap, Ashanti's face looked different—slightly disfigured with an unfamiliar frown. In real time, her muscles realigned and readjusted. Even the way her eyes moved in their sockets was noticeably different—slower. Her total disposition was different. Her new movements were more mechanical and stiff. Then she began to speak to me in a deep, rough voice, in a way that was instantly uncomfortable.

"Psst, pssst," she gestured for me to lean across the table. "I just got out the hole, how many more of us around here?"

"What?" I asked, confused.

"The hole, nigga. I been down sixty days for contraband, but fuck that charge, ya heard me? How many of us on this tier?"

"How many of us? What are you talking about?"

"You know?" she pointed at the back of her hand.

"Hmm . . . black people?" I took a swing at it.

"Yes, how many more?"

"Right now we're the only two, but Marcel will be here this weekend. Why?"

"You talkin' bout Big Marcel, with sexy panties?" Her arms extended apart in measurement.

"I don't know about all that, but yes, that Marcel."

"Fuck, we needed Marcel. You look a little light in the ass, but you'll have to do."

"For what?"

"If we're gonna make a break for it . . ." Ashanti looked both ways as if the feds were listening in. "The plan is set. Peep this, and we have to stick together. It's us against them."

"Ashanti, what are you talking about?"

"Why do people keep calling me Ashanti? The name is Alton. *Al-ton.* Got it?"

"Okay, Alton. Yeah, I got it."

"I counted two guards, but it's easy to catch them slipping. I will shank that broad at the desk, and you handle up on that bald-head nigga."

"Who, Phillip?"

"Yeah, Phillip, put him down quietly. We don't want to attract no attention when we break out of this bitch. Don't forget what we discussed."

"Got it, but just to make sure I'm clear, run it by me again." My cornflakes were soggy by this point because Ashanti—or shall I say *Alton*—had my undivided attention.

"*Slash then keys, nigga. Slash then keys.*" Her thumb slid from right to left across her neck. "Slash Phillip's throat then get the keys. After that, meet me at the end of the hall. You follow?"

"Yeah, I follow," I lied again.

"What's your name again?"

"Roderick, but they call me Rasta."

"Rasta? You got that blow?"

"I used to . . ."

"I get it, I get it, don't want to say too much in here because niggas hoes too—that's how I ended up in the hole. Had my bitch roll through with a few grams in the pussy, and one of these snitching-ass niggas got my lady popped on my charge."

I couldn't believe this was once Ashanti, just ten minutes ago.

"But back to the plan—*slash and grab*. It's our last chance— they got me down for sixty years on another robbery charge, talkin' bout I was the getaway driver. I saw my nigga Skeet Skeet at the bus stop and offered him a ride. Black DA worse than them white folk . . . that hoe! But anyway, I'm bout to give this time back because we bout to bounce out this motherfucka, ya heard me?"

Deep down I was amazed and laughing my ass off. "I heard ya, we have to stick together."

After Alton recapped the plan, he extended his fist for a bump, which turned into a grip shake, then another type of handshake I've only seen wannabe gang members complete seconds before a drive-by shooting. In her/his mind, this other person she called Alton was in prison and planning to make an escape, with my assistance.

I turned to look behind me at the nurses' station. DeShonta was bent like a folding chair in laughter. When I turned back to Alton, he didn't find it amusing.

"That's how it's gonna happen to that bitch over there. She's always cheesing in your face, but she gon' learn—it ain't no fun if the homies can't have none."

"Wait, what did you say?"

"That lil' thot DeShonta, at that nurses' station. I be checking her teething all in your face, even though I tried to holla at the bitch. She was all stuck up. I was like, fuck you then, funky acting hoe."

"Not DeShonta? She's sweet potato pie to me."

"I know, so peep this." Alton flicked his finger for me to lean across the table again. "Let's run a train on that hoe."

"Wait, what the fuck you just say?"

"Peep this, the bitch like you, right?" I nodded, just enough to hear the rest of this felony charge. "Let's drag her in your room, shut the door, and run a train on that bitch. I'll look out for you first, then you look out for me. And don't nut all in the pussy, ya heard me? Nigga don't rock like that. I've wanted to hit that for two years. You down?"

"Sure, I'm down, but look at the time, Ashan . . . I mean Alton. I'm late for my session with Dr. Morton. Let's pick this up later. Don't run that train on her without me, my nigga."

"As long as you don't snitch me out. The last snitch was ass up in a ditch. Ya heard me?"

"Yeah, I heard you."

"Then repeat after me: a snitch was ass up in a ditch." We said it together and did the gang handshake again.

On my way back to my room, I paid a visit to the nurses' desk.

"How are things going with you and Ashanti?" DeShonta asked, clearly amused.

"DeeDee, who in the fuck is Alton?"

"Just some convict who's been planning to shank Phillip and rape me for well over a year now."

"I think the gang rape is scheduled right before lunch. We're dragging you in my room."

DeShonta's eyes were soaked from laughter. "A gang rape with you around lunch? *Don't threaten me with a good time.*" She slapped the desk. "Dammit, I knew I should have worn my cute panties."

"Well I think she's serious. If I were you, I would watch my back and my front. Alton has it out for you."

"How about you watch my back?" DeShonta sashayed seductively to the front of the nurses' station. "Watch this; come with me." She walked back over to my breakfast table.

"*A-YO, Alton,* I heard you have a beef with me. A tier rep at the House of Detention told me I better stay strapped. Heard you planning to shoot up my momma's house in the Lower Nine. If it's on yo chest like that, we can go right now." DeShonta clapped her fist in her hand.

"Looka here, looka Lil Round, I don't have a beef with you; I'm tryin' to do my time in peace, ya heard me?"

"That ain't what I heard out on the street; they told me you were looking for me. Let's go, jump stupid."

"Look, Lil Round, niggas trying to kick shit off between us so they can move in on our set while we squeezing at each other. I'm not tryin' to catch no new charges, so you go your way, and I'll go mine."

"I thought so, and you better keep my name out your mouth." DeShonta laughed her way back to the nurses' station.

When I made eye contact with Alton, he mouthed out a threat

at me.

"*I knew you was a snitch, imma catch yo ass a Zulu Parade.*" Another throat slice with his thumb.

Back at the nurses' station, DeShonta grabbed a log book for Ashanti that was thick as two old Yellow Pages phonebooks. Unlike our progress logs, this book was divided into a front section for Ashanti and a back section for Alton. She flipped through endless pages of comments that dated back nearly three years until she finally landed on the blank section for this month.

"Ashanti has multiple personalities?" I asked.

"Dissociative identity disorder, and luckily for us, we're only dealing with one additional personality."

"What was the worst case?"

"When I first started here about six years ago, there was a five-personality patient, and we had to document each one! I was so happy when they transferred that little white girl out of here. Lord Jesus, she was a handful—and dangerous. Alton makes threats and plots, but Flower Child had to be monitored twenty-four hours a day. She actually had a few murder charges."

"A few murder charges! Where is she now?"

"Last I heard they moved her up to Shreveport after our budget was sliced. I also lost four coworkers as a result of that same funding crisis. That leaves six of us to do the work of ten. Thank God we have guests coming in a couple weeks who might get us the funding we need."

"Yeah, that's the presentation I'm a part of with Dr. Morton—"

DeShonta smiled at me with appreciative eyes. "If no one has said it then I'll go first—thank you for sharing your story. It's rare to have patients like you who can coherently communicate what we do here and how underfunded we really are."

"Since you're so appreciative, can I lock my door at night?"

"Hell no," she chuckled. "Only with me will that door lock." She winked.

From down the corridor, I saw Phillip's cock-blocking ass headed in our direction. Every time I try to make a serious move on DeShonta, here he comes, walking on tip-toes like a three-year-old. On some days I think she's serious about me, and on other days I think she's bored and I'm the only normal dude around besides Phillip. Do I think she would fuck me? Not while I'm here, but once I'm out—game on.

"Looks like it's time for my session; come see me before you clock out." I returned the wink.

"Umm, Mr. Ross, where do you think you're going?" Both hands rested on her curvaceous hips. "You can't leave until you fix what you broke." She pointed at Alton, who was Crip-walking in the middle of the floor singing Bone Thugs-N-Harmony.

"See you at the crossroads so you won't be lonely, so you won't be lonely . . ."

"You have to fix that," DeShonta gave me an amused smile.

"But I didn't break her."

"Yes, you did."

"How?"

"She came on to you, flirted hard at you, even offered to suck you off, and you rejected her. That's the trigger."

"Wait, run that by me again?"

"Whenever Ashanti is rejected, Alton comes out to provide protection. Think of Alton as a bodyguard. The only way to get Alton back in the bottle is to make Ashanti feel pretty and wanted. So I need you to go back over there and flirt with her."

"You're kidding, right?"

"Mr. Ross, it's either you bring back Ashanti, or Alton will be your cellmate. The choice is yours. But I can't put Alton in Amanda's room because Alton is a thirty-five-year-old man who would try to hump Amanda with a cell-made dildo."

I burst into laughter. "A dildo?"

"Oh you think it's a joke, huh? We caught Alton one time

about to insert this big-ass thing in this girl—it looked like a roll of salami from the meat market, and the girl was lying there spread-eagle ready. I got there just in time. Our Alton was going to break her off—literally."

"Alton thinks he has a dick?"

She flicked me away with her wrist. "In his mind, he does— and that's the part only you can fix."

"And it can only be the person who rejected her," Phillip smirked. "Only you can bring back Ashanti." Like Siamese twins, DeShonta and Phillip said, "You broke it, you taking it home with you."

"Fuck . . ." I grimaced.

"And you are fucked if you don't get Ashanti back here ASAP," Phillip chuckled. "Either go holler at her or Alton sleeps with you."

That wasn't happening, so I walked over to Alton and tried to get his attention, but he was distracted

"This is tha Carter muthafucka, yeah, yeah, yeah, yeah this is tha Carter, yeah . . ."

The song was from *Tha Carter* album, the one we listened to every Madden Night. Alton knew every word; even the hook was perfect. In an instant, I was back at Uncle Glenn's house with a pound of weed in the middle of the coffee table, surrounded by my dawgs. Laughing, sharing, hugging, fighting, loving each other through the difficult days of life. We were figuring out life as we lived it; no handbook, no point of reference, no daddys, only a father figure in the form of Uncle Glenn. Man, I missed my dawgs. It's like Alton was in my head.

An' I ain't got time to speak the history
I miss you an' I know you missin' me, gizzle but
Man, I miss my dawgs
Many nights, club hopping
Many nights we were blowin' trees
Many nights we were hustlin'

Man, I miss my dawgs
—Lil Wayne, "I Miss My Dawgs"

The place Alton took me to was so peaceful, so healing—I didn't want to bring back Ashanti.

Then Alton paused. "Hey lil' whoedie, you play spades?"

I pointed to myself.

"Yeah you . . . lil' whoedie, you play spades?"

"Yeah, I play."

"Where the cards at? Let's slap some spades."

"I'll get the cards later, after dinner."

"Then it's going to be me and you versus bitch-ass Phillip and that fine-ass thot DeShonta. Bring about three packs of Ramen noodles, and I got three. But we ain't losing shit, you heard me? We gon' flip that into twelve packs and split it. Ya heard me?"

"I heard you," I told him, but I'm thinking, *I could really chill with Alton; he reminds me of Crowd Noise.*

"*Yeah, yeah, yeah, damn I miss my dawgs, many nights club poppin', many nights we were blowing trees, many nights we were hustling . . . I miss my dawgs.*"

I half-turned to the nurses' station and saw Phillip pointing at his watch. DeShonta's arms were tucked tight across her chest. It was time to bring back Ashanti.

"Excuse me, Ashanti, I know you get this all the time, but wow, you're beautiful."

"*Nigga, what did you call me?*" Alton's face booted up tight as his hands formed into bricks.

At this point I'm thinking DeShonta and Phillip pranked me, but I continued.

"Ashanti, a little birdie told me you were single, and if so, I want to hold your hand and take you for a walk. A woman like you should have a man like me—someone who feels you are the most beautiful girl in the world. Can I hold your hand while we take a long walk?"

"Hold my hand? Dude, I don't rock like that, nigga!" Alton grabbed me by the collar and bull rushed me into the wall. Jammed against the wall, I looked over at DeShonta for instruction, but she replied with another flick of her wrist.

"It's just . . . you're so beautiful—you are the prettiest girl I've seen in here." I was distracted again by DeShonta.

"What do you mean, *the prettiest*? Ummm, hello!" DeShonta whipped her hair.

When I turned back to Alton, his eyes were closed. After about ten seconds, she spoke.

"I-I think you're pretty handsome too." She was soft and cute again. "I would love to take a walk with you," Ashanti said as she released my collar with a soft strawberry kiss on my lips.

"Sounds like we have a date right after my session."

"I'll wait for you," she said in an airy voice.

"See you in an hour."

"I know a place where we can be alone," Ashanti licked her lips.

"I look forward to it."

As I walked back to the station, Phillip and DeShonta struggled to keep the laughter inside.

"How will I get out of that?" I asked them.

"That's for you to figure out," DeShonta chuckled, "You never shot game at a woman, then had to let her down softly? So do it again, but cautiously—or Alton will come back and shank your ass."

As Phillip and I were getting ready to head over to Dr. Morton's office, Ashanti ran over and gave me another huge hug, then whispered in my ear.

"When you're done with Dr. Morton, I'll be in your bathroom waiting."

CHAPTER 13

Madden Thursday
August 3, 2017
9:05 a.m.

BIYELL

I knew she would come through for me; deep down I had that feeling. If I knew a year ago what I know now, I would have submitted GiGi's name to Uncle Glenn and would have long since divorced Tamera. That bitch was never down for me, she just used me to get her degree—but it's cool because I'm about to go the distance with GiGi. I'm not letting it end on this note. As soon as this divorce is final today, I'm going to Baker. I'm going to get my woman.

Called her all day yesterday, and every call went to voicemail, but that's understandable.

I saw those pictures.

I lost my head.

I did.

Those pictures of Tamera sucking that nigga's dick—they

hurt so bad. I try, but I can't get over that image; it's branded on my brain. She had this dude's dick in her mouth; her eyes were closed and she sucked it like it was delicious. Slob was everywhere. To her, maybe it was delicious. I never ran at her with a sweaty dick to suck—I would hop fresh out the shower, only to have her frown at my dick like burnt chitterlings. I didn't even know she could suck a dick like that. What was it about Mike that made him able to bring out that side of my wife? How was he able to get her to do something that she refused to do for her husband?

In the two minutes it took me to scroll through her phone, I was introduced to a woman I had never known. How was he able to release that freak in her?

I can't get it out of my head. I need to know, but I will never know. Now that I think about it, Tamera never really fucked me the right way—it was always me fucking her. I didn't get fucked the right way until GiGi. Sure, I've been with other women, but there were no feelings involved. The first real time I encountered intimacy and sex was with GiGi.

Why did I pick Tamera over her? That's right—Tamera had seniority. That's all.

Years married are worth about as much as a bucket of piss if the marriage is a fraud. A dude with a Mississippi license plate called *Big Mike* quickly proved I didn't mean shit to Tamera. But it's cool, she didn't have to suck my dick. I'll have GiGi to handle all dick-sucking duties, because I still have good dick.

Mike's dick has me beat by three inches at least, but my dick is still a nice size. But his shit appeared fatter than mine. I'm like a for sure nine-incher, but she held about seven inches in her hand with about five more inches in her mouth.

That bitch.

Why am I thinking about this all day?

Those pictures fucked me up, for real.

Mike is getting it all. From *week one* she gave him everything. And it's not just about a good dick sucking, it's the symbolism.

It's the principle—it's the fact that she felt he was more deserving of her inner hoe, but gave me the dry church pussy. I hate the dry church pussy. I hate to sound like *Waiting to Exhale*, but long before GiGI, I was the one helping Tamera get on her feet. I was the one putting in the twelve-hour days for Tamera. I was the one who kept us afloat when she needed to cut back on her hours to finish school, the one who kept her in a new car because she had a 480 credit score.

But she gave him the inner hoe and gave me this fake-ass church bitch.

I'm no angel, but if Tamera would have given me what she gave Mike in Week One, I wouldn't have needed so much outside lovin'. I wouldn't have needed the validation from other women if she had given me what she gave Mike. Would there even be a GiGi if my wife was the same nasty bitch I saw in those pictures? Anyway, it's over now. Today we're here to see the judge to end this marriage.

I told lies and Tamera was a lie.

The only thing I've lost is time.

Fuck it.

Tamera was a rent-to-own wife, and I missed a few payments—she's getting repo-ed today.

But why isn't Gigi answering this phone call? Glenn told me Tamera called GiGi and had a long conversation with her while I was in jail without bail—that's how evil that bitch is. She has a whole nigga in the bed with her every night and is still calling my lady trying to fuck my shit up in Baker.

That's why I had a dream last night where I ran over her ass with a streetcar.

Look at those two, seated over there like they've been together for twenty years. She probably just finished sucking his dick in the parking lot.

That bitch.

I warned the fellas the other night at Uncle Glenn's house—
If you think your woman is cheating, just end it, but whatever

you do, don't break into her phone. What she's giving you is not what she's giving him. You're not ready to meet her inner hoe for the first time on another dude's dick. But it's all my fault because I should have listened to my mama. She told me:

"Don't marry that girl."

Whenever your mom says *don't marry her*, you better listen. My mom detected something in Tamera that threw up a red flag. My mama said it:

"Tamera is going to use your ass like a Walmart gift card and toss you."

After Tamera made her come-up, that is exactly what she did. If she would have discovered GiGi prior to getting her degree, then GiGi would have been just a country chick who stole some dick. Tamera would have still been with me, faking she was happy—but today I'm taking away all power she has over my emotions. That's what sitting five days in jail, in the same clothes, with no bath, has taught me.

Never give a woman a reason to call the cops, especially if it's over another man. Walk away.

That's what I should have done, but I lost it, and she got the win. These past weeks have been filled with losses, but I've taken my *last L*, ya heard me? Here comes Telly from the judge's chambers—time to see what the gold digger asking for.

"How much does she want?" I cut to the reason we were here.

Telly shook his head left to right. "I'm fighting off $950."

"For one child?"

"I figured she would come in high then we would work it down from there."

"Telly, $950 is a very familiar number; that's car note, insurance, and cell phone."

"I figured that much. I told the judge that amount was out of guidelines with your salary, and your total number of kids.

I countered with $550 per month. I told her lawyer that the car is in your name and you would like her to return it as soon as possible. We'll have a ruling on that section and visitation when the judge takes the bench."

Suddenly I felt a pluck behind my head, and it made my day.

"I heard a dude was pimping you out in jail for a pack of Camels," Jarvis whispered.

"You heard wrong, it was a pack of Kool Filter Kings." We dapped and embraced. "Your court date is today too?" I asked as we stepped out into the hall.

"It was originally, but Monica's lawyer asked for a reschedule until November, which is cool with me. How much she got you for?"

"She's trying to get $950."

"Nine-fifty?! Ain't that much cable in New Orleans to pay $950 for one child."

"That's what I said."

It was then that Telly exited the courtroom all teeth on a call. He continued past us about twenty feet away.

"From that smile on Telly's face, things might go your way," Jarvis encouraged.

"You're forgetting that's Telly. If he's smiling that much on the phone, it doesn't have shit to do with me and everything to do with Megyn."

After about five minutes of Cheshire-cat grinning on my time, Telly ended his call and joined our huddle.

"Jarvis you're free to go, your new date is November 17."

"Did they say why we were rescheduled?"

"Yes, apparently Monica is in the hospital in Atlanta. It would probably be a goodwill gesture to call and check on her, or better yet, just send some flowers and candy."

Jarvis went from sunny to approaching storm all within five

seconds. I could tell he still loved Monica, and it was destroying him that he was out of her life. He backed out of the huddle with his phone to his ear. Shortly afterward, I heard him leave a voice message asking Symphony to call him. He continued to dial numbers one after the next, but no one answered.

"Man, I feel for my nigga—hate to see him go through this," Telly shook his head.

"If you don't take heed to what's happening—you're next," I warned.

"Dude, I'm not even in y'all category. Both of you clowns are married."

"Okay, just remember it's us today, you tomorrow. It catches up with you eventually, and I bet you a nickel to a muthafuckin'—you're next. And you're assed out like us . . . I ain't gon' feel sorry for you because I told you. Sit your ass down somewhere and chill."

"So you're Uncle Glenn, Jr. now?"

"Call me whatever makes you feel better, but you're next."

"I'm next? You two are in divorce court because you two niggas got caught trying to run weak-ass game. After I free you from this bullshit marriage you're in, I'm going fuck Megyn for the rest of the day, and I don't have to worry about Megyn calling Erica, because my shit is tight. I can teach you, but I have to charge." Telly started doing that ridiculous Q-Dog Omega Phi Pi dance.

"Still sprung out by that white girl I see?"

"Wait until you see her, then you will understand why we're off to Gulf Port right after court."

"I may be right behind you with GiGi," I said.

"Have you thanked GiGi yet?" Telly asked. "If it wasn't for her, your ass would still be on that concrete bench."

"I've called, but haven't reached her yet. I've been meaning to drive there to see her and my kids, but shit's been so hectic with catching up on work hours and this court date that it's been a while."

"Hmm, you haven't spoken with GiGi in how long?" Telly asked.

"I guess it's been a couple of weeks . . ."

"Nigga, don't come with the fuzzy math; it's been over a month. Sounds like you better find another chick for Gulf Port, because GiGi has quit your ass."

"I will get her back. Once this divorce is final in about an hour, I'm headed to Baker."

"You better head your ass back to work, if you know like I know," Telly suggested. "But if you're going out there, don't kick off no bullshit in Baker when you discover GiGi has moved on. I lost an entire week trying to get a bail reduction for you. I gave Judge Rant my word that this was a one-time occurrence, don't make me look stupid," Telly advised.

"No worries, but she's just angry. I will get her back on board tonight."

"Don't make me look stupid," Telly said again.

From inside the courtroom we heard the abrasive voice of the bailiff. The Judge was ready to take the bench, so we hurried back to our seats. After the bailiff made his announcement to turn off all cell phones, I couldn't help but notice Tamera powering down her phone—the phone with pictures of his dick all down her throat and her shirt drenched with saliva.

That bitch.

Our case was up first. On my way to the bench, Jarvis gave me a good luck handshake, but I wasn't going to need it, and he would soon know why.

The judge had an ash-gray afro and wore a no-nonsense expression like Mrs. Evans from *Good Times*. Her name was Judge Bernice Cain, and I could tell she took zero shit from the men who appeared before her. She was one of those stiff-neck judges who could make a grown man cry with the announcement of child support payments plus arrearage.

Tamera's lawyer was a young black chick with a face that pruned each time we made eye contact. Tamera sat on the side of her and never looked my way. The bitch knows she's wrong. I'm taking my lick for the failure of this marriage, but she should have to take her lick. She played a major role in our demise, and I believe she was cheating with Mike. I can't prove it, but I have that feeling.

"Attorney Ned, I have reviewed you client's tax returns and will rule as follows on the matter concerning child support. I'm awarding Tamera Baltimore $780 per month, which could increase to cover the cost of medical insurance should the custodial parent face a change in employment. The child support payments will conclude on the child's eighteenth birthday and are subject to periodic review in accordance with the rate of inflation. As it relates to visitation, all visits will be supervised for a total of thirty-six months, but visitation will not commence until Mr. Baltimore has undergone a mental evaluation. Attorney Ned do you have any additional comments?"

"Judge Cain, I don't have any additional comments, but my client would like to make a brief statement for the record."

"Objection, Your Honor, the ruling has been handed down," Tamera's attorney said.

"I will allow a two-minute statement to be entered into the public record."

That's when Telly whispered in my ear. "Dude, stay calm."

I cleared my throat. "Your Honor, I respect the ruling you've handed down and would like to say on record that I have never abused my wife nor have I abused my child. I did violate a restraining order and punched dude over there. I went to jail for that, and I take responsibility for my actions. The requirement that I have to take a mental evaluation just to see my child is the greatest insult to me as a parent. I ain't doing it. I protest this portion of your ruling because it has painted me as a child abuser."

"Stay calm . . ." Telly said again.

"I no longer want visitation rights. I no longer want any rights to my child. I am willing to pay the custodial parent the original amount of $950 a month until the child is eighteen, but I want both the custodial parent and the child out of my name today."

"Your Honor, may I have a second with my client, please?" Telly yelled.

"Mr. Baltimore, are you sure you want to waive your rights to visitation?" Judge Cain confirmed.

I turned to Telly. "Attorney Ned, this is my decision." Then I turned back to the judge. "Your Honor, that is correct. I will not be treated like an abusive parent when I have been the best father I could be to my daughter. With my other kids, I have full access to them as an equal parent, and those are the kids I will publicly acknowledge from today going forward."

I then reached into my suit jacket pocket and produced an envelope.

"I have come with a check in the amount of six thousand dollars, which is an advance payment toward my child support. Could you please ask the custodial parent if she accepts my offer and will remove my name from her daughter's birth certificate, with the new certificate stating *Unknown* for the father?"

Shock and awe erupted throughout the courtroom as the judge demanded silence. I know Tamera well enough to know she was hurt; she held her chest as if someone had punched her with a tight fist. I also know how money-hungry she is—and this was my way of showing the court what mattered most to the so-called custodial mother. Then her attorney spoke.

"Your Honor, my client will gladly accept the check from the father but has declined his offer to have the last name changed."

"Mrs. Baltimore, I can't order you to accept or decline in this matter, but his offer has been recorded on the official record. Therefore, I would like a resolution before we close out this divorce."

Her attorney whispered franticly in her ear while Tamera nodded.

"Your Honor, my client has accepted the offer and will have the child's name changed. She also accepts the defendant's offer to waive all parental rights to the child. My client also accepts the $950 a month payment."

"And *Unknown* must replace the father's name on the birth certificate," Telly confirmed.

After another brief consultation: "My client agrees to remove Biyell Baltimore from the birth certificate and replace it with *Unknown.*"

"Your Honor, if I may, my client has also requested that the vehicle Mrs. Baltimore currently drives is transferred out of her name and returned to him. Mr. Baltimore is willing to give her thirty days to return the vehicle."

"Your Honor, I object to my client losing her main source of transportation and ask that you include the vehicle as part of the property portion of the divorce," Tamera's lawyer countered.

Judge Cain read over the agreement for the car, then issued her ruling.

"As it relates to the vehicle, I am ruling in favor of the defendant because the car is not paid off, and Mr. Baltimore is still solely responsible for those payments. Your client was awarded more than enough money today to buy a car in her name. Also, Attorney Ned, once you have the paperwork prepared for the name changes, you can walk over to my chambers and I will sign it immediately. Attorney Ned, if you would approach with the check, that will conclude these proceedings."

After the gavel sounded, that was it—I was free. From the other side of the court came the sounds of weeping from Tamera; she was visibly shaken. Today I wanted to send a message loud and clear: If I can't pick my child up from daycare without a supervisor from the court, then I'm dead to this child . . . fuck it.

CHAPTER 14

Madden Thursday
10:15 a.m.

JARVIS

Uncle Glenn once told us there was something a little off about Biyell, but that was the understatement of the year. Dude's brain is on a different circuit, and today the entire court witnessed it. He strutted his ass out of here like he won a million-dollar judgment, pounding his chest like King Kong, but he just erased himself from his kid. *How could you, bruh?* It took Telly less than twenty minutes to draw up the paperwork to change Tamera's name from Baltimore to back to Willis; it's official. It took him even less time to change the baby's name. A court order carries a ton of weight.

Tamera's appearance was that of a woman who just left the funeral of a very close loved one—I mean tore up from the floor up. That was surprising to me at first. For most of the court session, she sat poised with an arrogant face, sporting a posture of absolute confidence, knowing the majority of the proceedings were fixed in her favor. She would have controlled the scheduling of the supervised visits and would've had a direct line to the judge the first time Biyell fell below her expectations. That was before Biyell removed himself from the equation.

She's emotionally devastated, and that's the win Biyell wanted. He knew having a child with an *Unknown* on her birth certificate was the best victory he could achieve, because when Tamera was a child, she was lost in the system with *Unknown* written on her birth certificate. She'd always hated it, and he knew it. If the goal of divorce court is to see who can fuck over the other spouse the most, then well played, my brother.

Mike had to hold Tamera upright as they left the courtroom. Biyell, as I said, just walked out of here content. In some ways, I can understand why Biyell would take that position—then, again, on the other hand, I can't. I couldn't have my child growing up without my name because of something that took place in court, but I can still understand his position. He was a great father. To require Biyell to undergo a series of mental evaluations and supervised visits was ridiculous. To be treated like a crackhead parent was some bullshit.

But that's how they treat us when we come to this court. The mother is automatically the custodial parent, even with the court knowing zero about what type of parent she was before they filed for divorce. The mother is automatically given the benefit of the doubt, as if ratchet hoes that leave their kids to watch themselves while they club-hop don't exist. You would think those examples are extinct, but they're out there—fucking over their kids while we're never given equal parenting rights.

But anyway.

I called anyone who I thought would answer the phone to get an update on Monica, but one answered. I pray she pulls through whatever this emergency is that has set her back. I do miss her tremendously. I also miss my kids. They refuse to accept my calls, but this morning Bri sent me a picture of her belly—she's showing bigtime. It's like this baby refuses to keep things on the low and is doing everything possible to make his presence known.

What is wrong with me?

Why not go be with her?

Because it's embarrassing.

Briana is embarrassing, this baby is embarrassing; to be with her would only add to the humiliation. But I will provide for her, and for the past four months I have gone to her apartment manager and paid her rent. But I can't be with her. To be with her would be confirmation that I am fucked up.

My skin is thin.

CHAPTER 15

Madden Thursday
7:55 p.m.

BIYELL

I'm on the road again to Parkwood Terrance subdivision in Baker, Louisiana. The skies have opened up, visibility is only about twenty feet, but driving through a storm is worth it for my GiGi. She's going to be so happy when she sees my divorce paperwork. She's going to want me inside of her all night. I know she misses me just as much as I miss her, and I'm fresh out of jail with rock-hard jail dick. We're getting it on like Marvin Gaye tonight. I wonder if I can talk her into wearing that wig?

If I don't get killed by a tornado first.

To my left, alongside the highway in Gonzales, Louisiana near the outlet mall, several cars have decided to pull over to the shoulder rather than brave the downpour and hail, but I'm not stopping. This rain is a representation of where I am in life right now: I'm in the middle of a storm, and I have to get to my woman.

GiGi still hasn't returned my text, but it's cool, I will thaw her out once I get to Baker.

Deep down, I have always known it was going to be GiGi in the end; she was always more down for me than Tamera. If I needed something done she would do it immediately; if I wanted something extra, she served it up on a platter. After what I've gone through with Tamera, I'm kicking myself in the ass that I didn't make this decision earlier. My marriage was stale, and Tamera knew it. We gave our lovers the hot shit and served each other the day-old bread.

Marriage licenses aren't worth the paper they're printed on. I feel like a marriage license should expire every six years with my driver's license unless we decide to renew. That *until death do us part* portion of the vows is bullshit. It shouldn't be until death does us part, it should be until *I no longer want to fuck with you* does us part.

No courts.

No lawyers.

No alimony.

Child support kiosk machine determines the payments.

My grandparents were together for seventy years, and every year for their anniversary, we would go to a church service in their honor and people would shower them with gifts and praise—but deep down, my grandmother hated his ass. Grandpa had a mistress with a whole family on the other side of town, complete with matching kids and grandkids. It wasn't even a secret anymore by that point. My grandmother knew, and she was mean as fuck; that's where I get it from.

At his funeral, his mistress and her set of kids weren't allowed to come. I felt so bad for Ms. Mable and how she was treated like garbage. My grandmother knew Grandpa loved her, but banning her and his other set of kids was done as retaliation. At the funeral, not a single tear fell for him; ushers were standing near in launch mode, and nothing. My grandmother sat there and nodded her head to a song only she could hear. Her resentment was like a cold fog that covered a swamp.

They were fucking miserable for sixty-five of those seventy years they were married, and the first five years he was at overseas at war. But as a couple they wanted that trophy—the one handed out at the end of life for enduring with someone you can't fucking stand—oh wait, there's no such trophy. If you ask me, I think Grandpa would have preferred to spend every day of his life with Ms. Mable. It's a shame he died married to the wrong person, even if that wrong person was my dear grandmother.

With Tamera, I was headed down the same path. I couldn't stand her five days out of the week, but she was the mother of my child, so I tolerated bad sex. Just based off the pussy she has given me over the last five years, if our marriage license was up for renewal yesterday, we would have still gone our separate ways today. But enough about the old—I'm free to marry GiGi, and that's what I plan to do.

Just as I was about to turn down her street, I saw a Baker Police car parked in front of her door.

Why is there a Baker Police car in front of her door?

I thought the warrant issue was resolved after it was proven that her mother lied? The last thing I need is another cop running my name through their system. They might create a charge and throw my ass back in jail.

The rain has reduced to just a drizzle. I decided to sit for a minute and wait. From this corner, I have a clear view of her house. Hopefully, he'll leave soon. I'm starving.

Suddenly, I received a text from Tamera; I knew how to hurt that bitch.

How could you be so cold blooded as to abandon your daughter?

My reply text was swift and razor sharp.

How could you sell your daughter's namesake for $182k? Materialistic bitch.

Yes, I added it up.

The cost to get rid of Tamera and her protective orders totaled $11,400 per year, minus the $6,000 advance I gave her today. It hurts that I will never see my child again, but she's young and will forget about me. If a nigga Tamera just met can be around my child unsupervised and with no mental evaluation, then fuck mother, child, and the entire fucking system. Delete me completely, and the three of you live happily ever after.

I've spoken on these matters.

Next.

Through my soaked windshield, I saw the cop exit GiGi's house and run through the rain to his vehicle. I waited for him to make the loop in the cul-de-sac, but he sat for a while. Then his brake light flashed, which was my clue that he just shifted his car into gear. Too impatient to wait until he had driven away completely, I turned down GiGi's street.

We came face to face, like the first passenger off the airplane and the first person in line to board. His eyes trespassed into my truck, and mine did the same into his patrol car. He was an African American cop who appeared around my age; I was expecting a Caucasian. He wore a white uniform shirt and drove an SUV unit. *I bet he's a supervisor.* His face was familiar.

Why was a supervisor from the Baker Police Department at GiGi's house?

His SUV snailed as if a magnetic force were preventing him from accelerating. *Why is he slowing down?*

Please don't pull me over.

Please don't turn around.

Please don't run my name.

Please, Lord.

In my rearview, I watched his brake light reflect off the soggy tar road. He came to a slow, rolling stop just as I came to a rolling stop in front of GiGi's home. Not until I exited my vehicle did he continue to the main road and make a left turn out of view.

Thank you, Lord!

I jogged through the drizzle to her door and attempted to unlock it with my trusted key, and that's when I noticed the brand-new doorknob and deadbolt. I knocked on the door for the first time in four years. Had she demoted me to a knocker? Were my key privileges revoked? When she gave me that key, it was in a card that read: *you have the key to my heart.*

GiGi came to the door with a huge smile that quickly turned flat; gleaming eyes that quickly faded to black. She didn't flinch to step aside. If I didn't know any better, I may have gotten the impression that she was trying to blink me away from her door.

"Were you expecting someone else?" I asked.

"The kids are at revival with my mother."

"Did I ask about the kids?"

"I assumed you were here to see them . . . ."

"And you."

She didn't reply. Her expression was as cold as the rain cascading off her roof.

"I can't come in?"

"No."

"Tyra, I just want to talk."

"I'm done talking."

"Tyra, just ten minutes."

"Not tonight."

"But you're not answering my calls. If not tonight, then when?"

"I'll call you when I'm ready to talk," she started to close the door.

I stopped the door with my foot. "Tyra, just ten minutes . . . please."

"Ten minutes and then you have to leave."

I walked past her and noticed that she didn't even bother to lock the door behind me; I could still hear the rain through the crack. I found a seat on the sofa. Tyra posted herself within arm's reach of the doorknob. Her face was empty like Monday morning church. Her arms twined into a knot. Her lips were glossy, but not for me.

A dog can smell a dog. I smell dog. Another dog has been here recently. He's pissed on my fence. He's marked my house as his house. Where are you? I can smell you—in here, on her.

She's trying to replace me.

"Tyra, I wanted to say thank you for getting that warrant cleared up. I would still be in jail if not for your actions."

"No need to thank me, it was the right thing to do."

"It was, and I appreciate it—a lot." From the sofa, I felt the heat from her exasperated sigh as her hip and head dipped to the left. "My divorce is final."

I approached her like a peasant standing before Cleopatra.

I offered her my divorce papers as if the sheets contained in the packet were silk garments from an undiscovered land far away. I handed them to her like a love offering, like a great sacrifice to my queen, but she didn't flinch. Her charcoal eyelashes were determined to blink me out of her life. Not even a congratulations. Not even a *that-a-boy.* Another band of storm clouds passed overhead, followed by the drum section from heaven and the sound of the last of me dripping out of her heart.

I'm so stupid.

I thought she would greet my divorce as the greatest news ever, but her cheeks were motionless, as if I'd just made a comment about the rain, or traffic in Baton Rouge, or described a sad video I watched on Twitter. But I have to tell her how I feel and what I want, and the plans I've made for our family.

"Tyra, it's written all over your face—you've tapped out on me, but hear me out. I want us to be a family, a real family. I know I caused you a great deal of heartache—"

GiGi placed her hand on the doorknob.

"Please . . . I know I fucked up, but all of that's over now. She's over now. There are no other children out there with my last name. I've even signed over my parental rights. And it's not that I don't love my child, but I know my temper and the stipulations to see my child would have landed me in jail every week. I'm not living like that. I want peace. I want to be here with you and my children every day . . . every night. I want to take care of you and love you the right way. It's just us—Biyell and Tyra. I know you're angry and disappointed, but I love you and came her to fight for you."

The door couldn't open any wider without smashing the wall.

"So just like that, you're kicking me out like I don't mean shit to you?"

"If you didn't mean shit to me, your ass would still be in jail."

"Then why handle me like this?"

"Like what, Biyell? Like what? Huh? Like I've had enough? Like I expected you to come here and say everything you've just said? Were you expecting me to jump into your arms because you finally became the lie you told? It appears you need a reminder of how we arrived at this point. You are a liar, who lied to get some pussy. That's all you are, and that's all you will ever be."

"Hold up, Tyra—"

"Hold up, my ass; you wanted to talk, so now we're talking." But she never closed the door. "Do you know what keeps me up sometimes? How I fell for it. I am so fucking angry with myself for not listening to the warrior inside of me who whispered every day, *Biyell is playing you*. I was scammed into a fake-ass relationship, with a fake-ass man who had a wife. When it comes to finding the right man, I fell for a Bernie Madoff; a man with a Ponzi scheme of bitches to replace the bitches he fucks over. That's all I was to you, so cut the shit."

After a blinding lightning strike, her voice lowered to a deep, blood-curdling rumble, like the drums up above. Then came another bolt.

"Our children are the same age. The same fucking age. Have you no decency? How fucking trifling are you? Over the past four years, I have gotten to know two Biyells: the lie and the truth. Fuck both of you."

"So, what are you saying?"

"I'll break it down a little bit more." Her face wore a smile that was unassociated with joy; only finality. "I'm saying you can see your children as much as you like—we can even split the month up the middle, two weeks with mommy and two weeks with daddy. I'm not putting you on child support to make you take care of the kids you made, and I'm not interested in this . . ." Her finger ping-ponged between us. "I don't give a fuck how divorced you are, those divorce papers are four years past due."

"Tyra, just hear me out right quick—"

"Biyell, there isn't anything you can say or do to change how I feel. I don't have any hard feelings toward you and I hope that we can have a great friendship for our kids, but other than that, this drama is over. *The end. Exit to the right. Watch your step.*"

"So you're not going to hear me out?"

"So you can say what? It was me you wanted the entire time? I was the reason you got the divorce? You loved me more than Tamera? What? Save all of that *game-ish* shit for the next naive bitch."

"Tyra, I'm not trying to run game—"

"Biyell, you are the Bob Barker of running game, but I'm not a consolation prize or a fuckin' vacuum cleaner. I am the grand prize: *A NEW CAR!*" She yelled like the announcer from *The Price is Right.*

Knowing all was lost, I turned to leave through a front door that appeared as wide as a garage. As I passed in front of her, she spoke.

"And another fuckin' thing: don't come to my house again without calling me first. We're clear?"

My body barely cleared the door when I felt it slam behind me. Then heard a loud *clack* from the deadbolt.

Before getting in my truck, I stood there for a moment, drowning in the rain, staring at a locked door, holding a worthless key.

As I removed her door key from my keychain, a flash of lighting turned night into day for a second or two, but I didn't care. I placed the key on her doormat. The message was clear.

It was over, and I was officially her ex—her baby daddy. It hurt far more than Tamera and Mike; seeing the two of them together only drove me to rage, but the determination in GiGi's face to get me out of her house was a horse kick to the chest. Last year around this same time, I had two beautiful women that I combined to make the perfect woman. Today, I have no one. I'm single for real and don't want to be. I'm cold, wet, and exposed. Just as I ought to be.

On the drive back to New Orleans I listened to R. Kelly's "When A Woman's Fed Up" on repeat, and that's when I remembered why that cop I passed looked so familiar. GiGi's mother has her daughter's prom picture up on her wall. He's the dude from the picture—the one GiGi never wanted to talk about, the one she apologized to in her sleep that night, the one who has pissed around my fence.

The dog I smelled was Julian the cop.

Her first love . . .

CHAPTER 16

Madden Night
11:30 p.m.

TIMOTHY

Today she finally caught me, and I was cold busted. Gazing at her. Following her around the room—not physically, but with my eyes. I can't help it. Discreetly, it's my favorite thing to do, but today she caught me and treated me to her adorable giggle, followed by a one-word question.

"*What?*"

"Nothing . . . just admiring my lady."

"Oh, stop."

"Can you stop?"

"Stop what?"

"Looking so beautiful."

"*Awwwww, Timmy . . .*"

Every time she says that, she always drops whatever she's holding or stops whatever she's doing and makes a straight line to my lips. Our love is a textbook love affair, and it couldn't have come at a better time. For me, this will be my second marriage. For her, this will be the first, so she has all the excitement that comes with the anticipation of a fairytale wedding. And I plan to give her just that: a wedding fit for a queen.

LaDeisha is my queen.

Sometimes I watch her sleep for hours; I'm still in disbelief. I still can't believe LaDeisha said yes, and that soon I will be her husband. From that first date at Brennan's Restaurant, this has been a Lifetime romance movie—not that I've watched the Lifetime channel, but this is how I pictured the perfect love story. That stuff Luther sang about; I have it, finally. My God, I love this woman. I love to look at her, everything about her is interesting to me. It's like having your dream car you park far away from other cars because you fear it getting scratched. You wax it once a week. You peep at it in the driveway.

That's LaDeisha.

Her hair smells like berries.

I won that challenge, and I did what I had to do to win. Just like on the reality television show *Survivor*, I eliminated the competition each week, because that's what winners do. And to my surprise, my competitors were knocked out within the first ninety days. A few due to my master plan, and some due to the implosion of their own houses of cards. When the smoke cleared, I had the girl. March 30 is the payout date.

I have proof that I won.

I want my money.

I need that money.

I need it for the life I've dreamed of with LaDeisha . . . but I do feel bad for Rasta. We go way back, all the way to third grade, but we're grown men now and he had something I wanted. I wanted LaDeisha. Nevertheless, I didn't want to hurt him, but he was in my way. Rasta was all wrong for LaDeisha, and her mother couldn't stand him. Her mother loves me.

I have been hired to document the last remaining days of her thirty years in Congress, and her passing of the baton to LaDeisha. In July, I traveled to the Capitol twice, and I'm also shooting a documentary of LaDeisha's campaign. They have made me the marketing director, and I handle all marketing and branding. That's how I won her mother's heart: they no longer have to outsource what I can do in house. Being that her mom knows everyone from here to the Oval Office, I have picked up a few extra projects from her friends in Congress, and three weddings this summer.

It was obvious that Rasta didn't fit into this world, but I fit perfectly. This is the life I wanted with the woman I fought for, and dammit, I deserve to be happy. When I was with Kayla, she avoided social events once she gained that weight, but not LaDeisha; she doesn't have weight issues.

Praise the Lord.

I served my time with a big bitch.

A marriage license can't make me like what I no longer find attractive; life is too short to settle. I wanted fine as fuck, and that's what I have, lying next to me. Just look at that perfect ass glistering under the flickering light from the flat-screen.

After we make love on nights like tonight, she buries her head under my armpit while I trace her fatless curves with my finger. Her skin looks so succulent she makes me want a snack; like a Jumbo Snickers from Walgreens or a slice of chocolate cake. I can eat her pussy for an hour and never come up for air, but she can only handle it for ten minutes.

This is the life.

Rasta, if you're listening, I'm sorry I forced her to call me after she broke it off with you, but you were in my way.

And no, she doesn't know that Rasta and I were friends. It's irrelevant. The only thing that matters is Timothy and LaDeisha, and our wedding.

My lawyer received a response from Glenn's attorney. He's

planning on fighting me, but in the end, I will win. I have that video, and I obeyed the rules. My lawyer asked for more flexibility to negotiate a settlement, and I agreed—only because our wedding is in April, which has us at the eight-month mark. Nevertheless, I still have the $25k from Glenn plus the $225k from my half of the sale of the house I shared with Kayla. Anything I'm able to squeeze out of Glenn puts me that much further ahead. I'm winning life right now.

Suddenly I see the love of my life raising her head.

"Baby, I almost forgot."

"Forgot what?"

"Can you move my photo shoot for Monday to after lunch?

"That's not a problem. Did something come up?"

"Yes, my mother has a good friend who is the director of a mental health facility, and he has invited her for a tour. From what she shared, they're having a major budget crisis, and he's barely hanging on. He needs my mom to lobby for him in Washington and at the state level, and she's dragging me along to show me how it's done."

"Sweetie, that sounds like a great photo op."

"It is, but not inside of the facility. Once the tour is over, then we will have a press conference to stress the need for mental health funding, and that's when I will need you."

"Anything you need, baby, consider it done."

"Can I have another kiss goodnight?" she asked.

I leaned into her lips and sucked the bottom one into my mouth, followed by her tongue.

"You better stop that before I catch my second wind," she warned.

"Second wind? Ha, after you cum, that's it for seventy-two hours."

"Oh, you're talking smack, I see. Just be ready for round two in morning," she threatened.

"I'll be right her waiting."

LaDeisha smiled and tucked herself back under my armpit.

I resumed squeezing her booty and playing in the valley of her back. All those miles she has traveled on that elliptical machine have chiseled an ass that sits up high and round; an irresistible ass. That's why she can't sleep or walk past me without a hard pop on the ass. Sometimes I grab a handful, other times she treats me to a ten-second twerk, but that's it. She says I will get the full *Back That Thing Up* on our wedding night.

Suddenly, LaDeisha lifted her head again.

"Oh, sweetie, I almost forgot to give you the name of the facility for the photo op. Are you familiar with the West Jeff Behavioral Medicine Clinic?"

"I can't say that I am."

"It's by West Jeff Hospital on the corner, looks like a plain office building. Please remind me to send you the address."

"That's West Jeff Behavioral Medicine Clinic?"

"Yes, babe."

"That's all I need; I will find the address. I love you, LaDei-sha."

"I love you too, Timothy. Goodnight."

"Goodnight.

CHAPTER 17

Friday, August 4, 2017
8:50 a.m.

I just ended a call with my attorney regarding this lawsuit from Timothy. They would like to settle, and that doesn't surprise me. My lawyer feels the reason they want to settle is because we're dealing with a money grab. I have to be honest with myself and admit that I want to settle this and get it over with; this entire ordeal was a bad idea. My wife doesn't agree with me. Diana is still having daydreams about stomping Timothy in the face until his gums are all that remains. In fact, she is racing across the room as we speak to make her position as clear as bottled water.

She snatched the phone out of my hand and informed the lawyer, "*we ain't settling shit.*"

"Diana, I'm ready to put this behind me. Things didn't turn out the way I anticipated. Why can't you let it go?"

"Because you're rewarding him for backstabbing my nephew. Why is that so hard for you to see? Timothy took advantage of your kindness. He waited until all the other guys were eliminated, then sent you a video of the woman *formally known as Tootsie*, aka LaDeisha."

"Why are you talking to me like I didn't live through it? I know he played me, but I'm tired of all the hostilities and threats. Look, it doesn't matter how he won the money, at least one of them won it . . . that's more than none at all."

Diana blew from the table and huffed to the bedroom.

She was so angry I could feel her breath as she moved about in search of her keys. Whenever my wife reached the peak of anger, she would go one of two places: the bedroom with the slam of a door, or to her sister's house. I knew once she found those keys that I only had a two-minute window to speak my peace before she was out the door. Her keys were on my side of the kitchen table, behind the salt and pepper tray.

"Diana, could you please come back? Let's finish this conversation."

She re-entered the room with folded arms.

"What if we lose this lawsuit and have to pay out the full amount plus legal fees? This letter says Timothy is willing to settle for one million dollars. Let's close this chapter."

"*Hell no!*" she snared.

"So you would rather risk losing just to prove a point? You're not making any sense to me right now."

"Here's what makes no sense." She moved closer to me with a tilted stare. "Why are you so passive?"

"You're calling me weak?"

"Yes—very weak, and timid. Why aren't you the one ready to kick some ass over how this went down? What happened to you?"

"So now I'm a pussy?"

"You called yourself a pussy."

"If it's not your way, then it's weak. You think confrontation makes you *a strong black woman*, but I disagree. It only makes you a black woman who I can't reason with."

"If I had a man who defended our interests I wouldn't have to be confrontational!"

"Then maybe you should go find one who defends your interests and has two working legs—that's what you should do."

I pulled myself up and hopped to the bedroom. It was my turn to slam the door. This only happens about once a year, so I slammed it with enough force to knock down the wall. Then I opened it and slammed it again in her face. I'm getting tired of Diana questioning my manhood. I don't have to take this bullshit from her.

"Glenn, open this fuckin' door."

"Hell no, go find you a man with two legs, and leave me the fuck alone."

"This doesn't have shit to do with legs, so don't project that excuse on me!" Diana yelled through the door. "Glenn, you better open this door."

"Or what, Diana? You're coming in here to kick my ass?" I opened the door. "Hit me. Get it out your system, just hit me. I'm not man enough for you, anyway. Go get the type of man you want and leave my weak one-legged ass alone."

"I never said any of that, and you know it. I have never put you down or criticized you."

"You don't have to; it's all over your face."

"Glenn, I'm challenging you, not criticizing you. There's a difference."

"There ain't no difference. You feel he took advantage of me because I'm too disabled to kick his ass. That frustrates you because you come from a family where the men settled every argument in the backyard like a bunch of pitbulls. I am not like them. I like peace."

"You know what, Glenn? Maybe you're right about one thing. I am confrontational, but it's because I will never stand around and watch someone I love get misused. That's the reason I am so pissed at you. It was Timothy who saw weakness in my husband and took advantage of that weakness. You will not make this about me wanting another man or about legs. I have stood by you when you didn't have two nickels and had zero hope—"

"Here it comes, throw it all in my face."

"Let me finish; I stood by you because I love you with two legs and one leg. Even if you would have lost all your limbs, I would still be here because that is what love is. You might not like how I respond to people like Timothy, but I'll be damned if he rides off into the sunset with money that came from your amputation."

"Diana, wherever you were going, I suggest you go. Your keys are on the table. I need fifty feet between us. Immediately."

Diana collected her keys off the table then snatched her purse off the sofa. A few seconds later, the front door slammed. I love my wife, but I'm sick of her feeling empowered to overstep me; this is a matter of respect. She doesn't respect my opinion because she feels I'm weak, but it shouldn't take fistfights with random people to earn her respect. She can take half of this money and go find the type of man she needs to feel secure.

Suddenly, my phone alerted me that she was calling, but I let it go to the voicemail. Diana called again, and I ignored that call as well. Then she called the house phone.

"What, Diana? What do you want?"

"You really feel I want another man?"

"Diana, I feel like the only type of man you're going to respect is someone who is your ideal body type. *I missed it by a foot.* I'm tired of you handling me like a child because you're upset. I'm not your child. Before I have you disrespect me, you can take half of that money and go find the one you need. With nine million dollars, two-legged dudes will line up around the Superdome to be with you. I'm about to hang up this phone because fifty feet also includes your voice."

I hung up.

I'm sick of her attitude and her thinking she can boss me around. My mother lives in the Seventh Ward, and she has raised me already. I'll show Diana better than I can say it—I am my own man, got-damn-it.

"May I speak with Attorney Aisola, please?"

Inaudible.

"When he's out of the meeting, could you give him a message for me? This is Glenn Braxton, please let him know I'm willing to settle with Timothy Feltus, and I can be in on Monday after my doctor's appointment to sign the paperwork."

Inaudible.

"Yes, Tuesday at three o'clock works for me. Thank you."

CHAPTER 18

Monday, August 7, 2017
4:52 a.m.

RASTA

There's no light shining through my five-inch-thick Plexiglas window, which means it's one of the wee hours of the morning. This is an hour when I would really prefer to sleep, if not for that upcoming concert.

"You want the sun to shine up your ass? Get out of that bed; we have rehearsal."

I knew the voice without opening my eyes. I also knew the next four days were going to be a living hell. Marcel the Walrus was back, and in rare form. DeShonta did give the heads-up yesterday that the group home was sending him in because he was having a bad reaction to his new medication, and warned me that for most of last week, he had been waking up at three in the morning for rehearsal. When Marcel was up early for rehearsal, he expected the entire group home to do the same.

"See, me and you, we ain't gonna make it . . . you too damn

lazy."

"Marcel, it's too early for this, chill out with the noise." I smothered my face in a pillow.

"This is how groups get booed off the stage; they don't rehearse because folk like to sleep all day. I know how to get your ass out of bed." From the foot of my mattress, Marcel snatched my blanket.

At night, these rooms are like the insides of new refrigerators, with AC vents determined to freeze the blood in your veins. I'd reached my breaking point. I popped out the box like my name was Jack and went after the big fat walrus in a voice I haven't used since I yelled at my son when he tried to quit on his football team in the middle of a game.

"Marcel, I've had enough of this shit!"

"What did you say to me? You trying to run this band?" Large, intimidating teeth bit down on his bottom lip. "The last fool who tried to take over my band left out of here covered in a sheet. You will play or lay. What's it gon' be?"

For real, I'm not one to fight a person with special needs, but Marcel is about to get a special ass-whipping.

"Give me this fuckin' blanket." I pulled my blanket with enough force to snap his shoulder out of the socket. "It's too early in the morning for this shit. Get your ass in that bed and stop disturbing this floor or I will fuck you up in here."

"Oh yeah?"

"Yeah, now try me, motherfucker." I started bouncing like Ali. "You bad, try me."

Marcel crouched in fear with eyes stretched from pole to pole. In that instant, he reverted to a ten-year-old shivering in the shadow of an angry father. I pointed at the bed. Marcel slid his back along the wall, then crawled in like a giant toddler. There I stood in the middle of the two twin mattresses in a blade of moonlight from the narrow window until Marcel cocooned under his blanket. Satisfied that I got my point across, I backed into my bed, re-tucked my feet, and fluffed my pillows. Then I heard the last thing I thought I would hear from his side of the room.

"*Sniff.* I just wanted to sing with you. *Sniff, sniff.* Why you so mean to me?" he whined.

"Marcel, go back to bed."

"People always yell at me. People always mean to me. So mean."

"MARCEL . . ."

"I told Mommy I was sorry, but she was so angry. I told her I didn't mean to do it, but she didn't believe me. I just wanted my ball. It rolled under the glass cabinet, but I didn't mean to knock it over and break all her fancy plates. MOMMY, NO! Don't take me to the stove. Please, Mommy, it was an accident. She put that big fork in that blue fire. She touched me with that fork, even though I didn't mean to break her fancy plates. It was an accident. Mommy, stop, stop, Mommy, please stop. It burns, it's hot. I'm sorry, Mommy, please stop."

I removed the pillow from my face. I've heard this story before. Was it in a dream? Is this a dream? It wasn't, but it was a never-ending nightmare for Marcel.

"Don't send me back to Belle Chasse State School, Mommy. I said I was sorry, please don't send me back. That man. That man with the scratchy face. That man is there, and he takes me to his house. Mommy, I don't like his house. If you send me back to that state school, that man . . . that man will take me to his house and make me kiss his birdie. Mommy, I'm sorry, I will never do it again."

I sat up with my back against the wall. Marcel had my undivided attention. I wanted to run to the nurses' station, but I couldn't move. I was suspended in horror with no intermission.

"Please, Mommy, come get me. I will sit still. I promise not to steal your cookies. Don't send me back; I don't like kissing his birdie. But if I kiss his birdie, he's nice to me. I'm a boy, I'm not a girl, but he thinks I'm a girl. I don't want to be a girl, I don't want to play his games. Please don't send me back, Mommy; I don't want to sleep in his bed. You said if someone touched my backside to tattle. I did. No one believed I kissed his birdie, and he kissed my birdie. Please, Mommy, I promise to be good. Don't send me back. *Sniff, sniff, sniff.*"

I have a lot of regrets in life, but yelling at Marcel in anger has sunken me into a dungeon of remorse. I gripped my temples and squeezed as tight as I could, as if the side of my head were a rewind button, and my life were a DVR. I wanted to reverse the last fifteen minutes and clip them like I cut my dreads. In the bed across from me, in a room with no pictures, carpet, or plants, was a man that I once knew as a bully—but the bully served an honorable cause. He was needed to protect the ten-year-old child deep inside of Marcel.

Listening to the ten-year-old cry shredded my heart into a million pieces. My bi-weekly roommate was no longer the psy-chotic schizophrenic in the stripper drawls; he was the little brother I never had. He was Marcel: a dual victim of the Loui-siana Department of Mental Health Services and a mother who never had the patience to love him the correct way. I didn't need to read the giant binder DeShonta kept open at all times to know Marcel had been severely abused; I saw it all. Like a horrible B-film on Turner Movie Classics, I watched it play on repeat.

It was 1989 when my mom clocked in for her first day at Belle Chasse State School for the Mentally Challenged, and every day, she came home with stories that made it difficult to sleep later in the night. It was her stories that introduced me to another type of abuse that was just as destructive as physical abuse; an abuse that was inflicted by those too detached from the suffering of their patients.

The other abuse she described was the administrative abuse brought on by budget cuts and overworked staff. She shared in-conceivable accounts of the dire fallout of a single doctor with one hundred and fifty mental health patients; far too many to care for. Far too many for the staff to care who lived and died, or to monitor how long patients were restrained to their beds.

In most cases, it was twelve hours a day.

"It was the longest year of my life," my mom always says when she looks back on that experience.

Then there were the stories of the sexual abuse; patient to patient, and even worse, staff to patient. Over eighty-nine cases were reported and investigated, but hardly anyone was held accountable. Instead, patients like Marcel were sent to live in group homes, where there were no more than eight men or women assigned to one private care provider. My mom was the whistle-blower who saved those patients, and I was now sharing a room with one of the victims she'd rescued.

"I guess God placed me there for a reason, and what a joy it is to serve when he calls your name," my mom said on her last day.

I feel like shit.

I just yelled at one of the patients my mom fought to protect. In that split second, I became an abuser of a patient with special needs. These patients are still suffering from a lack of resources and adequate care. I have just implemented myself in the abuse cycle.

I kicked off my covers and sat up just as the sun said good morning. Marcel's back was to me. His body was in a fetal position under the blanket; I could hear him sucking his thumb and mumbling. It was time to fix this the only way I knew how, so I opened my nightstand drawer and retrieved a notepad and a black Sharpie.

After five minutes of drafting a game plan, I shook Marcel.

"Dude, we have rehearsal this morning, get out of that bed."

"Huh?"

"Rehearsal, for the show on Sunday. Don't tell me you forgot about the show?"

He twisted toward me with an astonished smile. "That's right; the show is Sunday."

"That what I've been trying to tell you; the show is Sunday, and we need to make sure these songs are tight, so I made us a rehearsal schedule. Here's one for you and the other one is for me."

Marcel popped up with a burst of excitement as his eyes scrolled down the rehearsal schedule.

"Eight . . . eight . . . to-to nine af-ter breakfast. Rehearsal is eight to nine after breakfast." He looked up at me with a proud grin after sounding out each line of the schedule. Our new re-hearsal schedule called for a one-hour practice after each meal, and he could pick the song. There was only one song: "Look What You Done for Me."

As Marcel studied the schedule, my eyes were drawn to the wavy skin on the backs of his hands; his hands were ridged like the tops of brownies. My eyes panned down to his feet, which also showed scars from a series of bad encounters with a steak fork. The signs of his physical abuse at the hands of his mother weighed me down in sorrow, but not Marcel. Right now, his mother was a distant memory; temporarily forgotten as he taped his rehearsal schedule to the wall on the side of his bed.

After morning hygiene, we were off to the dining hall; break-fast and meds for Marcel and a bowl of cereal for me.

In the breakfast hall, I spotted Mary: wife of Joseph and mother of Jesus. She waved me over to her table. *Oh, what the hell*, I thought.

"Good morning, Mrs. Mary."

"Good morning to you too, my dear."

"Mrs. Mary, I've been with you over two months and have only addressed you as Mrs. Mary. If you don't mind me asking, what is your real name?"

"Oh, that's no bother at all, I get asked that question all the time." She paused in mid-sip of her coffee. "It's Christ."

"Repeat that for me?" I stopped in mid-chew.

"Christ. My formal last name is Christ."

"I sort of figured that, but just wanted to make sure. These days, some wives have hyphenated names, or keep their maiden names. You just never know for sure."

"It's interesting you would mention that." I could tell she was searching deep in her mind. "I haven't thought much about my maiden name in quite some time, but I would have you know that it's Brown."

I returned my spoon to the bowl for a second. "Mary Brown is your maiden name?"

"Mary Mitchell Brown. Then I married my wonderful husband over there; here he comes now." Mary waved over to the front entrance of the dining hall.

I chewed my cereal while my belly shook in laughter. From her expression, I knew Joseph had taken a seat next to me, and apparently he was not in a good mood this morning.

"Oh Joseph, there you go accusing me again of something nefarious when all we're doing is enjoying breakfast. And he's not the reason I returned to the room late last night," Mary explained as she was bombarded by a line of questioning from her jealous husband.

"Joseph, how many times do I have to say it—you're the only man I have known. I was a virgin when we met, and no other man has touched me since the last time we had this discussion."

In the brief silence between rebuttals, I made my best effort to appear disinterested in their quarrel and took in the sights of a room that had begun to feel like home. At the nurses' desk, DeShonta was busy entering check marks into logs that covered a range from midnight until thirty minutes ago, which was the sum total of the time she had been sound asleep at her desk. I hadn't seen Phillip yet, but I was expecting him to appear any moment from the stairwell, which was his secret sleeping place. At the table next to me were two cafeteria workers who were also assigned the task of feeding the cerebral palsy patients.

"Well, I never!" Mary Christ was insulted by one of her husband's accusations. "Joseph, I will not sit here and listen to you question my integrity. I have been faithful to you. Roderick and I are having pleasant conversation like we normally do. We are just friends." She turned to me with an appalled expression. "Mr. Ross, would you please tell my husband that I was not with you last night?"

"Joseph, your wife was not in my company last night, I can assure you of that. Now if you two would excuse me." I collected my empty cereal bowl and made my way to the trash can.

From my rear, I heard, "Joseph, why do you have to constantly bring up that cable guy? I told you that was a moment of weakness. I was caught up in curiosity."

Cable guy? I looked over my shoulder at the heated exchange.

"Okay, twelve times, but who's counting? I don't see Biyell anymore, and you will not constantly accuse me of cheating." Mary jolted from the table and stormed past me.

I laughed so hard I nearly fell over in the garbage can. *Biyell, wait until I see you—oh, you better not show up for Madden Night ever again, you nasty fucker, you.*

Once I made it back to my room, a very cheerful Marcel was seated on the edge of his bed, waiting. Just as I took my seat, two beautiful faces appeared in the doorway.

"Good Morning, Amanda and Ashanti."

"Good morning, Roderick," they said in a unified, dreamy voice. The clothes they wore were shrink-wrapped around their bodies; their lips shone like a coat of fresh paint on a Mustang.

"Would you join us for breakfast?"

"Sorry, I just had breakfast, but you can put me down for lunch."

"*Then we have rehearsal,*" Marcel blurted out.

"That's correct, Marcel . . . we have rehearsal."

"No problem, then we look forward to lunch with you,"

Amanda said.

"We need to ask you a favor." Ashanti gifted me a seductive wink followed by a pucker.

"Not a problem, ladies. I look forward to lunch with you."

"Bye-bye," Amanda and Ashanti called as they sashayed away.

Marcel looked at me with a *showtime* face. He was the lead singer, and I was the band. It was time for Al Green.

"You ready?"

"I'm ready, Marcel."

"Hit it then."

And so I hit it on the one. ***"Doom, doom."***

"Now that you're . . ."

"Doom, doom."

"Here with me."

"Doom, doom."

"I want tooooo . . . keep you free."

"Doom, doom."

"To do the thangs . . . that you want to do."

"Doom, doom."

"The joy in life . . . is loving you."

"Doom, doom."

"But now . . . the day has come."

"Doom, doom."

"To let you know . . . where I'm coming from—yeah!"

CHAPTER 19

9:50 a.m.

LADEISHA

When I think of mental institutions, the outside of this building is not what comes to mind. If it wasn't for the miniature sign, we would have driven right by this place—but there it is, hiding in plain sight. It's an office building. These facilities are so underfunded, they're housing patients in converted commercial buildings. That's not right. We can do better than this as a state and a country. I can't wait to get a view of the inside; neither can my busybody mother.

"Mother, will you relax, please? We're ten minutes early."

"Listen to me, young lady; if you are going to walk in my shoes, then ten minutes early means we're five minutes late," my mother said as she made sure my pearl necklace was symmetrically centered, and that my hair didn't hide my pearl earrings. "Are we clear?" My mother briefly looked to the side and spotted Timothy and his crew already in position. After gazing at him, she shot me a smile of approval.

"Yes, most honorable US Representative Celeste Barthelemy for the Second Congressional District . . . we're clear."

My mother pressed the white, ruffled collar of my blue congressional dress. I allowed her to prep and adjust my attire as she saw fit, because as my daddy always says, *the life she gave you at birth was actually her do-over.* He cursed me. Not only have I always been a carbon copy of my mother at every stage of her life, but she's downloaded everything that she's passionate about into me—like sufficiently funding mental health services.

During her retirement from Congress, when she's not serving in her CEO role of our new lobby firm, she plans to dust off her Doctor of Jurisprudence degree and target the state athletic associations, the NCAA, and the NFL over the issue of chronic traumatic encephalopathy (CTE.) in convicted felons. Her theory is that most healthy, able-bodied young men have played football at some level, and CTE may have contributed to the failure of their cognitive processes in the moments leading up to their felony arrests. My mother's teeth are sunk in, and she's ready to rain down fire and brimstone on football governing boards unless they agree to contribute to the mental health care of all former football players.

She has me tied into that effort as well, and I'm becoming familiar with all the congressional committees I could assume should I win in November. Filling my mother's shoes is a little overwhelming, but I am her do-over, and she's living her best life twice.

"Oh look, there are the state reps I invited; all fourteen of them are here as promised. Take notes, chickadee; a testament to your political power is who comes running when you need them," my mother said as she exited the SUV followed by her security detail.

She speed-walks as a sign of high energy and urgency; she's accustomed to this pace. I'm not. I typically have to work my way through her three muscle-necked guys to shake the hands of all the players in the political kingdom she has built over thirty years, but I normally get there just as she says, *And here is my beautiful daughter, my heir to the Second District.*

I'm already exhausted from campaigning, and I let myself cave to my mother's crazy idea that Timothy and I should have the wedding in September in order to dominate the news cycle leading into November. I'm barely standing, but I switched on the smile and charm, as my mother taught me, and greeted the state reps who accepted my mother's invitation to tour a facility in dire need of funding.

To my left is my future hubby with his crew, making sure every frame is picture perfect. He arrived out here an hour ago with two additional photographers and one camera whose job it is to focus on me the entire time as part of our documentary.

When the doors opened at ten o'clock on the nose, my mother shook Dr. Morton's hand as the camera flashed and the video guys captured the needed campaign footage.

Dr. Morton addressed the budget delegation. "Greetings to all of you and a special thank you to my friend and next-door neighbor, Congresswoman Barthelemy." They wrapped in a warm embrace.

I turned to blow a kiss at Timothy, and he caught it like a butterfly. I couldn't be happier with him as my man.

Once inside the first floor of the West Jeff Behavioral Medicine Center, we were introduced to a gentleman name George Rucker who served as Maintenance Supervisor. Unfortunately for Mr. Rucker, he was forced to lay off four janitors, leaving him as the lone person responsible for the floors and bathrooms. Mr. Rucker had just completed twenty-one consecutive work days without an off day. He revealed to us that Dr. Morton never asked him to work that consecutive run of days, but he'd felt compelled to. He referred to his job as his ministry. Mr. Rucker went on to share that there were too many patients upstairs with special needs to not have the facility sanitized every day.

"Did you smell that fresh lemon fragrance when those doors opened?" Mr. Rucker asked the delegation. "If I miss one day—just one day—you would've thought one of you had stepped in a pile of—"

"All right, Mr. Rucker, thank you so much," Dr. Morton chuckled as he led us to the administrative office.

The tour could have ended right there in the lobby with Mr. Rucker, but I had a feeling that by the end of the tour, we would meet more members of Dr. Morton's overworked, underpaid staff. Next, we entered the administration section of the facility, and there we encountered two exhausted-looking women doing the work of six staff members. They struggled to find a smile to greet us.

They wore faces of pain, brought on by the never-ending whine of the telephones in the background. Melinda and Vanity were the Swiss Army Knives of the building whose duties included, but were not limited to, patient processing, patient admitting, patient billing, warrant processing for unaccounted no-shows, patient alerts for law enforcement, family visitation scheduling, patient transfers, inventory restock including dietary, court filings, patient release, infectious disease management, reception of patient personal property, and last but not least, staff payroll.

I was exhausted just listening to them take turns explaining their daily tasks, yet they both told us they fulfilled them out of a sense of duty. They both said that their first pledge of allegiance was to the patients upstairs. I was also touched when one of the ladies handed my mother an envelope containing the names of employees who they wanted to rehire; some with nearly twenty years of experience in mental illness patient care. Even with the looming threat of losing their jobs, they were thinking of those who were laid off back in January.

Next, we moved from the administration area to the elevator.

"My distinguished guests, we've reached the portion of the

tour where we will visit the patient floor. I would like for you to meet the front-line heroes who have kept this facility functional in the face of grave odds. The second floor is also where you will find our patient housing and dining area," Dr. Morton explained as the group split. One portion opted for the stairs and while the other guests preferred the elevator.

Our first stop on the second floor was Dr. Morton's office. It was a closet compared to my mother's office in DC, but quite functional.

"And if you would follow me right this way, I will guide you to our patient housing area, where you will have the privilege of hearing from one of our suicide patients. I am so proud of this gentleman for how he has taken control of his mental wellness plan, especially after recovering from a devastating heartbreak. He is a textbook case of some of the patients we treat; those who are suffering from what Kubler-Ross describes as the Five Stages of Grief. It is true that pain experienced from a bad romantic breakup is the exact pain felt after the death of a loved one."

I was intrigued to discover that forty-five percent of the patients treated at West Jeff Behavioral Medicine Center were those who had tried to commit suicide; average, everyday people who decided they would rather end their lives than face another day of inner pain.

The path to the presentation site took us down a long corridor of patient rooms. Some patients curiously poked their heads out into the hallway, while others sat on their beds and watched the passing procession. Toward the end of the hall, two young ladies stood outside of their doorway and greeted us with handshakes and waves. I overheard one of them say her name was Amanda, and the other was Ashanti. The view into the next room over was blocked by a door that was opened to the eleven o'clock position. I couldn't see the patients inside, but I could hear a guy singing Al Green.

As we continued down the hall, I couldn't see my mother or

Dr. Morton because of my mother's security detail; I only knew we had arrived at the dining hall when the group came to a stop by a nurses' station. It was there that Dr. Morton introduced us to a gentlemen name Phillip and someone he referred to as *the real psychiatrist on staff*: a young lady named DeShonta. Dr. Morton threw an arm around DeShonta, who appeared very shy.

"Ladies and gentlemen, this young lady is my eyes and ears, and on many days she's also my brain. DeShonta has developed a revolutionary treatment system based on the individual profiles of our patients. Strategically, she houses patients with other patients based on how their conditions could benefit indirectly from close interactions with those who have opposite strengths and abilities. It's a natural healing strategy, and it's had such positive results that I drafted a scientific study on her behalf and submitted it to the National Association of Mental Health Physicians. After reading about DeShonta's alternative wellness strategy, the Association would like for her to come speak and receive an award—but we're short on staff and can't afford to have her out for three days to travel up to Boston. With your help, we can continue to provide this valuable service to our community and give my staff of heroes some much-needed backup and rest."

The entire delegation sounded a round of applause at the nurses' station for DeShonta and the staff who cared for the patients on the second floor.

"DeShonta, could you do me a favor and disturb that rehearsal down the hall? It's time for our main speaker to enlighten our guests from his point of view."

The sea of delegates parted to allow DeShonta to pass.

"While we wait for our guest speaker, this is a great time for me to answer any questions you may have about our facility."

"Yes, I'm State Rep for District 99, and I would like to know if this facility is available to patients in my district."

"That's a great question and one I'm glad you asked. There is a misconception among lawmakers that this facility only serves mental health cases in Jefferson Parish, but I'm pleased to inform you that we service patients throughout the state if a physician refers that patient to our care."

The representative nodded and thanked Dr. Morton.

"Any other questions?"

"Yes, I would like to know the average stay of your patients. Also, what is the longest inpatient stay?" my mother asked.

"Those are both great questions. The average stay is five to seven days. We also treat patients who are admitted intermittently for monitoring, and every now and then, we have extended stay exceptions for patients who may have been classified as TTO: Threat to Themselves or Others. Our specialty patients with TTO classification have especially benefited from the exceptional care provided by staff members like Phillip and DeShonta. One such patient has been with us for just over sixty-five days, and we couldn't prouder of his progress. As a matter of fact, he's standing right behind you."

My mother noticed him first. She reached for my hand to pull me forward.

It was Rasta.

Before me stood the man who was the love of my life for three years. The one my mother said I needed to trade in for someone on my level. The one who cut his dreadlocks for me. The one who gave up weed for me. The one who didn't fit into my mother's plan for my life.

I saw him, and he saw me. Our eyes conversed from across the room.

His Adam's apple sank twenty feet, then slowly climbed back up to the top of his throat only to sink again. He was tall, dark, and beautiful. Just looking at him caused a tingling sensation to twirl around my body. I watched the words he had prepared leave his mind one after the other, and I could not shield my face from the remorse starting to brew in my soul.

It was Rasta.

He composed himself long before I was ready to accept the

reality of the moment and began his presentation. He didn't have to say my name; he spoke to me. Timothy was the star of this horror story, and I was the leading actress. Every word he spoke was tragic. He didn't have to look me in the eyes for me to accept that I was the one who had penetrated his chest and shattered his heart. I also realized that I was the source of his grief. I drove him to swallow twenty-two Tylenol PM tablets.

Then he talked about the challenge put forth by Uncle Glenn, and spared no detail leading up to the day he tried to take his life.

"To discover that a friend that I trusted betrayed me was enough to push me over the edge, but I thank God for this hospital. Dr. Morton has taught me how to control my thoughts with positive self-coaching. I would not be here standing in front of you if it were not for this hospital. You may look around this room and see people who look crazy to you, but they're not crazy; they are my family. Before I was admitted here I never believed in mental health services. I thought they were only for extreme cases, but mental health services are for people like you and me. This place has convinced me that everyone could benefit from a thirty-minute conversation with a mental health professional. I'm living proof. If I never get out of here, then I'm okay with that too, because this is my new family, and for the first time in a while, I'm enjoying life."

I wanted to run up there and hug him, but the nurse named DeShonta beat me to him. My mom turned to check on me.

"I'm okay, but I need to make a phone call and get some fresh air."

I also need to speak with Timothy—right the fuck now.

CHAPTER 20

Ten minutes later

TIMOTHY

I'm set up in an area about ten feet from the front door of the West Jeff Behavioral Medicine Center, and my cameras have the best view position. We even beat out the three local networks. I checked my watch and the time was eleven-thirty; the sky looked like a clear blue ocean and the overhead sun provided the perfect lighting for my documentary team. And if I thought this day couldn't get any better, I just received some awesome news from my lawyer. Glenn has accepted our offer to settle, and we should have a deal signed by tomorrow afternoon.

To the left of me, I heard my camera guy yell, "Mount up and roll!"

That's the cue that our star has arrived.

At that exact moment, LaDeisha exited the front door, alone. My camera crew scrambled into position and started filming. It was LaDeisha—well it appeared to be her. I mean, I see her body, but not her face. I don't recognize this LaDeisha; she's pissed. She's never pissed. My best guess is that her mother embarrassed her or volunteered her to help at the facility. I bet that's what happened.

She continued straight at me like a cruise ship coming into port too fast to dock. Her stare was sharp with profanity and threats. It was then that I concluded this had something to do with me—but I have been the perfect man. Right?

Like the heat from a Thanksgiving oven, she blew in my face. "Stop filming."

"Sweetie, what's wrong?"

"Stop filming, now," she spoke through tight lips.

I turned to my film crew. "Guys, let's pick it up when the entire delegation is ready for the press conference." The two camera guys returned their equipment to the tripods.

"Where are you parked?" she asked, her lips still clenched around her words.

"On the side the building . . . why?"

With long angry strides, she headed to my vehicle without me. I unlocked the doors and followed. LaDeisha took her seat with her palms flat on her thighs. I barely had the chance to close the door and turn on the AC before she blew the top off her radiator.

"You and Rasta were friends?"

Not what I was expecting. Not the conversation I wanted to have, but I have a contingency explanation. I just need more information from her before I volunteer any information.

"Wait, I don't know why you're coming at me like this. What did I miss here?"

"Timothy, don't give me that bullshit. I swear to God, don't test me right now. Were you and Rasta friends?"

"I mean, I know him from around the way, but I wouldn't say we're friends. *Why all of the attitude?*"

"Timothy, I told you on day one—we will get along fine until you lie to me."

"LaDeisha, what's there to lie about? I know him from around the way, but that's it. I know him. I know a lot of people. What's the big deal?"

"Timothy, you and Rasta were friends; just as close as I am with my best friends. You hid that fact from me when you were pouring your heart out about how much you love me. You left that part out because you ran over him to get to me. Now, I will give you one more opportunity to come clean. Start talking." Her flat palms balled into fists.

I couldn't believe she was going to punch me. Her breathing was deep and heavy; lines of sweat raced down both sides of her face. Her eyes were the color of peppermints as she faced me head-on. In the background Luther Vandross was just about to sing the first verse of "Promise Me;" that was before she slapped the face of my radio. It's just me, LaDeisha, a lie, and the truth, all compressed together in my Lincoln Navigator. This spacious cabin is not big enough for all of us; someone has to go.

"Sweetie—"

"Lay off the *sweetie* shit and answer my question."

"Okay, okay."

It's obvious she's heard something, so I have to shoot straight with her from here, but I don't want to turn this conversation into a confession. I have to get her back on the defensive some way, somehow. That's it; I will answer her question, then get pissed off that she's questioning me about Rasta. Then I'll accuse her of still loving him. I need to flip this around right now.

Just as I was about to lie, we were both caught off guard by two EMS vehicles racing our way. Loud and rude, they bullied the traffic. As they drew nearer, a third EMS vehicle quickly caught up to them and join in the yelling. In my rear view, I saw the three news crews who were camped out with us for the press conference haul ass in the direction of the emergency room at West Jefferson Hospital. Even LaDeisha, as pissed as she was, became temporarily distracted by the panic-stricken EMS vehicles. Then, a fourth EMS vehicle raced our way.

Three hard knocks on my passenger window nearly gave me

a heart attack; it was one of my camera guys for the documentary. He gestured for me to roll the window down.

"Tim, I'm sorry to bother you, but my brother works for Channel 4, and apparently there has been a school shooting about three blocks from here."

"*A school shooting?*" LaDeisha incredulously asked PJ, my freelance filmmaker.

"Yes, it happened about fifteen minutes ago, and the scene is still active."

LaDeisha immediately started dialing her mother. Her conversation continued in the background of PJ's updates.

"From what I gather," PJ continued. "We're in a position to get footage that could help Representative Barthelemy make her case for mental health services. I say we get her to the school ASAP."

"I think you're right, but give me a quick second to confirm." I waited for the green light from LaDeisha. She ended her call with her mother and turned to me.

"My mother is coming out right now; the tour is ending. Let's get my mother in front of one of those news cameras."

"This is a gift from the news god to be three blocks from an active shooter at a high school," PJ said.

And just like that, PJ was off directing the film crews to get ER footage while we waited for LaDeisha's mother to join us outside. I caught a break.

"LaDeisha, can we pick this conversation up later this evening? This footage will all but guarantee you the win in November."

She stared straight ahead in deep contemplation, then half-turned back to me. "How many crew members do we have?"

"Three, plus me."

"Have one get the footage at the ER, get one over to the scene of the shooting, and ask one to cover the press conference when my mother exits the building."

Our plan was carried out with precision and focus. Our footage from the school scene as the kids were being led out of the building was the earliest coverage of the crisis. Then, LaDeisha joined her mother for the press conference with Dr. Morton and the state reps from the budget committee. LaDeisha was also interviewed by several news crews for channels aired across the country and around the world. Her clip was integrated into the footage for MSNBC and CNN. We scored a home run.

Whatever she was pissed about doesn't compare to the gift her campaign received from yours truly.

Once all the chaos of the afternoon died down, LaDeisha accompanied her mother and their security detail back to their family home in English Turn subdivision. Our agreement was to continue our earlier conversation around seven o'clock at her place. I'm here.

At ten minutes to seven, LaDeisha walked through the door to find me at her breakfast table. She didn't say a word at first, but walked past me to the restroom. After a fifteen-minute phone conversation with her mother, she finally joined me in the kitchen wearing a pair of jean shorts and a black sports bra. After getting a bottle of water from the refrigerator, she joined me at the table with an embalmed face.

"First of all, before we continue our conversation from earlier, my mother wanted me to thank you for your quick thinking today. To be three blocks away from the scene with a full film crew was more than we could have dreamed."

"I'm happy we were able to capture it all."

"With that out of the way—"

I cut her off. "LaDeisha, I'll go first. I'm sorry I didn't tell you I knew Rasta. I didn't want you to rule me out because I knew him—"

"Timothy, stop . . . just stop. I spoke with Uncle Glenn."

Oh, fuck.

"Really, when was this?" I tried to conceal the nervous energy that ran from my toes to my hips.

"During the tour, I stepped away to call him."

"Why?"

"Rasta shared how you stabbed him in the back."

"Stabbed him in the back? Now hold up, LaDeisha—"

"Yes, stabbed him in the back."

"When did Rasta start working at the mental hospital?"

"He isn't working there; he's a patient."

"*A what?*"

"Patient, and guest presenter. He shared the entire story. I know everything. Then I called Uncle Glenn, and he confirmed it. I should have connected the dots when you asked me to make that video for him announcing our engagement. I knew he was Rasta's uncle—I met him at their Christmas party—I was so caught up in everything that I didn't even question the *coincidence* that you knew him, too. I should have known then that you and Rasta were connected."

I forgot just that quick that I once called her from Uncle Glenn's cell phone. She saved the damn number. *Fuck, fuck, fuck.* Time for Plan B—accuse her.

"So while I was waiting in the sun outside, you were hugged up with Rasta?"

"Hugged up? You cutthroat motherfucker. I never spoke to him, and he didn't speak to me, but he saw my mother and me. We heard the entire story. We heard about the challenge and the money and how you submitted my name as the one you were going to commit to for a year. And all of this was going on while I was still trying to process things with Rasta. I even asked you to give me time, and you agreed—"

"LaDeisha, I know how this looks and I apologize for not being upfront with you, but I did it all for you."

"For me? You took advantage of his friendship. He trained you to take his job without knowing you were scheming the entire time."

"It wasn't a scheme, LaDeisha; you're looking at this through a negative lens. Can't you see? I love you. From the day I met you, I've loved you. I wanted you. Instead of judging me, why can't you see my effort? I felt you were worth it."

I reached across the table to touch her arm, but she jarred away.

"I called you the night I broke up with Rasta to tell you it was done and that I needed time; then you appeared like a thief in the night. That same evening, I wondered how you made it over here so quickly. You said you got here so fast in the name of *comforting me*? You were parked around here, that's the only way you could have made it so fast. You watched him leave my house, didn't you?"

My hands tried to reason. "LaDeisha, sometimes in life—"

"Didn't you?!"

"Yes, I was parked in the middle of the block."

A spring popped in her neck. Her eyes gazed up into nowhere. She leaned back in her chair with one leg across the other, her arms intertwined. The leg that straddled over the top of the other rocked her entire body, and I knew then that she was rewinding everything I had ever said. She scanned every past conversation through an internal lie detector that had never been powered up—until she saw Rasta this morning.

"You know what has me so pissed off right now?"

I shrugged.

"Not only did you use Rasta and Uncle Glenn, but you also used me. Because of you, people in that circle must think I am a heartless bitch to dump a guy then get engaged to his friend. Did you ever think about how I would feel on the day this all came to light?"

"Sweetie . . ."

WHACK! Her hand slapped the table.

"If you call me sweetie one more fucking time . . . I promise." Her fist was cocked and loaded.

"I'm sorry. Look, this is getting a little heated, so let's go to our separate corners and calm down—"

"Calm down? I'm sorry, you got the impression that I was irate? You think this is irate?" She started to stand.

"LaDeisha, please chill and hear me out." She lowered back to her chair. "I want to answer all of your questions. I was going to tell you later down the line after I won the money and we were living the life we planned. I didn't see it as using you, I saw it as competing to win your hand in marriage. That's all, LaDeisha, I promise. I'm sorry—I am—but I know we can get past this."

"You just don't get it, do you?" her voice softened as she leaned into the table. "Rasta swallowed twenty-two pills. That's what I walked into on a tour that was supposed to be a simple photo shoot. But here's where it required everything in me not to collapse on the floor. The pills were Plan A—he had a backup plan if those failed. Plan B was a pistol to the temple, but he wanted his mother to have an open casket. He read his suicide note out loud for us. I waited for him to say my name, but he skipped over it. He didn't mention me by name because of the delegation and my mother."

Every section of LaDeisha's face cried. A storm surge poured from her eyes to her mouth, then cascaded in a waterfall down to her chest and lap. As she spoke, her bottom lip trembled as if there were a sudden cold front in the middle of summer and her bare skin was exposed. With an index finger, she repeatedly pressed a button on the table only she could see. After every word she spoke in her broken voice, she mashed that button.

"Timothy, part of that letter was addressed to me. I was in that letter. In his dying words, Rasta asked a favor of Uncle Glenn—to get a message to me saying I wasn't to blame, and how sorry he was to disappoint me. Imagine that. You're sitting here feeding me all this hog shit about how much you love me, and how you did all this because of your love for me—"

"LaDeisha, I do love you—"

"Timothy, you don't love me. Today I saw what love is; for the first time love was so close I could've touched it. Rasta could have humiliated me. He could have ended my political goals with a scandal, but he didn't. He protected me. He covered me. You have no clue what love is, you selfish fuck. Love has the ability to crush a person but shows mercy. Love bows out gracefully. Rasta was love."

I watched as LaDeisha leaned until her forehead came to rest on the table top. Her arms sought shelter under her breast. Then came another band of torrential showers and hail from her eyes as her body swayed from sobs and an abyss of sorrow. I stood and walked around to her side of the table and placed my hands on her shoulders. When my skin came into contact with her skin, I felt something vital to our relationship leave her body.

"In my conversation with Uncle Glenn, he revealed that you served him with a lawsuit for the prize money. It left me speechless. How could you be so cold? So heartless? To hear I was involved with someone so slimy makes me want to puke."

"LaDeisha, I'm going to take this opportunity to leave . . . okay? We need to put this day behind us and resume this conversation tomorrow. I don't know how else to apologize, but I want us to survive my little mistake."

"Ummm, a little mistake? A little mistake? But you're right; there's nothing you can say that will make me feel better."

I kissed the crown of her head and headed for the door. "I will call you in the morning."

"Wait, don't go yet," she called out.

I froze at the halfway point between the breakfast table and the front door. A quick smile flashed across my lips before I turned to face her; somehow I knew leaving was going to help her put things in perspective. It's bad enough that I just sat there as she cried like a baby over Rasta. I plan to confront her about that on another day. As for right now, LaDeisha better calm the fuck down so we can put this behind us. That punk-ass nigga Glenn thought he was going to sabotage my relationship with LaDeisha, but what we have is bulletproof. Fuckin' cement!

I wiped the smile and faced LaDeisha. Her arm was extended

like she was in a classroom and knew the correct answer. "Please come back."

I slowly made my way back to the table, where her arm was still extended above her head.

"Before you go, could you do me a huge favor?"

"Anything, LaDeisha. I will do whatever you need me to do to help us heal."

Her head pondered slightly to the right. "Hmm, healing; I like that word."

"Yes, healing is what we need. I fucked up, and I accept full responsibility. I'm even willing to go to counseling. Whatever. It doesn't matter, just as long as we heal from this and move forward."

"And you're right; I couldn't have said it better if I tried. Before you leave, take this with you." Suddenly her hand opened. "Take this ring with you, and any thought you had of us getting married. I wouldn't marry you if you were the last man on earth and I were the last woman—the world would end."

"LaDeisha, are you serious? You're ending our engagement?"

"My mother pressured me away from a man who truly loved me. I know I will regret that decision for a very long time—"

"LaDeisha, please don't do this. We can work this out. Give me a chance to fix this; to fix us. Please."

"Glenn told me why you really divorced your wife. You told me you were both unhappy for years and were going to counseling to try to make it work. That was all bullshit. He told me you dumped her like a dog because she gained some weight, and you would've done the same to me. I know your type; you're the kind of man who's in love with the image of a woman and not the most important part of her. You would have traded me in the first time I gained a few pounds. I don't want to know a man like you, and I repent that I ever knew you."

"I can't believe you're doing this, after everything I did to marry you."

"That's right; I'm ending this scam of yours, and I prevented Uncle Glenn from signing those settlement agreements. As of twelve noon today, you were eliminated from the challenge. On behalf of Rasta and Kayla, leave my key, take this ring, and wobble your fucked-up ass out of my house."

Boom went the door as she slammed it behind me.

My marriage to Kayla and my plans with LaDeisha both ended in the same setting: karma is a kitchen table.

CHAPTER 21

8:30 p.m.

TELLY

Megyn is my love. She is my heaven, my everything . . . and that is why tonight is a special night. I purchased eight dozen red and white roses and eight long-stemmed candles with holders. I formed an aisle of roses and candles from the front door to the bedroom. I also cooked blackened trout with angel hair shrimp pasta and paid a visit to a local gallery for a bottle of Quintessa, her favorite wine. After our dinner, I plan to end the night by pounding her until it happens: the moment she cums and passes the fuck out.

While Megyn is knocked the fuck out, I plan to tiptoe out and drive home to end my relationship with Erica. That's the goal, that's the plan, and tonight is the last night I will juggle two women. It ends tonight, in a place I've called home for nearly a year, but I will let Erica down softly. I have already hatched out my break-up speech.

First I'll inform her that I'm not happy, and that it has nothing to do with her because that's the truth. Erica is a wonderful woman, but she's not my woman. When we met, she needed me. That was all it was supposed to be; I help her out, we stay friends, and after three-hundred pussy payments, it's over.

Erica has paid in full.

Time to close account.

Why?

Erica doesn't excite me physically. In the beginning, yes, but not anymore. She became too settled too quick. She went from sex doll to mom dull within the first six months, but I stayed because Megyn was drafted in the first round. Megyn made up the difference—a very obvious difference.

Take, for instance, this: I threw away the mom jeans and thought that was the end of it, only to have her dig through a box in the garage. Now she has two pairs of those ugly-ass jeans, one stonewashed and the other that looks like a pair of Gloria Vanderbilt's. It's shit like that—the maw-maw mentality—that I can't take, but with all things considered, she's a good woman. For that reason, I will let her down softly. I even deposited another five grand in her account. Erica will be okay, and getting out right now will allow her time to find a man who will love her Gloria Vanderbilt jeans.

I'm not the one.

Megyn is a better fit for me; it feels like she was born for me, but mistook Jacoby for me, only to realize that he wasn't the one she saw in her dreams. That was me. Tonight, I will fly the rest of the way with Megyn. Wait, I think I hear her car pulling up outside. She's here.

But why am I so nervous?

But why am I sweating like a hog?

But why do I feel like like my life is changing forever?

It's like Megyn has broken down a wall. She tore down a wall that took me twenty-five years to fortify. She demolished my wall in less than six months. She has to be the one. No other woman has caused me to fall in love so fast, and I feel safe. I have no worries. Megyn is my queen.

She used her key to enter my apartment. I heard the wind suck into her lungs. From the cracked bedroom door, I can see her, but she can't see me.

"Oh my God. Oh my God, Telly, when did you find the time?" She placed her purse on the counter next to the wine. Then she snapped a few pictures of the trail of roses that led straight to my heart.

"What am I going to do with you?" She entered through the bedroom door expecting me to be at eye level but found me on a knee.

I opened the little black box.

She took a knee.

"Ciara, I asked you a few months ago if you would consider marriage again, and your reply was . . . for me, you would. Since our first kiss, I have thought about being your husband. Since the first night we made love, I thought about a family with you. But after that night you shared that vision of our agency, I knew you were mine forever. Ciara, I invited you to our love nest tonight to ask you—"

Suddenly someone walked through the door.

We stood. I locked eyes with Megyn. In her excitement, she hadn't locked the door.

How could she not lock the door?

Dammit.

We both faced the direction of the living room, but the person who entered didn't reveal themselves, nor did they say a word. I quickly closed the little box and stuffed it back into my pock- et. *Don't tell me it's Erica. How can I get out of this shit and still keep Megyn? There's only one thing I can do, and that is to walk in the living room and tell her the truth. Deep breath, deep breath, shake the nervousness out of my fingers . . . here it goes.*

From the left side of the room, I stepped into the aisle of roses to see the last person I expected in my apartment.

"So you fucked over my divorce in order to fuck my wife?" It was Megyn's ex-husband, Jacoby Sincere.

"Jacoby, I don't know what you're talking about, but if you want to discuss this professionally, then I suggest you come to my office."

His eyes circumvented me as he stared into my bedroom. "Ciara, you can come out now, I followed you here."

I gestured for her to stay in my bedroom. "Jacoby, it's best you leave my apartment . . ." I held my arm behind my back and gripped my imaginary gun.

He frowned at every vase of roses all the way back to me. Then, his face widened in a facetious grin. "Nigga, from the looks of it, you appear to be in love. Are you in love with my wife?"

"She's not your wife . . ."

"That's right, you handled my divorce. *Ain't that some shit?*" Jacoby choked a batch of roses out of the vase on the right side of the aisle; an assortment I meticulously and lovingly arranged for Megyn. "I mean, you must have spent five hundred on this romantic evening?"

He was way off, because the total including the ring was $4,800, but who's counting? His eyes panned into the kitchen.

"And you cooked? Can a brother have a plate?"

"Jacoby, I'm asking you again to get the fuck out of my house."

"Did she tell you that I'm still fucking her?" He was lying. "*Hey-yo, Ciara*, you might as well step out here and face me."

In my right peripheral, Megyn timidly came into view and stopped at few paces in front of me.

"Ciara, he doesn't know you're still fucking me, huh? Get the fuck out of here. He doesn't know?" With the flick of a wrist, he instructed her to turn back and face me. She obeyed him.

"Ciara, is this true?"

She stared down toward the bulge in my pocket from the little black box that held her engagement ring. Then she nodded.

Jacoby was relentless. "No. No. No. You think I followed you all day every day for two weeks to let you get off that easy? Bitch, you're crazy . . . TELL HIM."

Megyn's head tilted back and tears ran into her ears, but she didn't have to say a word at that point because I knew it was true.

"I never ended the sexual relationship with Jacoby, and you never asked about him, so I never mentioned it. But I was—"

"Are currently," he corrected her.

"Still am sleeping with him. I'm sorry, Telly; I never meant to hurt you."

Over Megyn's shoulder, I could see her ex-husband moving up slowly. Even though he had been out of the league a few years, he looked like he could suit up tonight for Monday Night Football. We're the same height, but I haven't seen the inside of a gym in five years; this dude lives in the gym every day.

"Tell him where you were around lunch today." She was hesitant. "Ciara, it's better if he hears it from you, being that you love him and all."

"At Colette's . . ." she replied, and a whirlwind of bewilderment consumed my mind. I'd heard that name before, but I couldn't recall. *Colette's. Colette's. Colette's.*

"Ciara, I don't think he knows what that is—enlighten him a little more."

"Colette's is a club where partners in—"

"*Ciara* . . ." Jacoby growled.

"Colette's is a sex club for swingers; we met a couple there today for lunch . . ."

"And . . ." he couched her on.

"And, and, sex, with two couples. It's what we're into; it's what I'm into."

The *pssssssssssssssssssssst* sound that filled the room was happiness seeping out of my heart. It's like being the victim of a cruel magic trick where the magician vanishes into thin air with your wallet and watch and reappears on 41st Street in Manhattan. It's thinking you found the one only to discover that you found yourself . . . in the likeliness of a woman. I was just dick for her. I was a side nigga. I was expendable. But I was about to propose . . . would she have accepted my proposal and still maintained her sexual relationship with Jacoby? But I thought she loved me? She whispered in my ear *I love you*—she did. How could it be my pussy and Jacoby's pussy unless . . . unless . . .

"Telly, I'm sorry I didn't come right out and tell you. Things happened so fast . . . I couldn't stop it. Please find it in your heart one day to forgive me," she called timidly as she gathered her things and bolted out the door, leaving me alone with Jacoby.

"So let me guess how you got hooked—she finger-fucked you, didn't she?" he laughed. "My wife ripped the virginity out of your little asshole . . . didn't she?" He thought that shit was really funny, but it wasn't.

"Bruh, you got what you came for, just leave." He was right; I was looking forward to it tonight.

"*Telly, Telly, Telly*," he shook his head in pity. "Let me explain something to you." He took slow, threatening steps toward me. "I should blow your fucking brains out." He opened his blazer jacket to reveal a huge black pistol in a shoulder holster. My real pistol was in my glove compartment. Fuck!

"Ciara would never admit I was here, and Erica doesn't know you're here."

Fuck, how does he know Erica?

"At least that was my first thought, but then I said *naw, naw, naw*. Watching Ciara stomp your heart out with the truth was rewarding enough." Only the width of a flower vase separated us. "Here's the part that Ciara didn't tell you. When I was in the league, Ciara and I had regular threesomes with a cheerleader. She got pregnant. The child support was ridiculous. I didn't know how to stop my baby mama from raking me dry. Turns out, there's something about sucking a dick that makes Ciara's brain shift into overdrive. You wouldn't believe the ideas she comes up with when she has a dick in her mouth."

Well, I'm a monkey's uncle; when Megyn thought of the idea for the sports management agency, she was sucking my dick.

"There she was, going in on my dick, and it hit her: once I retired from the league, she would file for divorce due to my extramarital affair. Then we would move all our money over to her account, leaving me bankrupt. To make a long story short, on paper I'm broke, but thanks to the divorce, we keep it all, plus pension checks from the NFL."

He was so close I could smell the Hennessy on his breath.

"I said all of that to clarify that you can't take her from me—but come fifty feet around Ciara again, and I will fuck you over in a way you will never recover from."

It was then that he reached into his blazer pocket and held up something I recognized from law school: an ethics complaint to the Louisiana Bar Association.

Louisiana Bar Association Rule 1.7 Conflict of Interest: *A lawyer is prohibited from engaging in sexual relationships with a client unless the sexual relationship predates the formation of the client-lawyer relationship. Loyalty to a current client prohibits undertaking representation directly adverse to that client without that client's informed consent. Thus, absent consent, a lawyer may not act as an advocate in one matter against a person the lawyer represents in some other matter, even when the matters are wholly unrelated. The client as to whom the representation is directly adverse is likely to feel betrayed, and the resulting damage to the client-lawyer relationship is likely to impair the lawyer's ability to represent the client effectively. In addition, the client on whose behalf the adverse representation is undertaken reasonably may fear that the lawyer will pursue that client's case less effectively out of deference to the other client.*

"You fucked my wife while you were still my attorney during those divorce proceedings; if you ever contact Ciara again I will destroy your law practice. Then I'll fuck you up physically. Stay the fuck away from my wife."

On his way to the door with a fistful of my roses, he noticed the bottle of Quintessa.

"My brother, my brother, you went all out. Well, *trick*, you won't be needing this, but I will. We have another couple meeting us at the club for eleven, and I don't want to keep Mike and Tamera waiting. Small world, huh?" He didn't bother to close my door.

The next sound I heard was my cell phone alerting me of a text.

Guess what the girls and I made for you? See you when you get home.

A chocolate cake.

CHAPTER 22

Madden Night
Thursday, August 10, 2017
6:05 p.m.

The second batch of burgers and steaks is on the grill. I burned the first batch, but no one is here yet, so fuck it. The beer is iced down; it's Madden Night. That's the only thing that matters. Diana has been at her sister's house since Friday, and I don't give a fuck. We're playing the *who's calling first* game.

I'm not calling.

I only have one foot, but I put it down in this *mutha-fuka*. Glenn Braxton is not to be played with. If I don't put my foot down, then Diana will continue to run all over me like a track star. Not today, not in my house—she gon' respect me. That's right, Aretha; she can stay gone until I get some respect in my own *mutha-fuckin-house*.

And when I sat down and thought about it, I realized the only time some shit ever started in here is when Diana jumped stupid. I never wake up in a foul mood or come home and kick the cat. Not sure how I would kick the cat, but if I had a cat . . . you get my point. It's always me tip-toeing around her moods. Well, those days are over, and enough is *a-fuckin-nuff.* I told her when she came home Friday night to pack that overnight bag:

"*You walk out that door, don't come back.*"

"I'm leaving." Diana grabbed her bags and marched out the front door.

Then she opened the door again. "Now I'm back." She posted up in the hall with her hands on both hips. "Oh look, I'm leaving again." The front door slammed. "Now I'm back. Hmmm, I think I'm leaving your ass again." Out she went and then ten seconds later, "I'm back in this bitch, *whatcha gon' do, huh?* Call the police? I'll come back when I want to."

"That's what you think, but some locks getting changed to-night."

From the front hall, she yelled, "Glenn, if I put my key in this door and it doesn't open, some new tenants better live here. Now try me. You feeling gangster? Try me."

The door slammed for the final time, then I heard her car burning rubber out of the parking lot.

With her childish-ass-self.

As I said, I'm not begging her to come back because I didn't tell her to leave. I'm establishing some authority in this bitch; you will not handle me any kind of way.

Do you hear that, Diana? You will not dis-re-spect Glenn. Braxton. The Thirrrd.

I'm on my seventh Heineken, but fuck it. And it's way over-due that I back Diana *the fuck up* off me; over the years I have always been the one to *let that go.* Not anymore. It runs deeper than this situation with Timothy—that's over. This is about my manhood. It's a battle for my soul. This is about the crust of me, and it's going to be my way or the hard way. The choice is hers.

It's my fault. I always let her have her way. That's probably why she's stayed with me so long, because no other man would let her get away with it. That's why she's with me; she doesn't feel like starting over. When you remain with a woman after you've broken her heart, she may stay in the house with you, but it's not for the reason you think.

No, podnah.

It's to remind you annually—every year that day at midnight—that it was you who fucked up. I allowed Diana to treat me like a bum at the red light until she felt better, all because I was sorry about Derinda. Ain't that a bitch? Why did I allow myself to be her emotional punching bag for over thirty years?

Enough is enough; I wear the big drawls. You hear me, Diana?

"Who in the fuck are you talking to?"

The first person to arrive was Biyell; I could hear his feet dragging across my floor. He greeted me at the edge of the counter.

"Don't worry about it."

"What's burning?"

"Oh shit, shit, shit, hurry! Flip the meat for me. Hurry!"

"Dude I didn't come here to work—I came to eat and play *Madden.*"

"Boy, get your ass out there and flip those burgers."

Biyell made his way to the back patio. He looks like a before and after testimonial from a weight loss commercial; his pants are the *before* picture. If I didn't know any better, I would think he borrowed that work uniform shirt, but those clothes are his clothes; I've seen that over-washed shirt at least a thousand times.

"Oh, Glenn!" Biyell yelled from the patio.

"What's up."

"Glenn, how did you burn up all of this meat?"

"I, I . . . lost track of time. How bad is it?"

Biyell came back inside and slid the pan down the counter. "Do you see anything you can slap on a slice of bread?"

It was a total loss; the patties were so burnt I could have used them for charcoal. All the meat was black, all the way through—well beyond scraping the burnt parts off the top.

"Uncle Glenn, what's up with you? Need me to run you to the ER? Because I will do that for you."

"No, I'm good."

"No . . . you're not! I've been playing *Madden* here for five years, and you've never burned a french fry. What the fuck is up with you, Uncle Glenn?"

"Biyell, I just got a lot on my mind right now . . . that's all."

"Bruh, you've burned up one hundred dollars' worth of steaks; a whole cow died for nothing out there. What's up?" Biyell's fist banged the counter.

"It's Diana."

"Glenn, I know you're not about to tell me some bullshit." He grabbed his heart and backed away to the sofa. "Bruh, don't say it. Don't say it. My heart can't take it. She fuckin' on you?"

"No, she hasn't fucked on me, that I know of . . ."

"Who fuck on who?" Jarvis asked as he dapped off Biyell.

"She didn't fuck on me."

"Whoa, you almost gave me a heart attack." Jarvis was relieved. "Back up a minute, so you thought she did?" Like a breaking news reporter, he plugged in his laptop.

"She didn't step out on me, nor have I accused her . . ."

"Back up to the beginning."

"Jarvis, don't put me in another one of your books."

"Rewind all of this, please." Jarvis's fingers hovered over the keys.

"Uncle Glenn burned up two pans of steak and beef burgers—"

"What? Two pans? *You sick?* Do you need to go to the ER? I'll take you." Jarvis walked over to feel my head. "You feel a little warm."

"I'm not sick."

"You fell and couldn't get up?"

"Jarvis, it's simple, I have a lot on my mind—"

"If you burn two pans of meat, we demand a real explanation. What's wrong with you?!" Jarvis yelled at me. "Your mind should have been on this meat."

"All I know is when I came in, the barbecue was like, *hello mother-fucka, you quit?* Uncle Glenn, of all days to burn up the barbecue," Biyell complained.

"Biyell, I'm so fucking hungry, Glenn about to be legless. But we will have meat!"

"Somebody call Telly and ask him to pick up some chicken," I suggested.

"Uncle Glenn, I had my mouth fixed for barbecue, not Pop-eye's. I'm going run to the meat market before they close, and I dare you to burn this batch," Biyell insisted.

"Hold up, because Telly is already at the store getting some Hennessy."

"HENNESSY?" They were both surprised.

"What's going on with Telly? He only drinks Hennessy when the nigga hurting," Jarvis wondered.

"I'm not sure, but I just texted him to pick up some more steaks," I assured.

"Now back to you, Uncle Glenn—what's up, bruh? Real talk, what's up?" Biyell asked.

"Diana left me."

"WHAT?" they yelled.

"Left like went to Bingo?" Jarvis stood in front of me.

"No, left like moved by her sister."

"For a few days? Right?" Biyell huddled next to Jarvis.

"I don't know. We had a bad argument over this bullshit with Timothy. I wanted to settle and she didn't, but it's how she handled me that caused the fight."

"And you let her leave?" Biyell asked. "You let her walk out the door, just like that?"

"I told her if she left out that door, don't come back."

"No, tell me you didn't say that? Please say it ain't so?" Jarvis backed away to his chair.

"I said it, and I meant it."

"Stop lying," Biyell pointed in my face. "You said it, but you didn't mean it, and you know it, so *stop fronting*. Over thirty years married and you on some bullshit?"

"I'm tired of Diana handling me like a child. I feel like the reason we have lasted this long is because I've always been the *peace keeper*. I'm always the first one to make up, even when I wasn't the one who kicked off the fight—"

"What difference does it make who patched it up first? At least you worked it out."

"Biyell, you're saying that because you don't have a woman walking around your house talking to you like a fucking ten-year-old."

"Biyell wish he had a woman walking around the house. By the way, do you still have a house?" Jarvis cracked.

"Oh, oh I see, you jumping out the box on me? Huh? Did I say that when Monica stilettoed you in the throat?! Huh? When your ass was *walking back to New Orleans* like Fats Domino, did I say that?"

"You mad, bruh?" Jarvis crawled on the floor in laughter.

"You trying to cap on me? Uncle Glenn, remember when we picked him up in Shreveport? He was bleeding from places I didn't know a nigga could bleed. His hair was bleeding. His lips looked like two pieces of smoked sausage. *Monica beat your ass in the face with a meat tenderizer?* I had to ask. *Are you shot?* I had to ask. Jarvis's face was so fucked up his nose called the police. *Don't try and cap on me,*" Biyell retaliated as Jarvis rolled around on the floor.

"Nigga had tomato juice running out his eyes. Moaned and trembled all the way from Shreveport, five fuckin' hours this nigga moaned. Yeah, I took a brick to the face, but at least I drove my bloody ass home like a man. I haven't rescued a mutha-fucka since Katrina, until Monica red-bottomed the *fuck-out-of-you*. *Trying to cap on me. Brokeback Mountain mutha-fuka.* But anyway, Uncle Glenn, back to you," Biyell frowned away from Jarvis. "So when are you calling your wife to put an end to this nonsense?"

"I'm not calling her. If Diana would like to talk to me, then my number is 504-778-55—"

"Uncle Glenn, that's hoe shit, and you know it," Biyell cut me off. "As protective as your wife is when it comes to you? If Diana left this house, then you said something . . . you hurt her. Didn't you? Didn't you?"

"I wasn't the one who kicked it off—"

"Uncle Glenn, let me explain something. I don't have nobody." The laughter died down in the background. "I'm living in a little studio apartment in New Orleans East, taking some unwanted time to myself. I'm not good at relationships—I've accepted that—but you are. And if you and Diana can't get past this nickel-dime shit, then there's no hope for any of us."

"Biyell, I need to do what you're doing. Take some time for myself . . ."

"Uncle Glenn, stop talking crazy," Jarvis chimed in. "Why do you two wait until you're millionaires to fuss and fight? When you two were struggling, you were happier than a punk in a parade. And I still haven't heard what she said that was so disrespectful."

"I don't know how to get you two to understand, but—"

"Understand what?" Telly asked as he entered the house with the bags. "Where's Lil Wayne? Where's the weed? Who died?"

"Nobody died, but Uncle Glenn is killing me with this emotional shit he's on tonight," Biyell said as he hurried out to get the rest of the bags.

"Dah-fuck wrong with you, Uncle Glenn?" Telly was puzzled.

"Lady Diana left his ass, and he's filled with too much pride to go get her back," Jarvis provided the update.

"How long has she been gone?" Telly asked me.

"Since Friday . . ."

"Friday?" Biyell blew me off. "Wait until you've had to beat your dick thirty-nine days in a row. None of this dumb shit will matter. Having to beat your dick will get your mind right."

"Biyell, when have you ever had to beat your dick for thirty-nine days?" I asked.

"My dick has taken out a restraining order against my hand, that's how bad it's gotten. My poor-boy ain't never been this scratched up."

"How in the fuck you get scratches on your dick?" Telly asked.

"Calluses, nigga, calluses." Biyell presented his palms like a witness in court. "You never beat your dick and blistered it?"

Biyell had veered the conversation down a street called *ewww*, and we didn't appreciate his openness regarding dick-beating. Too much info.

"Dude, I have no point of reference for none of this . . ." Telly continued to the kitchen to ice the cases of beer.

"Not another restraining order?" Jarvis laughed.

"Bruh, fuck you both of y'all. The point is . . . once she leaves you and your dick is all dry and ashy, you will realize that your position is some bullshit."

"Ashy dick aside, Uncle Glenn, I'm with Biyell on this one; you need to fix this with your lady," Jarvis agreed.

I got his point loud and clear, but at some point my wife has to let some shit go. She holds onto everything for too long; she's the queen of grudges. Her inability to retreat to fight another day is one of her major flaws. Even when she's wrong, Diana will find a way to make it my fault—even if she has to dig up something that died long ago. I handle things differently.

I gave Timothy enough rope to hang himself, and he hung himself. The audacity of that little fucker to propose to LaDeisha after coaching her away from Rasta and throwing Kayla to the side like that. I wanted to call my wife and share the good news that Timothy had been eliminated, but I changed my mind. If Diana respected me, then I wouldn't have to demand respect. When I had two legs, I didn't have this problem. This is a side effect of being an amputee, whether she admits it or not. I don't disrespect Diana and she will not disrespect me. Not happening.

I'm too good to her to be handled like this.

"I'm not going to sit around and watch your marriage fall apart. I have so many regrets I can hardly sleep," Biyell shook his head.

"Enough about me, I've never seen clothes fall off you. You treating your nose?" I asked him.

"Fuck no, I get high on pussy, you know that."

"You need to get high on a pan of cornbread and some commodity cream and Farina. The fuck happened to you?" I had to ask.

"I'm hurting over GiGi. It's over; she's back with her first love. Never thought it was going to hurt this bad, but it feels like—"

Suddenly another voice shone in from the rear.

"It feels like someone you love has died. Kubler-Ross described it as the Five Stages of Grief."

When we turned around . . . it was Rasta.

CHAPTER 23

Madden Thursday
That morning

RASTA

What is that creaking sound? For the love of everything holy, please stop. I'm too tired to investigate the source of the creaking, but it never seems to fail. The moment I drift off into la-la land, something or someone wakes me up out of this wonderful dream, at the most inopportune second. Right before ecstasy, it starts:

Errrrin.
Errrrin.
Errrrin.

I could recognize her face in a crowd of thousands from a block away; her smile has been embroidered in my mind. I'm in love with her meekness, and the way her hair billows in the wind like feathers from a flock of doves. Her skin is the color of the time-worn pages of a romance novel penned by an author overcome with lust and love. She is available to me, and for me.

She wants me. She has come to me three nights a week with the same request:

Make love to me, Roderick. Take me.

I was a knuckle away from being inside of her; then came the squeaking. Maybe if I squeeze my eyelids tighter, I'll drift back to that wonderful place and slide it in this time?

And I know you think my dreams have been about LaDeisha, but they haven't—that surprises even me. I mean, seeing her on Monday damn near made me piss my pants—she was the last person I ever expected to see in the dining hall of this place—but I don't dream about her, not anymore. I still love her, but my heart is ready to love again.

Errrrin.

Errrrin.

Errrrin.

Before I move on completely, I have to admit: LaDeisha was so gorgeous in that blue dress—and those lips, man, man, man those lips. It was excruciating to stand there and deliver that speech, but Dr. Morton said the final phase of my coping plan required that I recite my suicide letter out loud. I can't believe I made it through that presentation on the day LaDeisha was in the crowd with her mother, but I got it all out, and that's all that matters. The really cool part was that her mother came to me afterward and whispered in my ear:

I have never been so wrong about a man in my life; please find it in your heart to forgive me. With that, she walked away and resumed her lifelong role as Congresswoman Barthelemy.

I didn't see LaDeisha again after that, and shortly thereafter, all of them ran out of the building like it was on fire. I thought about blending into the crowd and running out with them, but I changed my mind. With my luck, Dr. Morton would have admitted me for two more months on a stalking charge. In any case, it was good to see LaDeisha, even if it was from across the room. She was so close yet so far; still close enough to see the cloudiness in her eyes. All in all, I have accepted her decision, and I'm ready to go on with my life, as soon as I get out of the West Jeff Behavioral Medicine Center.

Errrrin.

Errrrin.

Errrrrin.

Errrrrin.

The creaking—can someone please stop with the creaking?! That was my thought before it dawned on me—there is only one reason a bed would squeak in my room, and it's not from fucking. The morning sun allowed in just enough light as I opened one eyelid. There he was on the edge of the bed. With the little wooden hammer. And a tiny New Orleans Saints football cap. Fuck, he just noticed my one open eyelid.

"Hello."

"Good morning, Levi."

"What's your name?"

"My name is Roderick."

"Rod-Roder-rick, Roderick. Hi Roderick."

"Hi Levi." I was determined to steal another hour of sleep if I could.

"What are you doing in here?"

"I'm in here because I tried to kill myself."

Just shoot me, somebody. Drag me into the hall and shoot me. NO, NO, NO—I TAKE THAT BACK. With my luck I'll spend eternity in here with Levi, and Marcel the Walrus in his black satin stripper drawls, and Biyell's side chick Mary, and Ashanti and Alton! Oh God, help me.

"Why would you want to kill yourself? Did you know your name means *king, the sovereign ruler*? Why would you want to kill yourself? You are a popular king."

DeShonta. I know her fingerprints.

This is the handywork of DeShonta. It was her all this time. She pairs Levi with me twice a month because he constantly repeats himself. After my presentation, I heard her talking to a couple of the delegates about her strategy, and I just realized that

I have been an unknowing participant in her pairing study. Levi has repeated the same positive reinforcement so many times that when it's quiet in here late at night, I hear his voice.

"You are loved. You are a popular guy. People like you. Why would you want to kill yourself? Do you like yourself?"

"Yes, I like myself."

"Did you know you were a king? Did you know your name means *popular ruler*? Don't kill yourself, people love you. What will your children think if their father, their king, killed himself for no reason?"

If you're wondering when the dark clouds in my mind blew west, it was just then. Right there, I was cured of suicidal intent, and was no longer a threat to myself or others.

During our entire session yesterday, Dr. Morton didn't ask a single question; he lectured for over an hour. With his students packed in shoulder to shoulder, a few of them tried to scribe every word while others look on in awe.

"Roderick, the thoughts will return, because suicide is a voice, and I expect that you will recognize when it speaks. It starts as a whisper then gradually increases with your stress levels, but the way we mute the voice is to shut it down with the positive self-coaching we've discussed since you arrived. *You have to speak life-changing words louder than the voice of death.*"

I heard him loud and clear—we had gone over those positive self-coaching phrases so many times they're burned like a CD on my brain—but all I could think about was the girl from my dreams. The one with the jewel eyes.

I want to live because I want to enjoy life with someone I love. I want all the shit I once thought was corny—the bike rides through the French Quarter, board game nights with couples, video blogging our life, learning something together . . . Mandarin Chinese?

It's time for breakfast.

When I stepped out into the hall, I noticed Mr. Rucker stripping the floors in Ashanti and Amanda's room, which was odd because the only time they strip our rooms is when—

"You guessed correctly, Mr. Ross; both of them were discharged one after the other after dinner last night. That's how it goes around here: one minute you see them and the next minute you don't. Puff."

They were gone.

How could they leave without saying goodbye? Not even a wave. I thought we were cool?

A sudden rush of sadness pitched across my body. My legs were weak, but I made it to my seat with my usual cornflakes and carton of milk. I have no appetite. I have no sense of awareness. But I feel my heart beating in my fingertips. My sense of normalcy is gone. The two people I talked to every day about normal things were gone. And though I never took her up on her many offers to steam it up in my bathroom, Ashanti was gone.

Ashanti and I had become so close; we formed a bond that was glued with laughter and conversations about Jay-Z and Beyonce. And sometimes I would bring out Alton just for the fun of it, then make her feel pretty again. I mastered her personalities in that short period of time. We had an intimacy that was deeper than sex because it lasted all day, and it was efortless.

Amanda was effortlessly funny, sensitive, and loving. She had her crazy days the same as all of us, because that's life.

"Roderick, this place taught me how to cope because I couldn't handle shit. I still have a health hurdle to battle, but I'm alive and as long as we keep living, anything is possible."

Those were the last words she spoke in our group session before dinner last night. Anything is possible. Even DeShonta. Though she placed an electric dog collar around my neck and only allows me to get so close, in the end I appreciate her flirts even if she isn't serious. She makes me feel wanted again. She repaired my self esteem. But I still wish she would have tapped my toe at three in the morning instead of Ashanti. Nevertheless, we're close. Not husband and wife close, but she's like that awesomely funny coworker that makes the entire work day fun. DeShonta makes the air in this place breathable, and Ashanti was my window to the life I nearly lost.

I'm worried about Ashanti. Will Alton come out at the wrong time again? Will she end up right back in here? God, I hope so. Listen to me.

That's fucked up!

That's selfish!

This is not a vacation resort; this is a mental institution. How could I wish for someone to return to this place? But I'm in this place, hidden from the real world. How could Amanda leave me and not say goodbye? I was the one who comforted her before she was paired with Ashanti, I was the one she affectionately adorned her *hospital husband.* How do you leave your husband and not say goodbye? Fuck, this hurts.

A deep sigh sent a gust that blew my cornflakes across the table like tumbleweeds. Suddenly, over to the left side of the room, I saw DeShonta and Phillip sprint from behind the nurses' station and begin to frantically attend to a patient.

"Get behind him, quick!" DeShonta screamed at Phillip.

Once Phillip moved to the back of the patient, I saw the reason for their life-or-death urgency: Levi was choking. I leaped from my favorite seat and ran over to assist Phillip. He struggled to gain the proper pressure on Levi's diaphragm. Levi's neck had turned dark red from strain, his eyes filled with water, and thick, swollen veins began to appear. Levi had something lodged in his throat and it wasn't moving. I shoved Phillip's weak ass out of the way and bear-hugged Levi until his feet dangled.

"Do you want me to call my son?" Mary suggested from behind me.

"Yes, call your son now!" I yelled.

Mary hurried out to the hall and called out, "Jesus, we need you! Hurry, my son, please hurry."

First thrust—nothing.

Second thrust—nothing but the sound of clogged air. Off to the side, I could see Mary and a few other patients running toward us as I fought to dislodge the blockage in Levi's throat.

On my third abdominal thrust, it popped out: a piece of breakfast sausage. A cheer erupted through the dining room, and everyone was relieved. I sat on the side of little Levi while he recuperated; the little guy was still shaken up. All of us were.

"Levi, my little man, don't scare me like that . . ."

"Hi, what's your name?"

"My name is Roderick. It means famous king—people like me."

"I like you."

"And I like you too, Levi. No more breakfast sausages for you. Agree?"

We shook on it.

"Mary, tell your son I said thank you, that was a close call."

"Well he's standing right there, you can thank him yourself." Her hand pointed to the empty area to the left of Levi.

"Thank you so much, Jesus, we really appreciate your help, dude."

". . . He said it's no bother at all, and if you need him again, he's right down the hall," Mary said after an awkward moment of silence.

No sooner did I make it back to my room dripping in sweat than Phillip was at my door.

"Mr. Hero, it's time for your session, you know the routine."

I've walked this route to Dr. Morton's office so many times I could close my eyes and still arrive on time. Once we made it to his office, to my surprise, Dr. Morton was standing outside of his door.

"Good morning, Mr. Ross. Thank you, Phillip." Phillip nodded a greeting and walked back toward the nurses' station.

"Good morning, sir."

"Did I ever thank you for that wonderful presentation on Monday?"

"You've thanked me every day since Monday and three times yesterday. But who's counting, right?" I shot him a smirk.

"I just heard back from Congresswoman Barthelemy. She has called in a few favors. Several pharmaceutical companies have agreed to expedite our grant request. Long story short, we can re-hire all the people we had to lay off and add twenty more beds."

"Sir, that is great news."

"I think your presentation made the difference, and by the way, Congresswoman Barthelemy has called me twice this week asking if you needed anything. You really made an impression on her."

"I'm so happy I could help."

"Take a walk with me, I would like to show you something."

As I followed Dr. Morton, I noticed that he swiped open the large red door—the one with the escape alarm. That door gave way to another long corridor, then he made another left turn and we were in the main lobby of the hospital. I felt like I had awakened in a strange land. An overwhelming feeling of retreat weighted my legs, and then I saw my mother and Aunt Diana. I felt happy, exposed, and unprepared to be outside among the general population. I wanted to turn around and go back to my room. I didn't feel safe. That's when Dr. Morton placed his hands on my shoulders.

"Roderick, the time has come for you to rejoin your life."

I looked down at my mother's feet and saw a bag stuffed with my books and clothes. Everything I'd accumulated over my two-month stay sat at the feet of my mother and Aunt Diana.

"So you're discharging me?"

"Yes, you're discharged. They are here to take you home."

"But I haven't said goodbye to the staff and Levi! Marcel's rehearsal schedule . . . who's going to *doom, doom* for him?"

"Roderick, your rehearsal schedule is in the bag with your things, and DeShonta will pair Marcel with a new patient. The band will continue to play."

"I'm not ready . . ."

"You're ready."

"But I need to say goodbye."

"We don't say goodbye, because we're always here. It's time for you to return to life. The fact that you have attached to people around you again tells me you're ready to care about those who are connected to you. When you were admitted under my care, all your intimate attachments were severed. In the short time we've stood here, you have looked toward that red door four times. There are people on the other side of that door that you care about, and that tells me you're ready. Your mother has your discharge instructions as well as our little exercises from our sessions. I'd like to see you for an outpatient session every couple of weeks for the time being, to check in and make sure you're staying on track. Just remember, we're always here for you, and your presentation on Monday has helped us more than we helped you."

And just like that, Dr. Morton turned and walked back to the large red door, and I watched him vanish.

My mom and Aunt Diana hugged me like I was returning home from Iraq. Once we made it back to the car, my mom handed me the folder from Dr. Morton. On the outside was a yellow sticky note that read:

In this folder, I've included your coping strategy checklist. Whenever you hear a negative voice, drown it out with positive coaching. See you in two weeks. Dr. Morton

There was also a card in the folder, signed by DeShonta, Phillip, Marcel, Amanda, Mary, and Ashanti. I couldn't help but look back at the hospital as we drove away. For so long I wanted to be outside, and now that I'm outside, I miss my room already.

"So where to, Roderick?" Aunt Diana asked.

"McDonalds," I replied.

Dr. Morton's Coping Strategy for Roderick Ross
Positive Self-Coaching—Drown Out the Voice of Suicide

1. This too shall pass, and my life will be better.
2. I'm doing the best I can, given my history and level of current awareness.
3. Like everyone else, I am a fallible person and at times I will make mistakes and learn from them.
4. What is, is.
5. Look at how much I have accomplished, and I am still progressing.
6. There are no failures, only different degrees of success.
7. It is okay to let myself be distressed for a while.
8. One step at a time.
9. I can stay calm when talking to difficult people.
10. I know I will be okay no matter what happens.
11. This difficult situation will soon be over.
12. Is this really important enough to become upset about?
13. Other people's opinions are just their opinions.
14. Others are not perfect, and I won't pressure myself by expecting them to be.
15. I cannot control the behaviors of others; I can only control my own behaviors.
16. I am not responsible for making other people okay.
17. I will respond appropriately and not be reactive.
18. I feel better when I don't make assumptions about the behaviors of others.
19. I will enjoy myself, even when life is hard.
20. I will enjoy myself while catching up on all I want to accomplish.
21. Don't sweat the small stuff—it's all small stuff.
22. My past doesn't control my future.

23. I choose to be a happy person.
24. Challenges make me grow.
25. I can see stressful situations as challenges.
26. Challenges bring opportunities.
27. I can choose a positive frame of mind.
28. I can handle whatever comes.
29. Today has limitless possibilities.
30. I can find balance in my life.
31. I can find love and support.
32. I can accomplish anything.
33. I can create inner peace.
34. My intention is for peace.
35. I am strong.
36. Peace is power.
37. My intentions create my reality.
38. Stress is leaving my body.
39. Today I choose joy.
40. I can make healthy choices.
41. I am doing my best.
42. I breathe in peace.
43. I am in charge of my life.
44. I have many options.
45. I can create positive change.
46. I am wise.
47. My happiness comes from within.
48. Each moment brings choice.
49. I can stay calm under pressure.
50. I choose healthy relationships.
51. I can find my happy place.
52. I can overcome this obstacle.
53. Through stress, I grow.
54. Tension is leaving my body.
55. My mind is at peace.
56. I have done all I can.
57. I can let go.

58. I am worthy.

CHAPTER 24

Madden Night
7:10 p.m.

I was last in the line to hug Rasta, but boy it was worth the wait. He looked good, in a zen kind of way. In a joyful and peaceful kind of way. His bald head had been replaced by a bald fade military cut. He was a little thinner, but not sickly looking like Biyell, and his face lit up with each hug he received. Though it had only been a little over two months, and I'd been visiting him in the hospital every week, it felt like forever since we'd all seen Rasta. For the first time in a while I had the entire crew minus one, but now that I think about it, Timotny was never really a part of the group.

"So, did I miss anything?"

"Nigga you missed everything!" Jarvis replied.

"Fire up the game and tell me about it," Rasta requested.

"Bruh, fuck that game, we need to catch up," Telly choked out before raw emotions clogged his throat.

"Telly, don't start that crying. You're gonna make me cry," I joked, but it was too late.

"Rasta, man, my brother . . . you just don't know, I, I—" Telly's head shook from worry.

"I know Telly, my mother told me."

A tear ran down Telly's face as he sipped his Hennessy.

"I missed you, dawg," Jarvis said.

"I missed all of you . . . more than you know. What I'm about to say is also part of my healing. A couple of you know, and a couple of you probably don't, but I wanted to be the first to tell you. I was discharged this morning from West Jeff Behavioral Medicine Clinic for a successful suicide—"

"You mean a suicide attempt?" I asked.

"No, it wasn't an attempt, Uncle Glenn. I was successful in what I intended to do, but thanks to you getting to me just in time, I wasn't allowed to die."

"Damn Rasta, I had no idea," Biyell said in a hushed voice.

"Same here, bruh. If you needed someone to talk to, I would have been there for you," Jarvis assured, a quiver in his voice.

"I know, but my decision wasn't made because I lacked support. I was trying to escape thoughts about LaDeisha. The more I thought about her and Timothy together, the more I hyperventilated. The pain was so bad it felt like my rib cage was cracking. I learned that it's okay to say *ouch* when you're hurt. It's okay to admit feelings of vulnerability. If any of you feel like you need someone to talk to, please get in touch with me and I'll be there. Deal?"

"Deal," the entire room agreed.

"So how does it feel to be out of there?" I asked.

"I can't lie, it feels weird. But the strangest thing happened this morning on the way home from the hospital. I asked Aunt Diana to stop at McDonald's—"

"Hold up . . . so Diana was with your mom this morning?"

"Isn't that what he just said? Let the man finish," Jarvis fussed.

"See, that's the shit I'm talking about right there. Diana could've told me you were getting out this morning—"

"UNCLE GLENN, CHILL!" The room yelled at me.

"We pulled into McDonald's but the line was too long, so I decided to go in and place my order. Once inside, there was this lady at the counter searching through her purse in a panic looking for her credit card. So I stepped forward and paid for it."

"There you go, just got out and tricking off money," Telly laughed.

"But check this out, check this out. A few days before I was admitted, I was in the same McDonald's with the boys and discovered at the register that my account was overdrawn. This beautiful girl with cream skin stepped forward to pay for my food. I was embarrassed as fuck, but she insisted. In the hospital, I thought about her every day. When I was first admitted, my thoughts were mainly about LaDeisha and a little about her. As time went on, they were all about her and a little about LaDeisha. Even though I didn't know her, she played a major role in my healing."

"Don't tell me that was the same girl this morning?" Jarvis's fingers clacked away at the kitchen table.

"I promise on everything I love, it was the same girl."

"Get the fuck out of here!" Biyell called out.

"I couldn't make this up if I tried. After I paid for her breakfast, she smiled. I smiled back. Then she was like, *this is the part where you ask me for my number*. Dude, my chick radar has been shut off for over two months. It was the same woman, and it gets better. We've been on the phone all day!"

"Dude, you just got out the hospital and reeled one in the boat already? Here I am with an available spot and can't fill it!" Telly complained.

"We're going out tomorrow, which reminds me, I need all of you to pick up a love offering for me to get back on my game."

"Man, we got you." Telly said.

"Actually, I've been waiting on you to get discharged to break the news."

"Please, no more bad news, Uncle Glenn," Jarvis moaned.

"It's not bad news, but our Madden Nights here are coming

to an end."

"What?!" the group asked.

"I'm finally ready to build me something from the ground up, and with Rasta and Biyell's background in construction, I would like you two to serve as my general contractors. I'll get you guy stocked on equipment, and my house could be the first house in your portfolio."

Biyell popped up from the loveseat and walked over to me with open arms.

"Go sit your-ass down, Biyell, I didn't ask for a hug from you. After the way you cussed me out earlier . . ."

"If Lady Diana ain't in this house by the time we leave, imma cuss your ass out again." Biyell forced a hug on me anyway.

"Rasta, we got you," I told him when Biyell sat back down. "When is the date?"

"Tomorrow, were going to see *The Color Purple* at the Saenger Theatre. She has an extra ticket."

"Whattttt? You're going to a Broadway show for your first date? This thing is off to a good start," I nodded.

"Uncle Glenn, I like her, for real. It feels like we've known each other forever. It was *fate*, I'm telling you."

"Then that's what we'll call her from today going forward. All in favor say *treat her right.*"

"*Treat her right!*" the group replied.

"Well, since we're all here, I have an update about this lawsuit," I continued.

"I thought the lawsuit from your leg was settled?" Rasta asked.

"Dude, a lot of shit popped off when you were gone, just sit tight and we'll fill you in later," Jarvis assured him.

"I received a call from my lawyer earlier saying that the lawsuit from Timothy has been dropped."

"It doesn't matter; I'm still fucking him up on sight," Biyell said.

"No need to, because he played himself. Not only did he lose out on the lawsuit, but I also spoke with LaDeisha—she ended their relationship three days ago."

"Timothy was the last one standing and was a for-sure winner," Telly said.

"Yes, but Tootsie took care of that little problem for us. From the way she described it, he got what he deserved."

"Not really, he deserves one tooth," Jarvis piped up.

"That boiled egg-ass nigga gonna *need some milk* when I'm finished with him," Biyell threatened.

"So in the end, no one won the challenge, and all of our lives are totally different. Jarvis lost Monica and Briana, Biyell is wiped the fuck out, I'm about to get something going with Fate, and Telly's with, with, with . . ." Rasta plucked his fingers as he waited for a name. "With? With?"

"*Erica,* I guess."

"What do you mean, *I guess?* Didn't she win the cake test?" I challenged.

"What is a cake test?" Rasta asked.

"I'll explain it later."

"Look, I don't trust *none of these bitches* out here. For real." Telly headed to the counter to pour another glass of Hennessy.

"So what happened to Megyn?" Jarvis asked.

"Like I said, I don't trust none of these—"

"*Man down! Man down! Megyn ran game on him . . . man down!*" Jarvis blurted out. "I knew something was wrong with you because that is your fourth glass of Hennessy. What did she do? You caught her doing bad?"

"Megyn, she has baby daddy drama, and I ain't got time for it. Her ex-husband is stalking. I almost had to shoot that motherfucker. I told that pussy-ass-nigga don't ever come to my house again."

"DAMN!" The group yelled.

"He came to your house? That's hoe shit," Biyell concluded.

"Didn't you go to jail for going to another man's house and kicking in the door?" Jarvis took another shot at Biyell.

Biyell leaped to his feet. "That was my fucking house—"

"Here we go again . . . I thought we covered this remedial shit," Jarvis joked.

"Wait, hold up . . . Biyell, you went to jail? Some dude was at your house with Tamera?"

"Rasta! A lot of shit popped off. It'll take a week to get you caught up," Jarvis interjected. "But anyway, back to this ex-husband who repossessed his pussy."

"Repossessed? Repossessed? I broke it off on Monday."

Jarvis raised his hand. "Who's translating this bullshit?"

"That's not what happened and you know it." Biyell walked over where Telly was braced against the wall. "That shit don't even sound right. So what really happened?"

"Mannn, fuck Megyn. I don't even want to talk about that bitch." Telly bottomed up the glass in a single gulp. "That's all there is to know about that. I'm now accepting applications for a replacement bitch!"

"I thought I was hurt but you're *URT, URT, URT!* Every other word is *that bitch and hoe*," Biyell's summary was followed by a chorus of laughter.

"Telly, why not take this opportunity to go all out with Erica? This is the perfect time to be one man with one woman. Blameless. The husband of one woman," I suggested.

Telly's back rested on the wall like a drunk guy propped up by a Bourbon Street pole. I could tell there was far more to that story than he shared, but this setting was not the setting to deal with it.

"My brother, you have been delivered from the stress of managing two women. I suggest you go full time with Erica or end it the right way, but enough of this man-whoring around."

"Speaking of man-whoring around," Rasta interrupted me. "Biyell, a lil' chick told me to tell you hi."

Biyell's face wrinkled as he searched the corners of his mind. "Bruh, who?"

"Mary. She's about this high, lily white, always over-dressed, lived alone in Algiers Point . . . ?"

"That name don't ring a bell . . ."

"Ball gowns . . . ?"

"I can't seem to recall a Mary."

"Mary Brown!" Rasta yelled. "Looks like Betty White, don't play dumb!"

Biyell yawned and stretched. "Man, look at the time . . . I have to cut out, fellas."

Jarvis hauled ass to the front door.

"Lock it, Jarvis," Rasta ordered, then stabbed at Biyell with his finger. "Oh, I've been waiting to catch up with you."

"What happened?" I asked him.

"Uncle Glenn, let me tell you about this barroom toilet-ass nigga here. This Draino-dick-ass nigga here. This nursing home gigolo . . ."

"Who he fucked?" Jarvis yelled out as he raced back to his laptop.

"Rasta, whatever you're about to say is old shit . . ."

"But it's new shit to us. Bus it!" Jarvis's nosey ass insisted.

Right as Rasta was about to tell his story, in walked my wife.

"Later fellas . . ." I called as my eyes met hers.

"Later, Uncle," they all said.

"Rasta, hold that story for Sunday; let's have an NFL Preseason Party."

Once the room cleared out, she spoke in a voice softer than rose petals.

"Hi, Glenn . . ."

"Hi, Diana . . ."

"I, I, I just wanted to say that—"

"Don't say anything. Come over here and show me . . ."

CHAPTER 25

Monday, September 4, 2017
11:30 p.m.

TELLY

The only thing that was exactly as I expected was the rouge tint that flowed throughout the building like a red sea. On television and on the porn sites I visited in preparation for this night, the members were fit, trim, and beautiful, but sex clubs are truly a reflection of the people around you. I peeped into their semi-private rooms through entrances draped with powder blue fabrics that felt silk to the touch. The first room we viewed was like entering into a giant spider web in which everything stuck to the web was fucking. Sex was literally everywhere my eyes came to rest. For those who weren't in the act of sex, sex was constantly on offer.

I'm at Colette's sex club, but I'm not alone. I brought sand to the beach. Not Erica—she's too wholesome-acting for a place like this—but a woman I met online after posting an ad. The personals ad I posted on Craigslist requested a dinner date and nothing more; forty-eight horny women replied.

WANTED: NEED SOMEONE SEXY TO BE MY DATE FOR A COUPLES ONLY MASQUERADE PARTY. ALL EXPENSES COVERED. SIZE, RACE, DON'T MATTER, BUT I NEED A PICTURE AND AVAILABILITY. PARTY IS AT A SWINGERS CLUB.

After I weeded out all the prostitutes, I was left with two thrill-seekers who were only interested in the sex party. One was a younger girl around thirty; she claimed to be in town on business and bored, but I later discovered she was a higher-end traveling sex worker. The other potential date was an older woman who lived in Slidell and had a banging body. I decided to go with the older woman. Her name is Heather.

To get acquainted, we started the evening with dinner before we headed over to Colette's. To my surprise, Heather arrived in a black leather mini, black heels, and a tight, three-button, see-through black blouse. Her hay-colored hair was pulled back in a ponytail; for the entire dinner all I could think of was how much she resembled my high school history teacher, only sexier.

Heather was perfect for my plan; visiting a swingers club had been a fantasy of hers for well over fifteen years, but she was too afraid to express it to her late husband. She told me that she had her first black man last week—a cable guy—and it was everything she'd dreamed of and more. From the man she described, it was definitely Biyell, but tonight we are a couple, and she loves the idea of it being just for a night. I am her man, she is my woman, and we are going to explore this world no one has ever invited us into.

After dinner, we arrived into a den of lust and moans.

I held her hand and led her through the club. Heather's ass swayed like a love song in that black skirt. She held the attention of the men and women who loitered along the walls as they appraised potential partners for the night. They all wanted to fuck

Heather. Me, not so much.

We continued up the middle aisle to the back bar. On the way back there, we felt their eyes on our skin like goosebumps. Every inch of our bodies was examined like a menu; we were the new couple, and I liked it. We sipped our drinks at the bar and tried our best to give the appearance of a couple in search of a little action, but not too much. I sat on a stool facing the open floor with Heather pressed tightly between my legs.

I rubbed her thick thighs and fingered her from the back of her black mini; Heather didn't mind at all. Her hips rocked to Janet Jackson's "Any Time, Any Place;" she knew every word of the song. On the other side of the room stood a row of lavender leather sofas, and each sofa displayed an active sexual act. I could tell Heather was enjoying the live show performed by a group of people who couldn't care less if we watched.

Suddenly, a woman with the same full-face kitten-style mask that Heather wore seductively walked toward us from across the room, then right up to Heather. She placed delicate kisses on Heather's neck, then on her lips, and finally on the other side of her neck. Heather squeezed my hand through the entire encounter; she was excited and afraid. Then a hand reached around Heather's waist. With little effort, the hand unzipped my pants and freed my pipe. The woman gently pushed Heather to the side, then sucked me into her mouth while I kissed my date for the first time that night. I gripped and released Heather's ass like a large stress ball; everything was moving faster than I'd anticipated.

"Thank you for inviting me," Heather murmured against my lips.

"Thank you for being the sexiest woman in the room."

"You make me sexy; I bought these clothes for you."

"Then I plan to buy the next outfit."

"What about the woman sucking you?"

"I wish it was you."

"Then maybe I'll form a line behind her."

For a moment I almost let myself get caught up in the haze of the room, but then I forced myself to refocus. I'm not here for sex, I'm here to see her; that's all I want. I have to see her because I love her . . . but Megyn is nowhere to be found.

Heather moved to the side of my stool and enjoyed watching the lady go to work on me before she started sucking my neck. Despite having one woman between my legs and another one licking my neck, my eyes still scanned the entire lounge area in search of any woman who resembled Megyn.

Maybe she's with another couple locked in a fearsome four-some in one of the semi-private areas, or perhaps she's in the ladies' bathroom riding a guy in the stall? I have to see her, even though I can't have her. Even though she belongs to Jacoby, I've never been this weak for a woman in my life. I've never stalked anyone, but tonight I'm on a prowl. I'm determined to find her. If only I could separate this swollen dick from the mouth of this woman. And don't get me wrong, she's doing a wonderful job down there, but I'm here for Megyn. And I don't want to be rude, but the longer we stand here, the hotter Heather is getting. I think she's ready to join in the action.

Suddenly, I felt my power and strength leave my body and blast into the mouth of the woman between my legs. This chick stole it; all of it. I nearly fell off the bar stool. After my convulsions, she tucked my manhood away for the night. Once she stood, I pulled her to me.

"You're really good. Thank you," I yelled over Marvin Gaye's "Let's Get It On."

"You're welcome. The pleasure was all mine," she replied. "Your wife is very sexy."

"She's not my wife."

"Well, I like her, so please let her know."

"I will, later can I have a second serving, maybe dessert?"

"You can, but I doubt if you'll get hard again."

I chuckled. "What makes you so sure?"

"Because I know your dick, and it's done for the night." The lady lifted her face mask.

"Ciara, it's really you. I've called you every—"

"Don't come here ever again. Jacoby is in the far left corner. If he notices you, then he will—"

"I don't care what he does to me; I need you to come back to me. I love you, and I still want to marry you."

"He knows where you live; he played football in college with Mike." The name didn't ring a bell. "Mike who's engaged to Biyell's ex-wife Tamera. They're here also, in the far left corner. He and Jacoby have been ploting against you and following you, too. Please Telly, leave and don't come back here unless you want him knocking on your front door—the door of your home with Erica. I'm trapped in this world; it's best for all of us if you forget about me. I'm sorry and I do love you."

"Ciara, how could you love me and leave me like this unless you never loved me?"

"I'm sorry, but I can't have this conversation with you. Please leave. Jacoby is looking. Go. Go."

Megyn disappeared behind her mask and headed to the corner to join her husband, who was having a threesome with an Asian couple. I watched as she prowled on all fours alongside the woman and started sucking her milk-drop breast while the woman sucked the Asian man into her mouth. I followed her advice and left the lounge area. As I passed the bar, I grabbed Heather, who was transfixed watching the action on the sofas. I pulled Heather with me through the hallways that dripped with pleasure. She didn't protest, but I still wanted to confirm whether she was ready to go.

"I am if you are," she replied.

I spoke softly in her ear, "This night was also about achieving your fantasy. Did you see anyone you wanted? Anyone who turned you on?"

"Only you, but that can happen away from here."

And it did.

Colette's wasn't anything we couldn't achieve in my apartment, where I used to enjoy Megyn. That's where we spent rest of the evening. The next day, a text from Heather:

Thank you for last night, you made me feel safe and special.
I replied back: *When can I see you again?*
That's up to you.
Today?
Yes!

Heather moved in quickly and hard and took over everything I felt for Megyn. The best part about Heather is I have no reason to lie—she knows everything and is cool with everything. I replaced Megyn with Heather and was still able to keep Erica. Life is good.

CHAPTER 26

Friday, November 10, 2017
11:55 a.m.

BRIANA

Momma this is Bri, I wanted to let you know that my water broke and I'm headed to the hospital. I'm not trying to bother you or cause any more confusion. Just wanted to let you know. I will be at East Jefferson Hospital if you would like to see your first grandchild. Talk to you later. I love you, Mommy. Hope to see you today.

Jodie this is Bri, I'm not sure if you will get this, but my water broke. Okay, bye-bye. Love you. Bye-bye.

Bethany this is Bri, I'm on my way to the hospital, your nephew is ready. I wanted to let you know, that's all. Bye-Bye Bethany.

Aunt Latrisha it's Bri, I wanted to tell you again how sorry I am about the dress and to let you know that my baby is coming today. Hope you can find it in your heart to forgive me one day. Hope to talk to you again one day. Bye-bye for now. Briana.

Daddy *this is Bri . . . oh well, never mind.*

My baby is low. Everything in my stomach feels wrong. My pants are soaked; I have to change and get to the hospital now. At least the contractions haven't started yet; that's a blessing.

My entire family has blocked my number, and all my calls go straight to voicemail. All my texts vanish in the space from my phone to my mother's phone, but I still reach out to her every day; I still try to text. And every day since that day in Dallas, I have left a voice message begging for her forgiveness and pleading for her arms. But I'm condemned.

Banished.

Sentenced to life as the prodigal daughter who can never return. My last text before I grabbed the handle of my maternity suitcase was to Jarvis; it probably vanished into thin air with the text to my father. I'm free to move to New York like Jarvis and I planned, but a change in scenery wouldn't free me from this solitary confinement. The harsh truth they spat at me did little in comparison to the torment of their silence. I hope Jarvis read my apology letter; it's been three weeks and still no reply.

I have no one.

I'm blocked on their phones and blocked out of their lives. It's what I deserve, that's what Jodie said the day they found out I was pregnant for Jarvis. But it still hurts that my mother has blocked me out of her life—her baby daughter. Surely this separation is hurting her just as much as it's hurting me? Surely she's grieving for me as much as I'm grieving the loss of her voice? Few people know the depths of her submissiveness, because she's a master of suppression, but my father controls her emotions. She likes who he tells her to like, and turns her back on those who have fallen out of his grace.

I've fallen.

When I fell the first time, my mother was there for me. She protected me and never told a soul—not even my father—that I had been raped. It was a man from our church; a man who accompanied my father everywhere, the one who carried my father's Bible to the pulpit, the one my father trusted even more than my mother. I was two years below the age of consent, and my dad was on the verge of becoming what's known as a mega-church bishop. It was my mother who made the executive decision that the momentum of the ministry was far more important than securing justice for her daughter, so she concealed that I was pregnant and allowed him to escape accountability.

She discarded my pregnancy at a clinic on Napoleon Avenue and discarded my father's first assistant pastor with one swoop of her hand. My reputation was left without spot, blemish, or wrinkle—but not this time. I am exposed, and cut off, and treated like a social pariah who's dripping with hazardous waste.

All because I wanted my baby.

And because I wanted Jarvis.

I used to feel sorry for him—for how my aunt emasculated him and belittled him to my mother, always because of his salary. In my aunt's mind, her salary and my mother's salary earned her the right to disrespect Jarvis while my mother cheered her on. My mother enjoyed living vicariously through Aunt Monica.

I remember that party Jarvis threw when Aunt Monica became the Regional Manager for Chase Bank; she hardly acknowledged him. She barely spoke to him, and only in passing, when she sparingly introduced him to executives from her company. At the party, Monica interacted with one guy more than any other—a handsome man he was, but so too is Jarvis. She was obviously smitten head over ass for another man. At an event that was meticulously planned by Jarvis in her honor, she honored someone else with her cooing and drooling. Monica gave zero fucks if anyone noticed her not-so-discreet admiration. It was disheartening that no one—not even my mother—lifted a finger to check her, or at least confront her off to the side, but I wasn't surprised. My mother has always lived through Monica. Monica was doing to Jarvis what she had always wanted to do to my dad, but my mom is submissive as a slave.

That event couldn't end soon enough, but I stayed until the end and suffered the humiliation with Jarvis. I'd long since fallen in love. *How could she be so cruel to such a wonderful man?* I wondered. As with her pursuit of her goals, my aunt was consistent with her castrations. Every time Jarvis grew another pair of nuts, she sliced them off.

Like four years ago, when Monica asked me to give her a ride to the airport for a four-day business trip. Jarvis wasn't happy about it, and she couldn't care less. She diced him like onions right in front of me—right before my eyes—for her entertainment purposes only.

"Yes, four days, you are correct. And two weeks ago it was three days. You're right about that, too." She rolled her luggage toward the front door while he followed from the bedroom. "Being that you love to count the length of my business travels, how about you subtract the difference in our salaries and go write a book about that? That should keep you busy until I return."

Before slamming the door, she left him with a parting suggestion:

"If you don't like it then you know what to do."

Before cancer knocked on her door, Monica was a bold, beautiful, businesswoman at Chase Bank, but at home, she was a blusterous, blunt bully and I watched Jarvis shoulder the bulk of it to keep his family together. With every insult he took, I fell deeper in love with him.

I also eavesdropped on some calls between my mother and Aunt Monica and heard my mother hand out advice to her sister that she wasn't strong enough to follow on her own:

"Girrrrl, sometimes people are for a season, and where God is taking you, maybe Jarvis was never in the Master Plan."

Inaudible.

"Monica, sometimes people outgrow each other, I mean look

at you. Your career has taken off, and Jarvis is still chasing a pipe dream. Talking about *he's a writer?* Not one book in seven years. You, on the other hand, are a go-getter. Those are the facts, and you shouldn't feel guilty."

Inaudible.

"Black men are like a crop of apples; by the time you shuffle through the rotten ones, the ripe ones, and the ones who also want a *big worm* deep inside them, you're left with a few who are ready for market. Nile Bivens sounds juicy and delicious; he will not be available that much longer.

Inaudible.

"But don't make any decisions too quickly without seeking God; if you feel he is your soulmate then what God has for you is for you."

That's my mother; she has a way of bending and twisting Bible gibberish to justify anything and everything, including trading in Jarvis for a Chase Regional Manager named Nile whose market was two states over.

Do you understand?

I had to do something.

So I intervened, because Jarvis is a good man. He didn't know Monica had tied him to the tracks and that the midnight train to Georgia was ahead of schedule. I wanted to free him. I wanted to save him from certain devastation, but unfortunately my timing was off, and I became the villain instead of his Superwoman.

How dare my mother judge me for falling in love with Monica's husband when she knew Monica Napoleon was in love with Mr. Bivens? It wasn't her love for Jarvis that kept her in the marriage, it was cancer. Once she could no longer travel to see Nile because of nausea, someone else scooped up that apple, and left Monica devastated on the sofa, determined to drink her life away. Like my mother, I kept Monica's secret. It's what we do; we hide things, and that's what my family is doing to me right now. They're hiding me because I brought shame on the family.

For the first time, I wasn't in the Christmas card photo that was mailed to all the church members, and no one has thought to check on me even though I'm sick and shut in. I had a baby shower where I was the only invited guest and the only one in attendance, not counting the child I'm carrying. I have attended at least a hundred baby showers—not one of those mothers sent a single Pamper for my son, but I'll be okay. Even though I'm all alone, I'll be just fine. Even though there's no one to drive me to the hospital, I'm believing God that I will make it. What better time to prepare for my new life? All alone, all by myself, alone with my son, a new mom—today I will become a single mom. How fitting is it that I have to drive myself to the hospital? But I will get us there the same way I got us through these last nine months; with love and determination.

Oooh, ooooh, awwww, ouch, ouch, that hurts so bad. I have to breathe. I can't breathe. Breathe. Breathe, Briana. Breathe as you were taught breath in Lamaze class. Oooohhhhhhh.

My baby is lower. I can't get up off the floor.

Everything is squeezing. I can't feel anything but squeezing. Is it squeezing or stabbing? Contractions or knives? I can't get up. *I have to get up.* Oh, thank God, it's going away, it's easing up. I don't have much time. I have to go now before the squeezing comes back.

God please, I know I have no right to call on you, but I have no one else to call. Please Lord, help me get to the hospital. If the pain is too great don't let me faint, Lord. Please clear the way for me. And if no one comes to visit my child, and if no one sends a single flower, I thank you in advance for a healthy baby.

CHAPTER 27

12:20 p.m.

JARVIS

I utilized my entire lunch break for the first of three phone interviews with a young lady who's a reporter for *Essence* magazine; she's excited about my book. If everything goes according to plan, then I'll be featured in the June edition, which kicks off their summer reading. She also plans to recommend a feature for me in the author showcase during the *Essence* Music Festival; if that happens, then I plan to retire early from the classroom.

All of this is happening at the perfect time, because I've just tossed the idea of getting a publishing deal. After six months of sending out hundreds of query letters to arrogant literary agents, I arrived at the conclusion that I will not devalue my art, and I refuse to kiss their asses another day.

I'm African American, and my book isn't about a white *girl on a train* or a white girl in a fucking window, the girl on a bike, the girl with a kite, or a missing white girl, or a white girl with a bow and arrow—nor is it about a cop trying to save the same white bitch who can't seem to figure shit out.

My novels are about the other stories that are taking place while the literary world continues its obsession with Holocaust stories and white girls in fucked-up situations.

The good news is, with the money from Uncle Glenn, I've launched my own publishing company. It's called Symphony Publishing—named after my oldest daughter—and I am the first author signed. This way, I am promoting my book directly to readers. Plus, I keep the majority of the sales after Amazon takes their cut, and that's cool with me.

After a relentless effort, I've also given up on trying to win back Monica and have grouped her in the same bundle with the literary agents. You can only kiss so much ass before you get herpes in the mouth. I've retired from ass-kissing. I tried, the answer was no; it's time to move on. And wouldn't you know it, I've just received a text from Brinna.

Water broke, and I'm on my way to East Jefferson. Just wanted to let you know.

Do I go or ignore the text?

And so it begins.

Time is up.

Decide.

If I go, what if her mother is there? The last time I saw her, she slapped me so hard I swallowed a wisdom tooth. What if her father is there? *Gangster Pastor* has put the word out that my ass is getting kicked the moment we cross paths. But she's having my son today, and she invited me to be there. The last thing I need in my life right now is more drama and bullshit, and Briana represents drama and bullshit—*represented*, I should say, because that hasn't been the case lately.

Briana has chilled out—all the way out. Our lives changed in Dallas for the worse, but I don't blame the baby. I set all these events in motion, and I destroyed my marriage—not Briana. Uncle Glenn always says:

Outside of your marriage, there is always someone who would like to fuck you, but they shouldn't get the opportunity.

I granted Briana that opportunity and destroyed the relationships in my household and Monica's family. From what I gather from Briana's texts, she was basically stoned by her father; her mother is barely allowed to speak to her without getting into a fight with her father. Neither sister has spoken to her since Dallas, and I have ignored every invitation to her doctor's appointments. I am guilty as charged for all of the above.

Then there's November 17, which is the date of my final divorce proceedings with Monica, and then it's over. Her cancer is in full remission. At our last conference to settle assets, she sat across the table from me looking fucking fabulous, if for no other reason than to taunt me. It worked. I wanted to snatch her by the arm, throw her over my shoulder, and go home, but her home is no longer my home—that conference made it clear.

I'm single, but married, with a baby coming today.

That's the definition of a dude in a midlife crisis if there ever was a dude in a midlife crisis. What do I do? Do I go be with Bri? I need to make a call. After a few rings, the person I needed to talk to answered.

"What's up, Jarvis? You've been on my mind all day. I was just about to call you."

"Uncle Glenn, I'm not sure how you knew, but the walls are closing in on me."

"How so? The last time we talked, things were looking up. What did I miss?"

"You missed the text a few minutes ago."

"From Bri-Bri?"

"Yes."

"The baby?"

"Yes."

"Today?"

"Bingo!"

"And you're calling me to get my opinion on whether or not

you should go?"

"*Blackout Bingo!*" I yelled into the cell.

"Jarvis, I can only tell you what I would do in your situation. Tomorrow will mark thirty-four years to the day I was escorted out of the hospital by police after holding my daughter one time, and there's not a day that goes by that I don't think about her. Sometimes I think about my daughter all day. Like you, I was in a situation, but on that day, I was there when my child entered the world. Here's the litmus test. Are you deployed overseas?"

"Huh?"

"Are you deployed?"

"No."

"Are you in Angola State Prison?"

"No."

"Has Briana invited you to be there?"

"Yes, several times."

"Then do what I did—be there for her. It makes a statement of accountability to the mother of your child and your child."

"You're right."

"Jarvis, I know you're embarrassed, and I know you don't want another confrontation, but you're not the first person in the world to fuck up. The true measure of Jarvis is in how you support Briana."

"Thank you."

"Now get your ass to that hospital and celebrate the birth of your son. The situation surrounding the child is fucked up, but the child is a gift from God. Go!"

And just like that, he hung up the phone, and just like that, I notified my principal that I needed to get to the hospital immediately: my son is coming today.

"Your son?" Her face filled with confusion because she knows my wife; they're from the same Pontchartrain Park neighborhood.

"Yes, my son. He's coming today, and I need to leave early to be there when he arrives."

Less than five minutes later, I was back in my car and hauling ass to East Jefferson Hospital to be with Briana. After my chat with Uncle Glenn, it felt like a world of shame lifted off my shoulders. Never again will I hide the fact that I have a son outside my marriage. No one should have that much power over my life to make me feel the need to conceal my son. Fuck them. I'm going to this hospital to witness the birth of my baby and support the woman I love.

Damn, I can't believe I said that: *the woman I love*.

I love Briana.

I do.

That's how I ended up in this mess. It wasn't the sex; I can say that for sure because some of the texts that hurt Monica the most were the ones in which I confessed my love to Briana. I fell into this hole because I fell in love with a woman outside my marriage; I fell in love with Briana. And I still love her. But I'm forty years old and she's twenty-seven years old, which is a difference of thirteen years. She's young.

But she wasn't too young to edit all my manuscripts without charging me one dime. She wasn't too young to write my media kits and distribute them to Oprah's Book Club, the *New York Times*, and *Essence* magazine, just to name a few. Is she too young? How is she too young? Uncle Glenn once asked me:

If your wife catches you with that woman, is she someone you could be with after the divorce?

Yes, Uncle Glenn, I could be with Briana after my divorce is final.

On the way to East Jefferson Hospital, I made one quick but very important stop. A few red lights later, I arrived in the parking garage.

Well, little man, you couldn't have picked a more perfect day in November for a birthday.

Following all the ceiling signs to the labor and delivery unit, I finally arrived outside of her door and knocked.

"Come in."

When I entered the room, Briana was on her side facing the sunshine. She never turned to look at me, nor did she know it was me.

"You can set the ice chips right there, I will eat them a little later."

On the side of her bed was a printer that coughed out pink and white pages which recorded the sound of my baby's heart. It sounded like my son was playing the bongos. I heard his sounds of life for the first time. In that split second, I became angry with myself—angry that I was hearing his heart for the first time, angry that I hadn't been more active during the pregnancy. I'd missed him kicking in her belly and satisfying her late-night cravings. Then I heard Uncle Glenn's voice again:

Now get your ass to that hospital and celebrate the birth of your son. The situation surrounding the child is fucked up, but the child is a gift from God.

I will never miss another day of his life; I have a son.

Softly, I approached her bed and placed a remorseful kiss where her tears dripped off the bridge of her nose. "How long before our baby arrives?"

She didn't turn, but she pulled me over her like a warm blanket on a winter morning. Then she wept. At first silently, then out loud.

"I drove myself here; no one would take my calls. I drove here in labor praying I didn't have my baby in the car. I was so scared. Everyone told me I deserved to be abandoned and I accepted it. I accepted that no one was coming to see my baby." Her body shook from a pain that was far greater than labor.

"Briana, first of all, I am sorry I wasn't with you during this pregnancy, but I'm here now and I will be here. It's time that we forgive each other and enjoy today."

As I covered her, she held onto my arm with both hands,

scared to let me go as if I would leave and never return; she was traumatized by loneliness. Not even when the nurse came in to check her dilation did she release her grip on my arm.

"Well hello, I am Briana's delivery nurse . . . and you are?"

"I'm the baby's father. Jarvis Napoleon."

"Nice to meet you, Mr. Napoleon. I estimate she will deliver within the next two hours; I'm happy you made it in time for the birth of your son."

When the nurse asked Briana to roll flat on her back, I decided it was the best time to get down on one knee. The nurse immediately backed to the wall in shock as Briana's hands clasped over her lips.

"Briana, when I was stranded on the road that day in Dallas, you sent me a text that said: *You're all the family I have left. I love you.* If you still want us, then I want to be your husband. Will you marry me?"

In between the sobs, I heard, "Yes, yes, yes!"

Over near the door, eight nurses fanned their teary eyes. As I slid the ring onto Briana's finger, they let out a cheer. Shortly after that, my son was ready to make his grand entrance two hours ahead of schedule.

Jarvis Napoleon, Jr. was born eight pounds, eight ounces with all his fingers and toes. He entered the world healthy, pissed off, and cold.

And I was there for it all; it was just the three of us. The only balloons came from my friends and me; the only visitors that arrived were my friends.

Biyell.

Telly.

Rasta.

Uncle Glenn.

CHAPTER 28

Friday, November 17, 2017
9:30 a.m.

JARVIS

I'm back in the same court. Today is the day Judge Cain will preside over the demise of our marriage. It ends today, and internally I am a band of thunderstorms rolling one after the next.

"Next case, Monica Napoleon versus Jarvis Napoleon."

The weird part about divorce court is you still love the person you're divorcing, but a decision was made either by either you or collectively to end the relationship part. Even in cases where two people leave out of divorce court physically severed, it's only a partial separation, because the bang of a gavel is futile in the face of real love. Why lie to myself by saying I don't love Monica; why think childish thoughts?

I do love her.

The reason we're in this court this morning has zero to do with love and everything to do with insecurity, self-esteem, and the anxiety of losing my manhood. Recently, I pulled all the pages of notes I've stored over the years at Uncle Glenn's house and noticed a few traits we guys have in common. All of us crossed the age of forty within a year of each other, and with the exception of Telly, all of us had been in long-term marriages since our early twenties. All of us experienced challenges remaining faithful. The thing that helped me understand the issues facing Biyell, Rasta, Timothy, Telly and myself was Telly's health issue.

Last month, Uncle Glenn asked Telly to give him a lift to a doctor's appointment, but what Telly didn't know was that the planned appointment with the urologist was his appointment. Telly had his first prostate exam and also had lab work drawn. Remembering how opposed he was to a rectal exam back in March, surprisingly, he didn't protest at all.

Quite strange how he matured.

When the results came back, we discovered that not only was he suffering from an enlarged prostate gland, but also extremely low testosterone levels. The doctor ran additional tests for prostate cancer; Telly hasn't revealed those results. Scared shitless, the rest of the brothers made appointments for exams. Telly's cancer screening aside, we compared results and discovered that Telly was the only one of us with prostate issues and had the lowest testosterone levels, but low testosterone levels were present across the board.

Unbeknownst to us, that plentiful hormone which made us feel confident and bullish was depleting every day; fucking was our only athletic activity, the only time we felt like ourselves. Some of us only experienced pre-sex arousal when the sex was with someone new. Unfortunately for our wives, our twisted minds associated those brief spikes in our testosterone levels with the new chick. Consequently, we wanted more sex with the new chick, because she had the good stuff. It was all the same stuff, but our bodies were transitioning. This resulted in an outbreak of midlife crises—we all wanted to recapture the vitality of a twenty-year-old.

Exhibit A: Briana.

Telly's results also helped me understand why we were always sharing the latest dick pill from the convenience store or energy drink to help you *fuck all night long*; our bodies were changing, and out of the many conversations we had, prostate health was the least of them all. I can speak first and say that I experienced a power outage in my dick, and I thought it was Briana who opened the breaker box and flipped the switch. My problem was, I didn't understand the reason for the power outage.

I'm not making excuses for our behavior, but when I reflect on the challenge posed by Uncle Glenn, I think about how Telly didn't lift a finger to change. It turns out that medically, he's the one in the worst shape—something is going on here. Consider this: how many marriages would have avoided this place if we knew in advance that these changes were inevitable? What if we were taught how to embrace these changes as men? Would I be here if I'd had prior knowledge that somewhere between age thirty-eight and forty-two I would start to feel less like the man I used to be? Guess we have to finish this chat another time; the bailiff just entered the courtroom.

Seconds later, Judge Cain was back on the bench and *showtime* began.

"Attorney Ned, is this a deja vu moment or did I just see you yesterday?"

"No deja vu, Your Honor, sometimes people are lining up outside my door for divorces; not sure if that's a good thing." They share the professional smile.

Monica and her sister Connie were sitting in the same row as me on the left side of the courtroom. War was painted across their faces, but I greeted them with a full-tooth smile and wiggly fingers. For being too ill for court back in August, Monica looks great. She's put on a few pounds, and her hair has grown. It would be my luck if she fully recovers after our divorce is finalized. I could see that happening; for no other reason than to twist that knife in my gut. But hey, I'll take my lick for what I've done.

A little transparency.

I'm in no mood to fight with Monica.

Briana has made me happier than a fat boy trapped all night in a Popeye's. I've only seen my daughters once since that day at the Shell gas station; four days ago was Lyric's birthday. The good news is they only spent the summer in Atlanta, but even though my daughters are three miles away, it has made little difference. They're giving me the silent treatment, and the pain is unbearable. Uncle Glenn suggested that I not force them to talk but advised me to write them a letter twice a month. *This way,* he said, *they have a tangible record of how you feel.* I can't help feeling like all is lost, but I still mail the letters as he prescribed.

I'm not here to fight. I simply want to marry Briana and get on with our lives.

Even though I've lost everything because of my decisions, I do reserve the right to catch a Biyell Spirit and flip this whole court upside down. I'm just saying.

Monica's lawyer is a white woman dressed in a sky-blue pantsuit who appears to be in her fifties. For the first twenty minutes, she proceeded to make me look like the worst *son of a bitch* on planet Earth, and a lot of it was true. My affair with Briana was public and painful; I not only lost my wife, I also lost my in-laws, my principal is trying to fire me, and my very own mother just started speaking to me again last week. It's been a rough run for me, to say the least.

Monica's lawyer just ended her massive character assassination of me and Telly didn't object one time—NOT one fucking time did he stop her. I think that wop-head nigga agreed with every word. He should've objected to some of the bullshit in the name of love at least, but he seems distracted, I can tell. I'll take that up with him later.

It's Telly's turn to repair some of this damage and make me appear human, at least. Being that I was at fault for destroying our marriage, chances are I am going to carry the bulk load of the financial responsibility, but our argument is she makes more money than I do, therefore that should be considered.

Telly addressed Judge Cain. "Your Honor, with bonuses plus base salary, Monica Napoleon makes one hundred and eighty thousand dollars a year—that's fifteen thousand dollars per month. Your Honor, my client is an English teacher at Warren Easton High School. Jarvis Napoleon takes full responsibility for his actions with a consenting adult, and he has offered to pay a dollar amount which we feel is fair. My client has agreed to pay one thousand dollars a month for his daughters Symphony and Lyric until they reach the age of eighteen. Your Honor, if you would review the tax returns for the last three years, you will see a consistent level of earnings that fall in line with the suggested monthly payments."

"It says here your client makes forty-two thousand per year?" Judge Cain confirmed.

A little snotty *haha* came from Monica's side of the room. It was Connie.

Of course, Monica's attorney countered by belching out a child support payment of $2,100 per month. In addition to that ridiculous dollar amount, Monica also wanted an executive position within my publishing business to monitor all sales, of which she demanded half.

"Your Honor, the amount that the plaintiff is requesting in child support is more than half of my client's monthly salary. He wouldn't be able to afford that, and it's not necessary when you consider her yearly salary. I also object to the plaintiff attempting to gain ownership of a publishing company that is still under development and has not yet produced a profit. My client will agree to pay $1,200 a month and maintain full ownership of his publishing company and all royalties from his manuscripts."

Judge Cain took several moments to review documents from both sides before she addressed our attorneys.

"As it relates to matters of child support, I'm awarding the plaintiff $1,000 a month; this is taking both salaries into consideration. I am also awarding joint custody with unsupervised visits. Being that the publishing company was established during the course of the marriage, I am awarding fifty percent of all sales and royalties to the plaintiff."

And that's when I felt the Spirit of Biyell come over me. I leaned over and whispered into the ear of my attorney. "Do it now."

"Your Honor, may I approach?" Telly requested.

Monica's attorney followed Telly to the bench, and things immediately became contentious. The judge was presented with the secret that Connie knew and Briana had overheard. I wasn't going to go there, but since she targeted half of my publishing company—my dream that she never believed in—it was time to take off the gloves and get bloody. Telly returned to our bench and gave me a fist bump.

"The attorney representing the defendant has introduced evidence to this court that we must verify, therefore we will take a thirty-minute break. Mr. and Mrs. Napoleon, as well as their legal counsel, will join me in my chambers after the break." The gavel banged.

Judge's Chambers

The heat of anger transformed the Judge's Chambers into a sauna. Monica was fighting mad and I was appalled something awful. I was willing to go along with a reasonable payment for the girls, but she showed her ass in court. That's why I played the card Briana handed me; the card Monica's sister knew was out there, a card I never knew existed. The plan was hatched right after Briana revealed it the day my son was born. After she told me the truth, I immediately called Telly. The next day was Lyric's birthday, so I made arrangements to take the girls to dinner, but Symphony refused to come. First, Lyric and I stopped at a bookstore, and then we went to Cheddar's, her favorite restaurant.

And yes, I had to tell a little white lie to my daughter to swab the insides of her gums, but it worked. The lie was that I needed the swabs for their dentist to see who might need braces. Lyric agreed to let me do the swab, after which I put the stick in an individual tube, briefly excused myself, and handed it to Telly in the parking lot. Shortly thereafter, the waitress returned with our food, and my daughter never realized that I'd conducted a paternity test right there in Cheddar's.

As for Symphony, luckily, I had a hair tie of hers in one of my suitcases, so getting a DNA sample from her was easy.

After he obtained both samples, Telly contacted a buddy who was able to rush the results for us in time for court. Monica was just given the update by her attorney, but she wasn't surprised. My youngest daughter Lyric is not my daughter. Therefore, if we're talking child support, we're only talking child support on one child. Only our attorneys stood between us, so what better time to demand the truth?

"My only question . . . if I'm not the father, then who is?"

"I don't owe you an explanation."

"On the contrary, I believe you do," Judge Cain interjected.

"Your Honor," Monica's attorney stepped in. "I object, under the grounds of badgering. We will continue the proceedings based on the child that we have confirmed is Mr. Napoleon's daughter."

"With all due respect, here's how we're going to proceed," I interrupted. "I love both of these children—that's why I requested this meeting in private. Your Honor, my wife knew I wasn't the father of one of my daughters, and she was still prepared to take me for every dime. I have been in Lyric's life since she was a baby, and I don't want her to know that I'm not her father un-less her mother insists. Your Honor, I will continue to raise her as my daughter, because I'm concerned about the impact that this information would have on her emotionally. The sisters are very close. If Monica will agree to forgo any rights to my pub-lishing company and agree to $800 per month, then the results of the paternity test will remain in this room."

Monica and her attorney exited out of the Judge's Chambers to consult. Until Briana said it, I never questioned whether I was the father of both of my children. I figured Symphony resem-bled me and Lyric *sort of* resembled her mother, but I never, ever questioned her paternity. Now it turns out I'm not her fa-ther, and that hurts, because Monica was first to commit adul-tery. Monica was first to step outside of our marriage. But this is not the time for a victory lap, because I love that child more than the air I breathe. I may never know who her real father is, but as far as I'm concerned, Lyric is my daughter.

All of this could have been avoided, but Monica had to take shit too far; she wanted to execute me publicly. In requesting a chamber meeting, I spared her the public humiliation of having her affair revealed in open court.

Monica and her attorney re-entered the Judge's Chambers. It was time to hear their decision.

"Your Honor, my client would like to make a counter request of $900 per month for Symphony, and she still would like half of the defendant's publishing company."

"I see. I will hand down my ruling in the courtroom within ten minutes."

I left the Judge's Chambers furious that Monica was still was trying to take a portion of my publishing company—a business that hasn't produced a dime, not one dime. *She is so fucking evil. She just wants half of it because she knows that would piss me off. At this point, all the gloves are off.*

After the ten-minute delay, the bailiff called us all back, and Judge Cain entered the courtroom.

"I've taken the necessary time to review both sides of the matter concerning Mr. and Mrs. Napoleon. Mr. Napoleon went far and beyond to resolve certain matters privately due to the sensitivity of the children's issues involved. However, Mr. Napoleon's offer was rejected in its entirety by Mrs. Monica Napoleon. I for one cringe whenever situations like this surface in my court—this is not the *Maury Povich Show*. However, it has come to my attention that the defendant hired the same paternity testing firm that we utilize here in civil court. We have verified the results as accurate, and here is my ruling. It has been determined through paternity testing that Jarvis Napoleon is not the father of Lyric Napoleon."

There was a rumbling throughout the courtroom as the judge tried to restore order. I looked over my shoulder at Connie and called her a hypocrite with my eyes. I had tried to work with Monica, but this is the end result she wanted.

"The publishing company was formed during the marriage, so all profits are considered shared. Based on the findings of this court, there appear to be two cases of infidelity that have resulted in a destruction of this marriage, therefore, I'm placing both parties at fault. Regarding child support, I am ordering Jarvis Napoleon to pay $600 per month until his child, Symphony Napoleon, is eighteen years old. Based on the salary of Monica Napoleon, I will grant Jarvis Napoleon's request for monthly alimony payments of $2,400 with full entitlement to all pensions and investment accounts. As it relates to the home, I have ruled that the property will remain in the name of both parties unless a buyout is reached. Let the record state that Jarvis Napoleon is not responsible for any monetary support for Lyric Napoleon because he is not her biological father." The gavel sounded.

I turned to Telly. "But I never requested alimony?"

"I know, but I did."

"I don't know what to say other than thank you."

"You gave her an out, but she decided to bet against the house—I am the house."

As I made my way out of court, I could feel Monica's eyes stabbing me in the back of my head. Once outside the courtroom, she made a hard left with her lawyer, then suddenly stopped and turned. Standing in the middle of the packed corridor, she couldn't pass up the opportunity to deliver one final lick.

"Jarvis, the answer to your question is Nile Bivens." With that, she turned and stiffly walked away.

After thanking Telly, I headed out to the parking lot. Just as I was about to drive home, I received a photo and a text from Monica. The photo displayed my daughter Lyric standing with Nile Bivens. The text read:

Here's the reason we were late that day at the gas station: Lyric was meeting her real father.

Sure enough, the date on the photo showed June 5, 2017 at 10:52 a.m., taken at Six Flags in Atlanta.

CHAPTER 29

4:30 p.m.

JARVIS

I *offered you a bite, because it was sweet to me. I offered you a bite, to open your eyes and see. I offered you a bite because I wanted you to have all that I have.*
I eat when you eat.
I laugh when you laugh.
To see how much you enjoyed that first bite made me proud.
Who could be so selfish to chew, and not offer any to you?
Who could be so heartless to not split it in two?
Not me, not the woman I am, not ever—we're going to eat now, together or never.
As you read this, just know I would offer it to you again.
Even though it was forbidden, and I'm technically kin.
But we're not the same blood—more or less a friend?
That's why I saved my fruit for you, and wiped the juice drip off your chin.
At first bite, we both became naked and ashamed.

218 / TJ SPENCER JACQUES

And I've repented over and over again, Briana to blame.
I am a score and seven years but don't be deceived.
Long before you took the fateful bite, I planted the seed.
Out of a storm of chastisement came my beautiful child.
But I would never starve you, then sail up to Nile.

Enjoy my apple.

Yours truly,
Eve

I found those beautiful words inside an envelope taped to the front door of our apartment. This explains why my manuscripts come back to me in better shape after I hand them over to her to proofread; Briana is a writer. I never knew she was such a bold, courageous writer. She does more than proofread my thoughts; she knows my thoughts. She knows what I am trying to say: she studies me.

Before I maneuvered my key in the doorknob, the aroma of a garlic-based meat sauce with onions and green peppers tickled my nose. When I entered the apartment, Briana was at the stove stirring with a wooden spoon. I closed the door softly like a thief and tiptoed closer to her and the three pots puffing on the stove-top. Briana was wearing one of my button-ups and a pair of gym shorts. She was so beautiful standing by that stove. Strangely, I don't remember her cooking like this when I used to creep here late in the evening—but then again, in those days, I was coming here to eat her.

"Hi baaaabe . . ." she purred her way over to me. "How did it go?"

From behind my back emerged a dozen of roses. Her jaw dropped.

"Oh, thank you! I have never received this many roses in my life." She placed the glass vase of flowers next to the other four dozen.

"Exactly the way you expected it to go. I gave her the easy way out, but her pride dragged us back to the main stage in the courtroom. They awarded me some monthly coins in alimony. I can see Symphony, who doesn't want to see me, but I can't see Lyric, because Monica doesn't want her around us. In winning, Monica made sure I lost in the end."

"I don't know what to say . . . I could understand her not wanting Lyric around me, but you?"

"It appears Lyric has busy getting to know her biological father. Hey, I'm divorced."

From the bedroom, I suddenly heard a cracking sound that gradually increased in volume.

Immediately, Briana bolted to my son. "Sweetie, could you turn those pots off for me?" she yelled from the bedroom.

I killed the flames under each pot, then joined her in the bedroom with my son. My little man was latched on the same as yesterday, latched on like a champ. The entire scene was worthy of a selfie if it hadn't been for her huge tit. *Stop lusting for her tit.* Seeing her breasts function in their true purpose is still a major adjustment for me, and the way they leak when he cries is puzzling as fuck, but I am enjoying every minute of my new family.

I lounged across the bed in front of Briana and give my son a finger to hold while he enjoyed his dinner.

"Are you ready to talk about it now?" I asked.

"Talk about what?"

"You know what."

"The wedding?"

"Yes, the wedding. What do you have in mind?"

"Like I said last week, I don't want a big wedding. Let's go to Vegas or the Justice of the Peace. There's one right around the corner."

"You looked it up?"

"Yeah, it's pretty boring sitting here while your son feeds."

"With the money that's going to come in from my book, I

want to give you the wedding you've always wanted."

"Jarvis, my family cut me off, and without my mother there and my father to give me away, I don't need the reminder that I'm the black sheep."

"But other people will come, and someone else can escort you halfway."

"No one will come from my side of the family."

"So, Justice of the Peace?"

"Yes, it's what I want—to get married and get on with our life together."

"If that's the wedding you want, then your wish is my command."

"What I want more than a wedding is New York. We've talked about it, and you should be in Manhattan where the action is for writers. There isn't anything keeping me here."

It was then that I understood the depth of the fallout between Briana and her family, and the severity of the severed ties. During sex when I'd said *let's run away*, she'd retained every word. In real life, my life is in New Orleans. My daughters—daughter, I guess, but Lyric is still my daughter no matter what—and my mom, and my entire support system lies in New Orleans. I couldn't imagine moving that far away from Uncle Glenn; he's all I have in terms of a father figure.

Suddenly, there was an angry knock at the door.

Bum-bum-bum-bum-bum-bum-bum.

"Are you expecting someone?" I asked.

"No . . ." she shrugged.

"Who in the fuck knocking on my door like that?"

"That's right babe, go handle that," she giggled.

I flexed a bicep for her, then headed to the living room to answer the door.

Bum-bum-bum-bum-bum-bum-bum.

"Hold on hold on, I'm coming."

When I opened the door, my blood pressure nearly blew the scalp off my head.

"*I would like to speak with my daughter.*"

"And hello to you too."

"Shacking up with my daughter?"

"Nah, this is our home, and in a few weeks she'll be my wife."

"Umm . . ." Connie rolled her eyes.

"Being that we weren't expecting guests during dinnertime, wait here and I'll ask her if she's up for company."

"This is not your house to tell me where I should wait to—"

I slammed the door.

Bitch will not disrespect me in my house. She was the gatekeeper when I wanted my wife back. I worked day and night to fix my family only to have that witch shut down everything I tried—even made me stand outside and wait like the UPS guy. It's her turn to wait outside.

I reentered the bedroom to find Bri pacing around the bed, burping the baby across her shoulder.

"Who was it; Jehovah's Witnesses?"

"No, worse."

"Who could be worse?"

"Your mother."

Bri pivoted, then faced me. The blood drained out of her face. "My mother . . . is at the door?"

"Yes, I think she's here to see the baby."

Briana started hyperventilating.

"Look, if you can't handle this right now, I can ask her to come back another time."

"Breathe. Breathe, you have to breathe," she coached herself.

"I'll have her come back another—"

"No wait . . . she's my mother, invite her in."

"Are you sure?"

"Yes . . . I'm sure."

I returned to the living room and opened the door just as Connie was turning to leave. I gestured for her to come in. She narrowed her eyes at me in disgust. I closed the door behind her and stood guard like a bouncer at a nightclub.

"Hello, Momma," Briana said from the doorway of our bedroom.

"Is that my grandson?"

"Yes it is."

"May I . . . ?"

Briana eyes moved around her mother and found me for approval. Her mother followed her eyes all the way to me as I nodded. Only then did she walk the baby over to her mother. As Connie reached for my son, she shot me another look over her shoulder.

"His name is Jarvis Napoleon," Briana told her.

"Jarvis?!" her mother hissed.

"Yes . . . Jarvis."

"Ummm . . ."

"I called you, did you get any of my messages?"

"Yes, but you know how your father is."

"I know, but I'm your daughter."

"Briana, this has been a lot to deal with. Be understanding of your father's position. You know how it is."

Right there is where I bit my tongue.

"I didn't ask about my father, I asked if you received my messages."

"I received all of them."

"And you didn't return one phone call?"

"Briana, this scandal has torn our family apart. You can't expect me to act like it never happened—"

"I expected you to act like a loving mother and at least acknowledge me."

It was then that I heard the cracking sound again. I also noticed the discomfort in Briana's face from her overflowing breast. She lifted the baby from her mother's arms and placed his greedy ass back on the nipple. Bri stood nursing with a tight face. I held the door open.

"I see, well it looks like I have overstayed my welcome. How long do you plan to play house with Monica's ex-husband?"

"Finally the truth—you didn't come here to see my son, you came here to see if Jarvis and I were still together."

"This is sin, you know. God will not bless any of this."

"If this is sin, then the sins of the mother have passed to the daughter. How many people have you scorned in the name of Jesus? How many marriages have you destroyed with your bad theology? How is it you were willing to hide Monica's sins with Nile, but were immediately ready to usher me to hell? Please explain how one sin was worse than the other. Please share the Gospel according to you."

"You watch your mouth; I am still your mother."

"Not according to the holiday cards you mailed to all the church members. You only have two daughters. If I had a mother, she would have been here to drive me to the hospital."

I opened the door wider.

"My future husband and I were just about to have dinner." Briana held up her hand to reveal her engagement ring.

"Bling, bling!" I couldn't help it.

"But the ink hasn't dried on his divorce!"

"It doesn't matter. Jarvis proposed, I said yes. As soon as I'm able to walk a city block, I will marry him in the courthouse."

"Don't do this, Briana. What did I ever do to you to deserve this? You have nearly killed your father—his heart is so broken."

"Mommy, this is not about you or my father. You have made it clear that I'm no longer a part of this family. I have one person who I know for sure loves me and my son. Unlike my parents, his love is unconditional. Since you're so ashamed of me, I would have you know that Jarvis has announced the birth of your grandson at his job. What about you? What about my father? Have any of you announced the birth of your first-born grandson? It's amazing how you can't forgive me, but you forgave Monica for deceiving Jarvis for thirteen years."

Connie turned and hauled ass out of our house, and I made it a point to slam the door with all my might.

"Honey, are you okay?" I asked?

"No, but I will be. As long as you hold me, I will be."

We returned to the bedroom, where I wrapped my arms around her as she finished nursing our son.

"I'm proud of the way you stood up for yourself. I know that was hard."

"It was, but she's gone. Let's get married next week."

"Next week?"

"Does the offer still stand?"

"Of course, Briana, next week it is."

SIX MONTHS LATER

CHAPTER 30

Madden Thursday
May 3, 2018
10:01 a.m.

TYRA

I'm sitting at my desk this morning, but I'm not here. The box is, and it's calling out to me. I should sign out and go home, or go get my nails done, or visit that little mom n' pop bookstore where they remember your name and know every book on the shelf intimately. I think that's what I'll do. After all, I have the vacation days, and if I don't use them, then I lose them. So why not use one to simply fuck off? Aren't I deserving of a *fuck off day*?

I'm raising two kids, but I'm not by myself. I have my mother; she drives me bat-shit crazy, but she loves us. I also have someone who loves me with all his soul, and he's a wonderful father to kids who aren't his kids. That alone should be enough to make me run up and down those matted gray cubicles out there singing *I'm walking on sunshine and it feels good,* but it doesn't. My mind is across town with my children, swept up in this world of uncertainty I've delivered them into: a world in which they're loved by two men, but only one of those men is active in their lives.

Yesterday, my son Brennan walked from me to Julian for the first time while my mother captured it all on her cell phone. I sent Biyell a copy of the video. He didn't reply. It was stupid of me to send the video. I wasn't thinking; what man wants to see their son run into the arms of another man? Right after I sent it, I apologized. Lord knows I wasn't trying to hurt Biyell; I guess I got so excited that I forgot the rules of this breakup. I wanted him to be a part of that moment, but he has opted out of his children's lives in every way but financially.

Every month, he sends an eight-hundred dollar check for child support. After I make a copy of the check, I send it back to him un-cashed. I am not Tamera, and he will not treat me like Tamera. If he doesn't desire to be active in my kid's lives, then we don't need an act of kindness from a stranger. I can take care of my kids without him or any other man, but it still hurts, because my daughter hasn't forgotten her father. I thought after a year she would stop climbing on the sofa to open the curtains in search of his cable truck, but she still does it. Even after I moved the sofa away from the window, she still opens the drapes and calls for daddy. Even as we're driving down the street, if she spots a truck with that bucket lift in the back, she calls out:

"Mommy stop, that's Daddy."

That hurts me more than his cheating or the lies, or the day he left the hospital and never returned. Watching my daughter cry for someone who may not ever show has dulled the wonderful days I have had since Biyell left.

Then there's Julian.

He has been the best man any woman could ask for, but he's Julian, so there's no surprise there. The surprise, or shall I say the disappointment, has been Biyell. All the women around me, including my mom, have said the same thing:

Girl, don't worry about Biyell; you focus on the one who God sent you and let him raise those kids.

It all sounds good, but it all feels like bullshit to me. I feel guilty every day, and though Julian was willing to step right in for Biyell, something doesn't seem fair about it—as if he could only get me back after I went through hell with Biyell, became impregnated twice, and devalued myself by having dinner with his Biyell's wife only to come full circle like a humble fool and say, *yes I will marry you.* That's not how it went down, but that's how I feel. I feel like I don't deserve Julian, like I should suffer a life with Biyell as punishment—that's the guilt I wake up with every morning. But I can't go on leaving Julian hanging because my guilt is not his fault. The longer I avoid what my heart is telling me to do, the longer I'm punishing Julian for the sins of Biyell.

Our new relationship feels like we never broke up. Julian is the man I have compared every other man to. I compared every other dick to his—even the penis pictures that we float around the office and the porn videos we *oh my goodness* about at work—every date, every kiss . . . I compared all of them to Julian. He's right at the tips of my fingers—literally.

When I opened the little black box with the wedding ring that night, all the wind left my lungs. I haven't looked at it since the day he placed it on the table, but today the box is open just as wide as my heart. I want to remove the ring from the pink interior grip, but I'm resisting. I want him to remove it, but first I need to ask myself three questions before I let him slide it on.

Can I be the wife to Julian that he deserves?

Can Biyell or any other man steal me away from Julian?

Can I give Julian a child without feeling compelled or pressured?

I opened the box, then powered up the camera on my cell phone. My answers to my own questions were:

Yes!

No!

Yes!

My answer to Julian's proposal is yes. I'm not going to keep him waiting a day longer. I have to remind myself that I am still a good woman, and he deserves nothing less. The answer is yes. Nearly a year after he handed me the box, I finally sent the photo.

It wasn't even an hour later that I received a buzz from Bella, our receptionist, who notified me that there was a guest for me at her desk. I know Bella; usually before she buzzes anyone in, she'll ask them to have a seat while she sends me a heads-up text, but not this morning, and I knew the reason. She sent the visitor straight to me, and he knocked on the frosted glass portion of my door.

"No one can make it from Baker Police Department to downtown Baton Rouge that fast."

"When you have a patrol car with sirens, you can." Julian held a dozen white roses, which still had the $29.99 price sticker on the glass vase from Rouses Grocery Store.

"I take it you received my picture?"

Julian walked around my desk and lowered to one knee. "Yes, I've waited for that text every day. Just when I was losing hope again, it came this morning. Tyra, I know how you feel about spending the rest of your life in Baker—I'm willing to live wherever you want to live as long as I'm your husband."

He had left the door open. All the nearby cubicles were empty because every woman on my floor had managed to sardine in front of my office.

"Tyra, I don't care what brought us back together or how it happened, just as long as I am the man you want. I love your kids, and if we never have another child, then I will continue to love them as my own. Tyra, will you make me the happiest man on Earth . . . will you marry me?"

Of course, I cried like a baby, of course, my staff cried like a bunch of babies, and of course, *I said yes.* After I said yes, he slid the ring onto my finger, I fell to my knees with him, and we kissed behind my desk until the cheers became too loud to ignore.

"I'm going back to work; I'll see you later for dinner," Julian told me as we stood.

"Girl, you better than me—I would hop on his back and *giddy up* out the door!" Bella yelled.

I waved Bella away. "Okay baby, I still have a full day as well, but I'll see you tonight." I lifted myself onto my tiptoes to kiss him.

I only followed him to the door seal of my office, but the crazy ladies I work with followed Julian all the way back to the elevator, clapping like a church on Easter Sunday. Once I made it back to my desk, I called my mom to break the news.

"Momma, what do you mean you already know?"

"He called me on his way to you to ask for my blessing." She was giddy like a child with a new toy. I have never heard my mother this elated.

"*Tyra, let me tell you . . . let me tell you!* I have already called everybody in the city of Baker—even Mayor Clark. We're having a wedding!"

"Please slow down. This just happened, I haven't set a date yet."

"Well, everybody I spoke with is free next Saturday," my mother giggled.

"Momma, we'll discuss it tonight, but Saturday is out of the question!" I giggled with her.

CHAPTER 31

Madden Thursday
11:10 a.m.

JARVIS

D amn right, she's pregnant again. I did wait the six weeks. Chances are I impregnated her in the parking lot after that six-week postpartum appointment. I'm pretty sure I did.

My wife shivered when the doctor applied the cold gel to her moon-shaped belly, and less than a minute later, I was looking into the face of our second child. Well, it wasn't actually a clear image of her face, but it was enough to make out all of her little features; she looks just like Briana. I don't care how many times I've sat in a room like this, it's always special to hear the heartbeat of your child. Unlike Briana's pregnancy with my son, I've been here for all of this, and it's been amazing.

If we for some reason had any doubt whether Briana was the mother of this child in her belly, all doubts were cast away once the 3D ultrasound captured the baby sucking her thumb. I still catch Briana sucking her thumb from time to time, though she plays it off like she's biting her nails. Lies!

"Do you see your baby sister? Isn't she precious?" I asked my son, who was more interested in grabbing the wand the doctor held.

On the way home, Briana could hardly control her excitement; our second child was a girl, and she would soon no longer be the only girl in the house. Over the last six months, I couldn't have asked for a better wife than Briana. With her, I've found everything that was missing from my first marriage. We're lovers, she's my best friend, and our publishing business is booming. But few things for my wife and I came without a fight, especially things involving my ex-wife.

Three months ago, I received word that Monica married her baby daddy Nile and was moving to Atlanta. The problem was, she wanted to sell the house we once shared, but I refused unless she gave up all rights to my publishing company. Last month, she returned the certified paperwork waiving her rights to the publishing company Briana created for me, and the timing couldn't have been better.

This morning, my publishing agent notified me that Lionsgate is interested in a movie deal for my book, and they're willing to give me a huge advance for the option rights. That's right—I've hit a lick from the sale of my home with Monica and my advance from the movie deal. I'm feeling like life is finally going my way.

Once we arrived home, I immediately saw her car parked in front of our door.

"What is she doing here?" Briana asked me.

"Your guess is as good as mine," I replied.

We exited the car and unsnapped my son out of his car seat. Monica exited her car at the same time, and I could tell something was wrong.

She greeted me first. "Good morning, Jarvis."

"Good Morning, Monica."

Monica turned slightly to the right to acknowledge my wife. "Good morning, Mrs. Napoleon."

A very shaken Briana replied, "Good . . . good morning."

"May I have a word with you? I promise not to take too much of your time," Monica asked as she turned back to me.

I looked at Briana, and she nodded her approval. "I'll take the baby inside and get him settled." We transferred the car seat handle from my hands to hers. From the car seat, my son smiled at Monica, and she smiled back.

Once the front door closed, I cut right to it. "So, to what do I owe the pleasure?"

"Oh, cut the crap, Jarvis. You know you shit in your pants when you saw me parked here."

"Yeah, you're right, shit is running down my leg as we speak."

She managed a slight chuckle, but not too much, as if she were trying to conserve her energy.

"I never had the opportunity to say this, but congratulations on your marriage. I wish you and Mr. Bivens nothing but love and happiness."

"Thank you. This is still a ton to get used to."

"I understand."

"Do you?"

"Yes."

All the legal fighting Monica and I have engaged in since the divorce has been carried out through our lawyers, so today is my first time seeing her since that day in court. Even visitation times with my daughter have been arranged through a mutual friend. As soon as I saw Monica, I knew something was wrong. She has a familiar look on her face; that dreaded absence of hope look she wore during the last three years of our marriage. She didn't have to say it, because I could tell. The floral-printed head wrap confirmed it.

234 / TJ SPENCER JACQUES

"So, when did it return?" I asked.

Her eyes watered. "About three months ago, and this time it's far more aggressive than before."

"Monica, I'm so sorry to hear that. When I was trolling your wedding pictures on Facebook, you looked so happy and healthy. What happened?"

"Cancer returned that week. I asked my husband if he wanted to put off our plans, and he said no. But it's back, and that's what I'm here today to talk about."

"Can I invite you in?"

"This will only take a minute." Monica gazed at a wreath on my front door that welcomed all to the Napoleon home. "Jarvis, I wanted to say I'm sorry."

"Monica, you don't have to apologize to me, I was the one who set these events in motion."

"That's what I led you to believe, but I was the one who had an affair long before you and Briana. I only recently saw the error of my ways—my daughters got me to see how horrible I was to you. I never knew how much they absorbed, but they heard it all. Lyric recently asked me how I could treat Mr. Bivens with more respect than I ever showed their dad. They still refer to you as their dad, you know."

"Even Symphony?"

"Yes, even Symphony. On my wedding day, she cried the entire day. As angry as she appeared to be, I think deep down she was holding out hope for us. When I married Nile, it hit her like a sack of bricks. She misses her dad."

It was my turn to struggle and fight back tears.

"Jarvis, your forgiveness matters to me."

"Monica, all is forgiven. I'm hoping we can be friends going forward."

"I'm not going that much further than now."

"Monica, are you giving up? Is that why you're here? You can't give up, Monica; you still have the girls."

"I wouldn't say I've given up, but I'm tired of fighting something that's determined to kill me. Tired of waking up not knowing if I'm dead or alive. I'm exhausted."

"Please don't give up; you have to keep fighting."

"What I have to do is hope for the best but prepare for the worst. Part of preparing for the worst means drying my eyes and making accommodations for my daughters."

"Both daughters?"

"Jarvis, I don't want them separated, and if I close my eyes today or tomorrow that could happen, unless . . . unless—"

"Unless I agree to take them both?"

"Yes."

"But what about your husband?"

"It was hard to convince him, but I asked him as a dying wish to keep my daughters together. He says if you would be willing to give him summers with them, then he would agree. This way, the girls will travel together and will never have to separate."

"Monica, of course, I would be willing."

In that moment, Monica became overwhelmed with grief for something that hadn't happened yet. In her mind, I could tell she had given up. This visit today was part of her estate planning; that was the reason she needed so desperately to sell the house. There were college tuitions to plan and all the little things she wouldn't be around to see to account for. This was, in fact, goodbye.

"Can you please discuss things with my niece?" Monica caught herself. "Sorry, I mean your wife. Confirm if she's okay with being the custodial parent of my girls?"

"Monica, it goes without question that she will agree to it . . ."

"I'm sure she will, but could you ask her for me before I leave? That will give me peace of mind. You know I have a fear of a bitch burning my children with cigarettes. Briana loves them, and so do you."

"I do, we do. I'm going ask her, but would you like to come inside at least?"

"No, I'll wait here."

I entered the house to find Briana seated on the sofa in the one spot where she could have watched us through the window the entire time, but of course, she played it off.

"Briana, there's something I need to ask you."

"Is it about the reason she's here?"

"Yes, it's serious."

Briana walked over to the stove, killed the flames under her red beans, then returned to the sofa. Sheer terror of the unknown consumed her face; I could see her hands trembling in anticipation of devastating news. Her lips could barely touch as a result of the tormenting thoughts; I could practically see them race across her face, one after the other. I read her mind as she coached herself to breathe and fought off a full panic attack. As if Monica had come to reclaim me; as if the clock had struck midnight, she was Cinderella, and all of this was just a wonderful dream. That was the look of trepidation in her eyes and the rumble of turbulence in her gut. I could tell, because I know my wife.

"Monica shared some bad news with me about her health—"

"*Her cancer has returned?*"

"Yes, and it's more aggressive than before . . ."

"Why didn't you invite her in?"

"I did, but she wanted to stay outside. She wanted me to ask you if we can take both girls full time if she should die."

"You mean, she's offering both girls, to live here with us? To raise?"

"Yes, because she doesn't want them separated."

Briana lifted my son up off his play mat and handed him to me. Before I could say another word, she stormed out of the house in a straight line toward Monica. The one thing that I never wanted to happen was about to happen—*Briana and Monica in a face-to-face confrontation*, I thought. So, I followed Briana out of the house and saw Monica's head raise as she approached.

"Monica, I'm sorry for my role in what happened." Briana's voice was weighted with tears. "But woman to woman, I want you to know that I have always valued the trust you had in me as it related to your daughters. I will honor that trust should the day come when our home has to become their home. Yes, they can live with us—"

Before Briana could finish her sentence, Monica threw her arms around her, and they hugged and cried. I snuggled my little man and left them outside hugging and crying as we went inside and played with our trucks on the floor.

When Briana returned, she was still very emotional; she continued to our bedroom where she fell across the bed. We followed her, and it was there that I saw my wife unload all her tears into the bedding. I placed the baby on the floor on the side of the bed and tried to pull her to my chest, but she refused.

"Bri, I don't understand. What has you so upset? I thought the talk went well."

"Apparently she didn't tell you everything."

"There was more?"

"Yes . . ."

"What did I miss?"

"My mother also has the same aggressive cancer. No one called to tell me. It's like I'm dead to them."

"Bri, no."

"I don't know what else I have to do to prove to them that I'm sorry. How many times do I have to say it? Jarvis, how many times? They have made their point crystal clear; I am no longer a part of that family. The only reason Monica told me is because, because . . ."

"Because what, Bri?"

"Jarvis, Monica has less than six weeks to live. That's why she came today, and that's why she refused to leave until you spoke with me. Her body is no longer responding to the treatments."

"Oh, my Lord . . . six weeks?"

"Less than six weeks."

CHAPTER 32

Madden Thursday
2:05 p.m.

TYRA

I think I've answered seventy-eight consecutive questions about Julian—from the time the elevator beamed him down and all throughout lunch, they wanted to know everything. None of them could believe he had waited for me all this time. Hell, I couldn't believe it, but he waited—like a night watchman.

"*Gurrrrl, tell me he has a twin brother?*" Bella asked.

"*Gurrrrl, then he set the ring on the coffee table and said you let me know when you're ready? Shit like that doesn't happen to me. I had to buy my own ring!*" Laura yelled in laughter.

I'm happy he waited, and I'm even happier that I eventually came to my senses; it doesn't get any better than Julian. Oh, look, another text from my mother. That makes fourteen since the proposal this morning. I'm going to grant her this moment; her oldest daughter is getting married, and this may be the only wedding she attends for her daughters. My younger sister is gay and happy, and she doesn't believe in marriage. I was my mother's last hope.

Since lunch, I have been sitting here gazing at this ring. It's beautiful. It's heavy. *I should clock out early today and go follow my future husband around Baker for the rest of the day.*

Just as I grabbed my purse, I saw my assistant speed-walking in my direction. I knew whatever was in that file she was carrying just canceled my plans of stalking Julian.

"Knock, knock, are you busy?"

"Never too busy for you, Laura, come on in."

Laura quietly closed the door behind her. "Tyra, I'm sorry to bring this to you, considering the day started with such wonderful news, and I would have handled it on my own, but—"

"Laura, what is it..."

"Well, well, we just received an abuse report from our New Orleans district that was escalated up to you."

"Why would they have to escalate an abuse case to us? Is the media involved?"

"No, that's not the reason. Not yet at least."

"Then what's going on?"

"It's an abuse case involving one of our employees."

"Who is it?"

"Well, a daycare owner reported that she noticed the child victim—age three—bleeding from her vaginal area. When she asked the child if anyone had touched her, she told the worker that the man in the house had penetrated her with his finger. The case was escalated up to the district manager over New Orleans, who in turn escalated it up to us when the child gave a statement to the doctor at Children's Hospital: *I told mommy.* Then she noticed the mother's name. That's when I got the call."

"Do we know the mother?"

"I'm afraid we do."

She handed me the file, and I saw that the case was against a Mike and Tamara Reynolds. A quick look through the file confirmed that Tamera Reynolds was formerly Tamera Baltimore."

"Tyra, the police would like to know how you want to proceed." Laura sat on the edge of her chair.

"Where are the parents at this moment?"

"They're at Children's Hospital. The staff is keeping them in the dark until we send word on how to proceed."

"Has a statement been taken from Tamara?" I asked.

"Yes, she has confessed that the child did mention the abuse to her once before, but she didn't take her seriously. Our caseworker onsite feels that Tamera is defending the husband, saying that he would never harm her daughter."

"Have you pulled a background on the husband?"

"You know I have." Laura handed me a document pulled from the Louisiana State Police database. On top lay a printout from Jackson, Mississippi.

"The reason I dug into the Jackson database is that my sister works for CPS in Jackson, and Mike Reynolds is originally from Jackson. He was arrested in 1997 for lewd acts with a child under the age of fourteen. The child in that case was six years old."

"Have NOPD arrest Mike Reynolds for the molestation charge."

"What about Tamera?"

Here is where I hesitated slightly, only because Tamera didn't know her husband was a pedophile—but her daughter did notify her about the lewd acts. There was only one thing left to do.

"Tamera is free to go, but she will lose custody of her child while this is under investigation. Also, notify her that she has been placed on unpaid leave until this case has been resolved in court. If we cannot trust her to protect her own child, then how can we trust her to protect the children she's assigned?"

After Laura closed my door and I was alone, I became so angry with Tamera. *How could you let love blind you from your first responsibility, which is to protect your child? How could you take the word of a new husband over the voice of your daughter?* I shuddered in rage and disgust.

Then my mind fell on Biyell. What's going to happen once he finds out Mike molested his daughter, and Tamera knew? This will get ugly before it gets better; I just hope I can get to Biyell before he hears about this on the news.

I sent Biyell a text:

I know I'm the last person you want to talk to right now, but all bullshit aside, I need you to call me ASAP. One of your kids is in the hospital.

I pressed *send* and didn't get the chance to place my cell on the charger before he called.

"Come again? My child is in the hospital?"

"Biyell, are you in a private place where you can talk?"

"I'm on a construction site for Uncle Glenn; we're finishing up his house. What's this about one of my children in the hospital?"

"It's Bylisha."

"What?! What's going on? What happened?"

"Biyell, I need you to promise me that you will remain calm after I say what I'm about to say."

"Tyra, I will do my best . . ."

"Biyell, I received an escalation in my office from New Orleans; it was about an abuse case involving Bylisha."

"Abuse?"

"Yes, sexual abuse."

"Tyra, what are you saying to me on this phone?"

"Biyell, I just issued a warrant through the State Police to apprehend Mike Reynolds for lewd acts committed against Bylisha." I could feel the heat of rage through my phone. "He has been apprehended, and we have stripped Tamera of custody until after the matter is settled in court. I know you're listed as—"

"Did Tamera know?"

"It's hard to say for sure . . ."

"Tyra, you've never lied to me, so don't choose today to start. Did Tamera know he was molesting my daughter?"

"Yes, your daughter told the daycare worker and the doctor

at Children's Hospital that on three separate occasions, Tamera knew and she failed to act."

I could hear Biyell crying on the other end of the line. His cries were filled with pain for what his daughter had experienced, and regret for not being there to protect her. *This crisis just escalated.* I figured I'd better choose my words correctly, or Bylisha could lose both parents.

"Biyell, I need you to listen to me like never before, because right now your daughter is in my care. There are three people that Tamera listed for emergency care—two of them have had cases in our office, and the third person flat-out said no. I feel better turning her over to you, but you're on record rejecting her in court."

"I know I did, but . . . but I love my daughter. I love Bylisha; you know that, Tyra. I can go pick her up right now, where is she?"

"Biyell, with the statement you signed in court, you are not an option for me."

"But Tyra, you know I would never hurt my child . . ."

"Biyell, I know you wouldn't, and that's why I'm trusting you to provide me with someone who can care for her while we sort this out."

In the background, I could hear what sounded like a huddle of men around Biyell as he explained to them what had happened. His grief was nearly inconsolable, but the men I heard in the background tried to get him to pull it together. The entire conversation broke my heart, because I knew the day Biyell signed that statement waiving his rights as a parent in divorce court was going to come back and bite him in the ass—today it just bit him in the ass.

Tamera was once a child in the system, therefore she doesn't have a family unit intact to respond to a crisis of this magnitude. So often, people take their family members for granted—even I have been guilty of it—but I know if I were in the same position (though I wouldn't be, because I listen to my children), my mother would be there to take my kids. Such was not the case for Tamera. No family members had stepped up to save her and her siblings from foster care, and there was no one today willing to step up for her daughter.

Just then, I heard:

I will fucking kill both of them; they will die together for this. On everything, I will kill that nigga for molesting my child.

The men in the background couldn't get Biyell to calm down, and I was running out of time. I had to place Bylisha within the hour—thank God the next voice on the phone was a calm one. It was the voice of the man I had spoken to briefly, heard so much about, but never got the opportunity to meet—the one who tried to teach grown men how to be better men; how to be the husband of one wife.

"We're sorry to keep you on hold but I will take the call from here. Tyra, this is Glenn Braxton."

"Hello, Uncle Glenn. We have to stop meeting like this."

"We sure do. We're almost finished with my house, and I'm inviting you to the housewarming. I want to meet, okay?"

"Yes, I hear you. Uncle Glenn, I am trying to prevent Bylisha from falling into state custody, but I can't quite sign her over to Biyell—"

Uncle Glenn cut me off, "Well my wife and I will take her right now, where is she?"

"Great, all I need is some basic information, and if all comes back clear I can provide you with a pickup location."

When I ran a check on Uncle Glenn and his wife, everything came back spotless.

"Uncle Glenn, you still there?"

"Yes, I'm here."

"I am awarding temporary custody to you and your wife. I don't have an issue with Biyell seeing her, but she can only sleep at your residence. I will contact you within three days with instructions from the court. Her mother is not allowed around the child, and that also includes phone calls. If you agree, then I can text you the pickup location."

"Yes, I agree. The baby is not at Children's?"

"Bylisha has been discharged from Children's Hospital, stand by for the pickup location."

"Thank you so much. My wife is here, she would like to speak with you."

"Okay, put her on."

I spoke with Diana Braxton; she was overjoyed to have Bylisha and gave me her word that everything would go according to my orders from the state. Suddenly, I heard a commotion as several voices in the background screamed at Biyell.

"Tyra, we'll have to call you back . . ."

"Mrs. Braxton, what's going on?"

"My husband and the boys tried to stop Biyell from leaving but they couldn't. He's gone looking for Tamera. Biyell just purchased an AR-15 this morning. He said it was for protection, and now this. The boys and my husband drove off after him, but I'm available to get Bylisha."

Oh no, Biyell. Please keep your head.

CHAPTER 33

Madden Thursday
2:58 p.m.

RASTA

At ninety miles per hour, we drove directly behind Biyell, but he refused to answer his phone. I know he's angry and hurt, but I cannot allow him to throw his life away in a fit of rage. If you've ever wondered what makes a person pull out a gun and shoot another person, then look no further than Biyell.

He doesn't give a fuck.

He's determined to defend the honor of his daughter, and in many ways, I agree with him. Somebody should die for this today—but that's my irrational side. My rational side knows that violence is not the way, but somehow I have to convince Biyell. If we fail to stop him and his murderous plan, then two people will certainly die, and I cannot have that because Biyell is in my wedding next month.

Of all the times for this to pop off, of course it would be just a few weeks before I plan to marry Fate. I proposed to her on Christmas Eve, and she said yes. We are both ready to give love another try. She accepts me as I am. At first, I was nervous about sharing my episode in the mental health clinic, but Fate is a true believer in mental health, and I was encouraged to find out that she also visits a therapist twice a month. The funny part is, her therapist is in the same building as Dr. Morton's outpatient clinic.

Fate is also a no-strings-attached giver who does not keep a ledger of every little thing she does for me, nor do I keep a running ledger on her. We give freely and genuinely support each other.

We're getting married on a Saturday afternoon in June and I can hardly wait, but first I have to get my buddy through this day. We're so close—this construction project for Uncle Glenn has been the best thing that could ever have happened to our confidence. From the money we've made so far on the build for Glenn and Diana, we were able to buy another house to flip. Then my beautiful fiancée helped us set up a construction company, and her friend Tiffany found us a first-time buyer for our house—but Fate didn't stop there.

Last month we had a late evening barbecue at the construction site to celebrate finishing Glenn and Diana's trim ahead of schedule, and Fate invited Tiffany for the sole purpose of introducing her to Biyell. Tiffany was tired of being alone and looking for a good man. I didn't suggest Biyell, but Fate knew he was single. That day, I pulled Biyell to the side and threatened his life.

"Listen up, nigga; my girl is going out on a limb by introducing you to her best friend. Don't fuck this up!"

"I won't fuck it up," Biyell assured me.

"Biyell, I'm as serious as an HIV test. My girl doesn't know your past; I didn't tell her. She formed her opinion of you based on her interactions with you, and she highly respects you, Biyell. Don't make her regret it by being the dude Jarvis wrote about in that book. This is your chance to settle and enjoy where we are in life; God has been good to us."

"Rasta, there's no need to worry. I'm done with that life, and besides, her friend looks like Gabrielle Union! I couldn't pull one like her if I tried."

"Biyell, don't make me kick your ass."

"I give you my word, brother; I will not fuck Tiffany over. I have retired from whoring."

And he meant it. Dude even accompanied her to a Christian singles conference in Atlanta where she was a guest speaker. When he got back from that conference, he told me something which confirmed to me that he was serious about his retirement:

"Rasta, this is gonna sound crazy, but when I got to that conference, the first speaker started with the same quote Uncle Glenn showed us in that video. That quote from Timothy, of all the fucking books in the whole Bible:

1 Timothy 3:2: A bishop then must be blameless, the husband of one wife, vigilant, sober, of good behaviour, given to hospitality, apt to teach.

"When I heard the speaker recite that quote nearly as soon as I sat down, I knew this shit was more than a coincidence. This is my chance. I want the peace of being blameless, and I want Tiffany and no one else."

My dawg is smitten with Tiffany the real estate broker; the hookup was perfect. Everything was going according to plan, then today happened. Instead of us chasing the next real estate deal, I am now chasing Biyell across the Mississippi River Bridge.

"Where do you think he's going?" Uncle Glenn asked from the passenger side of my truck.

"Your guess is as good as mine. I do know Tamera lived in the Lower Ninth Ward, but t looks like he's headed toward the Orleans Parish Jail."

And he was.

Biyell slammed his brakes by the rear entrance of the jail—the entrance where those who have posted bail are released. Then he ran across the street to a bail bondsman's office. I parked and ran after him.

I entered the bail bonds office just as the agent was greeting Biyell, but I interrupted.

"Sir, please pardon us for one second." I grabbed Biyell by the arm and tried to pull him outside.

"Rasta," he growled. "Let me go, bruh."

"Not until you step outside and talk to me."

"Rasta, I won't say it again. Let me go."

"I will, but let's have a quick word in private. Let's step outside."

"Is there a problem, Mr. Baltimore?" the bond agent asked.

"There's no problem, but I do need my partner to stay out of my business," Biyell said.

"I can't have you two pushing and shoving in my office. I agree with the gentleman: it seems like you guys have something to discuss outside in private. After you work it out, then we can post the bail for Reynolds."

"What? The bail for Reynolds?" After hearing that, I dragged Biyell toward the door against his will.

"Gentlemen, I need you two to step out of my office—final warning."

The other staff in the bail bonds office got into defensive positions; their hands disappeared under their desks or behind their waists. Thank God Jarvis arrived. Together we forced Biyell outside.

"Biyell, you're posting bail for Mike Reynolds?"

Biyell didn't answer me.

"Dude, if you planned to post that bail to kill him . . . that ain't happening."

"Rasta, you don't understand, it wasn't your child he raped. That bitch has to die first."

"First? Then who's next? Huh? Tamera's next? Then you?"

He didn't answer.

"So you're throwing it all away today?"

He looked away from me as if I wasn't there. With my hands clutched to his collar, I drove his back against the exterior brick wall of the bail bonds office.

"Get your head out of your ass, bruh; I'm not gonna let you kill anyone unless you plan to kill me too."

"And me too," Jarvis said.

"And me too," Uncle Glenn echoed as he hopped over to us on his custom crutches.

"Unless you plan to shoot all of us . . . that's the only way," I said.

"And you can say goodbye to that AR-15 rifle in my trunk; you're not getting it back," Jarvis added.

"Dude, that's not my only gun!" Biyell raised his shirt to show a Glock stuffed behind his buckle. "You rape my daughter, you die—that's the fucking rule. Then that bitch will die for bringing that piece of shit around my baby. She was so busy trying to show off with that nigga she didn't even Google the motherfucker's name. I did, and it was right at the top—he raped a child in Jackson, Mississippi. Bitch wanted to show me how fast she could find a man and brought a pedophile into my house. My child support was providing this nigga shelter and lights to rape my daughter. He has to die, bruh."

No. 28: I can handle whatever comes.

No. 52: I can overcome this obstacle.

No. 25: I can see stressful situations as challenges.

"Biyell, listen to me."

"Rasta, ain't shit you can say to save him; I'm about to put up this ten thousand dollars for his bail and when he steps out, I'm beating that bitch down, then blowing his fucking brains out."

"And Biyell, you have every right to, but hear me out. That ten grand you're about to waste is money you worked for night and day. I know how much you have in the bank because I have the same amount. We have plans for that money; Tiffany won a bid at the auction this morning, she needs all that money, plus all I have. You told me when we started on Uncle Glenn's house that I will never have to look for you because you will be right by my side. Dawg, you promised me. I love you too much to let you go out like this on a molester who will get shanked in prison anyway."

No. 9: I can stay calm when talking to difficult people.

Through the glass window, I could see the bails bonds agent growing anxious for ten grand.

"Pussy-ass nigga raped my baby; that's my baby he did that shit to—"

"Diana is on her way to pick up your baby, and from what Tyra told us, it will be a long time—if ever—before Tamera can regain custody of Bylisha. For me, please calm down and help us help your daughter. If you kill Mike and Tamera and get yourself thrown in prison, that leaves your daughter in this world with neither parent. An orphan. Do you want Bylisha to be an orphan?" Uncle Glenn asked with tears in his eyes. "Do you, Biyell?"

In a weak, defeated voice, Biyell finally replied, "No, I don't."

"Then chill with all this ignorant bullshit and handle this the correct way. Let's get Telly to get you back in court to reverse that waiver you signed. Bylisha has a room at my house, and you can live with us. We have five bedrooms. Be the daddy Bylisha needs," Uncle Glenn pleaded.

"I agree with Uncle Glenn; Bylisha needs you," I affirmed.

"We need you," Jarvis added.

It was then that a black Mercedes 550 came to a rolling stop on the shoulder of the street. It was my Aunt Diana. She parked and walked around to the back passenger door, and out came Bylisha. The three of us stepped to the side to allow Biyell a full view of a child he hadn't seen in a year. Bylisha took care of the rest for us.

"*Daddy, Daddy, Daddy!*" She ran to him as if no time had passed. Biyell ran to her.

Biyell picked up his little girl and tossed her in the air. Once

252 / TJ SPENCER JACQUES

she came down, her arms wrapped around his neck. With his daughter glued between his arms, Biyell waltzed along the sidewalk under a perfect ray of sunshine—a daddy and his daughter. Bylisha was safe again.

Biyell turned to face us, and we waved bye-bye. Shortly after that, my aunt handed him Bylisha's booster seat and he snapped her into his truck

"Go enjoy the rest of the day with your baby, I will finish up at the work site," I told him.

Once Biyell drove off, my aunt walked over with a smirk and substituted herself for one of Uncle Glenn's crutches.

"Don't come grinning at us, we had it under control before you got here," Uncle Glenn said as he wrapped his arm around her.

"Yeah, sure; it really looked under control." Aunt Diana tickled Uncle Glenn under the arms, causing him to drop his other crutch.

"Lady Diana, your timing was perfect," Jarvis exhaled. "How did you know it would work?"

"When my husband asked me to bring her, it made perfect sense."

"Because we know how much Biyell loves that little girl," Uncle Glenn added. "Every day he didn't see Bylisha, a part of him died. Biyell isn't as tough as he portrays; his weaknesses are those kids. That little girl gave him a new reason to live, and all it took was for him to hear her say, *Daddy, Daddy, Daddy.*"

It was then that I opened the door of the bail bonds office to give them an update.

"Sir, we appreciate your patience with us, but you can cancel that bail for Mike Reynolds."

No. 1: This too shall pass, and my life will be better.

The agent appeared confused. "So his brother changed his

mind about posting the bail?"

"That wasn't his brother, that was the father of the child Mike Reynolds molested."

"I see . . . so in other words, if we had posted that bail, then chances are Mr. Baltimore was going to—"

"But thank God it all worked out," I cut him off.

"Yes, thank God," the agent replied.

CHAPTER 34

Madden Night
Thursday, May 31, 2018
6:30 p.m.

It's our first Madden night in the new house, and Diana has threatened to throat-punch each one of us if she smells weed . . . but she didn't say anything about the back yard. On the game, Biyell is stomping Crowd Noise, and to no surprise, he's silent as a church mouse. Crowd Noise isn't the only one losing games; all of us are rusty from the long layoff periods when life was too hectic to game up.

From room to room, Bylisha and Braylyn are running throughout the house looking like cute little twins. Diana has fallen in love with Bylisha, and it has been an intoxicating joy to have a child in the house—a joy neither of us ever had the chance to experience.

An monumental moment occurred when Tyra and her fiancé brought Braylyn and Brennan over: all of them and Biyell embraced without the drama. It was more than I could have prayed for; the rest of us looked on in complete awe. Tyra didn't stay long, but she wanted to come in and say hello. It was during this time that we witnessed Biyell and Julian share a man-to-man handshake. I'm still in a state of shock. We're so proud of Biyell for getting control of his emotions. He even called Tyra to apologize for leaving her in the hospital; that one apology healed many lacerations between them.

The new house exceeded our expectations, and I can't say it's a dream house because we never dreamed anything like this home. Rasta and Biyell were the general contractors on the entire project, and we didn't have to worry about a single nail being out of place. And then there are those mahogany kitchen cabinets—my Lord. Those mahogany cabinets. My wife stands off to the side and gazes at her kitchen for hours, focusing especially on those mahogany cabinets.

"It's too new to cook in," Diana told me as she admired the kitchen.

"*That's buuuuuullshit!*" I laughed.

Just when I thought he couldn't top his craftsmanship, Rasta walked us over to a little side compartment he'd built at the entrance of the kitchen. Inside stood two custom crutches that match my cabinets. I started crying like I'd won Miss America.

With the wedding on Saturday, we extended tonight's Madden Night to include our significant others. All the brothers brought someone except Telly, but I know why. It is time for me to have a word with him about the creeping.

"Telly, what happened that you didn't bring Erica? We were looking forward to meeting her and the girls."

"Uncle, I wanted to bring her, but we're beefed out right now."

"Over what? What did you do?"

"Man, she's been tripping lately."

"That's not what I asked you." I know Telly like a book, and when the issue is something he's guilty of, he'll deflect to Erica.

"What did you do to piss her off?"

"Since she went through my phone and saw those pictures from that threesome, it's been hell in that house."

"The pictures Rasta told me about with Heather and the other woman? In your old apartment? So, you still fucking Heather?"

"Ummm, yeah!"

"Telly, Telly, Telly. Brother, you will be forty-two this year—when will it stop?"

"It's just sex. I told her it was a fantasy; no feelings were involved. She didn't buy it. But it's not like I can get that type of sex from her. I don't even feel right asking her for a threesome."

"Why would you think she wouldn't be okay with that? You could have at least talked to her about your fantasy."

"Erica? Please . . ."

"But you didn't give her the chance to decline before you powered up *Silicone Doll* to do it for you."

Somehow the guys started referring to Heather as Silicone Doll, because she reportedly has an ashen complexion and pencil eraser nipples. That's the only rationale I have for the nickname.

"I know Erica, and if I were to ask her for something like a threesome, she would cry for three weeks straight. It's easier to keep someone I can fuck on as needed and warehouse Erica for the wholesome shit."

"Telly, it's obvious you will never commit to one woman, but why not let Erica go?"

"I'm not doing that! There are some things about Erica that are priceless."

"Like what?"

"Her pussy and her pancakes."

"Telly, her pussy and her pancakes?"

"Yes, pussy and pancakes. She makes the *best fuckin' pancakes* you have ever had in your life. Each bite is like a wedding cake with eggs. And her pussy is tight like new socks! Not letting her go. Fuck that. Erica is golden."

"You can't continue fucking her over; at some point she will get tired."

"My hurdle with Erica right now is getting her over the heartbreak of seeing those threesome pictures; once I'm over that, then things will get back to normal, and I know just the way to do it."

"And that is?" I wondered aloud about his scheme.

"I can't tell you that right now, but you will know real soon."

"Telly, just let her go. I have never met the young lady, but from everything you have described, my heart breaks for her. You're never going to do the right thing—"

"And what is the right thing, Uncle Glenn? Leaving myself exposed so a bitch can fuck me over? Not happening. Fuck that, all day. I have felt that sting before, and I'll never give another woman a chance to hurt me. Fool me once shame on me, but twice will never happen. That's how I treat all women, regardless of who it is."

"But Erica never gave you one reason to think she would cheat on you. At what point do you toss that dumbass mindset and realize you have everything in Erica?"

"I know I do, but I also keep a Geico girl."

"Geico girl?"

"An insurance bitch, just in case I have a wreck with an eighteen-wheeler."

"An eighteen-wheeler? Telly, what the fuck are you talking about?"

"An eighteen-wheeler is what Biyell ran into in his kitchen, when both women collided head-on. When debris is scattered over the pavement of my life, my Geico girl underwrites—she gets me back on the road again," Telly explained as he offered me a blunt.

In that moment, it became clear why Telly would never commit to Erica or any other woman: his self-esteem was shattered. Yolanda was the eighteen-wheeler, and now Erica is paying for it. When Yolanda wrecked Telly, Erica became the underwriter for Megyn. It's one of the most delusional mindsets I've ever heard of, but that's Telly's reality and why Telly will probably cheat on women until one of them shoots his ass.

Sailing from one end of my new pool to the other were little candles; about ten in all. On the other side of the pool stood a swing Biyell had built for his daughters, and to the right of the swing was green space cut to golf course height. Everything was serene in my back yard except Telly; this dude is a burning house with locked burglar bars, and I have to find a way to rescue Erica.

"Uncle I need to take a piss, I'll be right back," Telly called as he strolled toward the house.

"When you get inside, ask Rasta to step out, please."

Less than a minute later Rasta came outside, smiling at our view of the pool. For the first time in a long time, I needed some honest advice, and he was the perfect sounding board.

"Why didn't you ask Jarvis to be your best man?" I asked him as he sat down next to me.

"I thought about it for a while, but decided on Telly because I have known him longer."

"But his life is still out of control, and he is the only one out of all of us who's ratchet. My worst fear right now is another hoe outbreak within our group. I can't have that."

"Uncle Glenn, you don't have to worry about me. I've seen what's out there, and none of them can match my queen."

"But what about Telly? What do we do about him?"

"All we can we is encourage Telly to do what's right by Erica—that's it."

"After the wedding, I want to break the code."

"Break code? Why?"

There were these unwritten rules in our group that we lived by like a doctrine. And I'm not sure who created most of the rules, but there exists a protocol that we follow. The protocol includes not dating each other's sisters or tampering with the main lady or wife. But one of the rules that we consider a capital offense that's punishable by death is disclosing the existence or whereabouts of a mistress to a leading lady or wife. Under no circumstances is it allowed, tolerated, or justified. Even if you're friends with his wife and it hurts you to see her getting fucked over, you hold your peace. But I can't watch Erica suffer like this; I have to break the code.

"I want to reach out to Erica," I said before taking a long drag off the blunt. "I want to tell her she's getting played so she can protect herself."

Rasta stared at me like an algebra problem. "You mean, tell Erica he's fucking her over?"

I nodded. "Break code."

"Naw, naw, naw," Rasta's head shook in objection. "I can't go with you there. I feel just as bad as you do for Erica, but I can't, and you can't do that."

"But Rasta—"

"But no, Uncle Glenn! I can't go along with that, and you should get the thought out of your head right the fuck now. We don't stab each other in the back, remember? That's what landed me in a mental institution."

"Then what do we do? Huh? As respectful men who love our wives and take care of our families, trying to live like a little something, what do we do? Stand here and watch this innocent flower get chewed up and spat out the side of a lawnmower? This is a real question, Rasta, what do we do?"

"How did this become *we*?"

"Because you're in this shit with me. How do we save Erica?"

Rasta stood over me, and there was no shelter from his downpour. "*WHO SAID WE HAVE TO?* All the signs are there for her if she really wanted to stop fucking with Telly. She saw the threesome pictures. She opened his bank statements. She's seen the hotel rentals in the middle of the day. As we always say, *a dawg can smell a dawg,* and *a bitch can smell a bitch.* Short of us taking out a billboard on the interstate that says *GIRL, HE FUCKING HEATHER*, there isn't anything we can do to convince her to run from Telly like he's shit on a stick."

"So stay out of it and let her get crushed?"

"Uncle Glenn, I know it grieves you to see Telly dogging Erica, but stay out of it. I don't like it any more than you do." Rasta pointed toward the large back window, through which we could view inside the kitchen. "Look at Briana, Fate, Tiffany, my aunt, and my mother in the kitchen talking and bonding together. Soon we will all vacation together and do life as one big family. If Telly can't shape up, then it hurts me to say—because that's my boy and all, and we grew up together—but we may have to love him from a distance. I will not have my new wife thinking I'm *slinging dick* because he's *slinging dick.*"

"You're right, but I hate to see—"

"I hate to see it too, but you're damned if you do, accessory to a hoe if you don't. The reason you can't get involved is because this is where we come to work shit out; you are our safe place where we can speak freely, and it stays in this room. That is the reason you don't see Timothy despite the fact that I have forgiven him. I saw him in Home Depot and extended my hand like a man—not because I fully respect him as a man, but because I am one. You taught me that the night we watched the video. As men, we don't turn on each other. Once that confidence in you is broken, it's broken forever."

It was at that moment that Telly leaned out of the door and yelled that I was up next to play Jarvis. I was overruled in my quest to break the code, so I said a little prayer for Erica and plucked the flame out of my blunt.

Erica, if you can hear me, Telly is the devil. He means you no good.

CHAPTER 35

Saturday, June 2, 2018
3:30 p.m.

TIMOTHY

The call came in about a month ago; a request for an additional wedding photographer. Boy, I tell you, this wedding couldn't have dropped in at a better time—I needed the business. Things have been really slow, and at this point, I'm pretty close to having to pick up a part-time job to stay afloat. This gig today is easy money because I'm not the primary photographer for this job; it appears they mainly hired me for backup photos and video. Being that this is the only gig I've had in weeks, I'm early and already in position.

To prevent the photographers from stepping over each other and fighting for the perfect shots, the wedding planner told me to stay off to the side and wait for her command. Then, I am to capture the surrounding images. I figured this would be the case with two photographers fighting for the photo of the day, therefore I'm dressed in all black with a low-brimmed hat. I blend into the background. With the month I've had, I can't say I mind working second fiddle as long as I'm working, but when she said *off to the side*, I didn't know it would be all the way over by the organist. In any case, my gear is primed and ready, so let's get it on.

What a beautiful day for an outdoor wedding; it's early June and the sun is shining brightly between white cotton clouds. On both sides of the aisle I can see about two hundred white folding chairs with a peach cut of sheer decorating the backs. From what I can gather, the color theme is peach and metallic, because that combination is splattered just about everywhere.

A company hired me for this shoot—some organization called Lost Keys Entertainment—and the woman I spoke with, a Ms. Deebee, paid me in full. Since then, I've had several conversations with the wedding planner, who kept calling to confirm the same instructions: all additional photographers will remain out of the main shot until given the cue. By the sixth time she called, I was like, *Lady, I got it, how many times are you going to say the same shit?* I didn't want to lose the gig, so I smiled and agreed through each unnecessary formality.

From the sound of the soloist, I can tell the wedding has started even though I can't see shit from this ally. I'm not sure what song the lady is singing, but her voice is fantastic. I think it could be a gospel song.

Suddenly, the wedding planner gave me the cue with three snaps of her fingers. I knew the bride was at the top of the aisle, because I heard over two hundred people take a deep breath at once.

"On my command, I need the pictures of the bride at hand-off," the planner instructed.

She's cute and about my height, but gorgeous like a six o'clock news anchor; the type who's only passing through on their way to the big networks. I will definitely approach her at the wedding reception, but for now, I need to focus. I am here to capture the most critical moment of the day, and unlike the main photographer, I only have one job: get the shot.

"Go, go, go!" The wedding planner waved me out like a director of a Broadway play.

From the back shoulder of the groomsmen, I approached for the handoff shot, and it didn't take me long to figure out why I'd been positioned out of sight. I know three of the six groomsmen.

This is a setup.

I can feel it.

From tallest to shortest stood Jarvis, Biyell, then three guys I didn't recognize, and finally Telly, who stood next to Rasta. On the other side of the groomsmen were six bridesmaids in peach gowns that flowed down in a leggy split. *Rasta is getting married?*

All of them appeared equally stunned to see me; I knew immediately that whoever hired me was not one of the guys I used to call my friend. From the first row of chairs, Uncle Glenn stared at me as if he had just seen a ghost. I was the ghost. I moved to the mark where the planner wanted me for the handoff, but a thick cloud harassed the sun and caused my autofocus to go berserk. I only had a few more paces before the handoff, and I was still miles out of focus.

From outside my viewfinder, I watched as Rasta greeted the gentleman escorting the bride down the aisle. Suddenly, the cloud moved just in time for the exchange and the removal of the veil. After the handshake, Rasta gently removed the veil from his new bride's face.

I caught my camera just in time before it hit the ground.

"Isn't Kayla beautiful?" a lady in the first row, just to my left, asked in a cheerful voice.

When I turned to see who had spoken to me, I saw that it was Diana. I knew then that she was the one who had hired me to capture the moment Kayla walked down the aisle to marry a guy who was once like a brother to me. I wasn't hired to capture special moments; I was hired to watch Rasta and my ex-wife become husband and wife. Up close and personal. Face to face. Someone wanted me to have the best view of the wedding. Someone wanted to rub their wedding vows in my face. That someone was Diana, and no one can tell me otherwise.

There was nowhere to run and nowhere to hide. Then I heard the smirks from Jarvis and Biyell. I heard everything they said.

"Boy, I was going to fuck you up if I ever saw you, but I'm good now," Biyell whispered under the voice of the pastor.

"Diana, did you do this?" I heard Glenn ask his wife.

"*Maybe? Maybe not?* But you can never have too many photographers at a wedding."

I know it was her; it all came back to me. Lost Keys Entertainment, hired by Ms. Deebee, who was actually Diana Braxton. How could she be so fucking low as to hire me and force me to stand here, to listen to every vow and expression of their love for one another? How could Diana be so cruel?

Soon, the wedding reached the point where the pastor asked for the ring. Telly handed the ring to Rasta, who in turn placed it on my wife's—I mean Kayla's—finger. I felt my heart leak out of my chest. She was so beautiful, thin, and tall; she looked the way she had back when she played volleyball in college, like the model she was when I first met her during that photo shoot. It wasn't fair, but I did my job.

"Here it comes, Timothy—Rasta is about to stick his tongue in her mouth, make sure you get that shot!" Jarvis heckled under his breath.

Rasta kissed the bride, then the happy couple trotted down the aisle between rounds of thunderous applause. Then came pointing and more heckling as the word spread around the wedding. Before long, all eyes were on me. The cute little wedding planner found me just as I was about to take some photos of the newly married couple waving from the Rolls Royce.

"Mr. Feltus, that is all we need. Thank you so much, and I'll await the photos."

"But I was paid for the reception as well?"

"Yes, you have been paid for the reception too, but there's been a change in the plan. Ms. Deebee wanted me to pass on that you are dismissed."

That was the second to last thing I heard as the guests started to make their way to the reception. As I turned to walk away, Telly 'Crowd Noise' Ned took one final stab as the guests turned back to observe the spectacle.

"Timothy has sold ass cheap out here today, bay-bay!" His laughter was amplified and ear-piercing. "Timothy wasn't man enough for Kayla, so Timothy left Kayla for LaDeisha, then LaDeisha quit Timothy for back-stabbing Rasta, which left Timothy with shit on a paper plate, served up by Lady Diana. Ass on sale, ass on sale, Timothy got ass on sale for how much, fellas?"

I knew it was coming—for the first time in five years, I was the subject of the Madden Night roast.

"Hear ye, hear ye—Humpy Timothy has ass for five ninety-nine a pound!" Biyell called out.

"*Aww, hell naw . . . that's too high.*"

"Three ninety-nine a pound?"

"*You smoking flakka? That's still too high for some cheap ass.*"

"Two ninety-nine a pound?"

"*There you go!*" Telly started doing the robot, then they all said it in chorus:

"Ass on sale, ass on sale, Timothy selling ass . . . only two ninety-nine a pound!"

My former crew departed the altar area in a thunder of hysterical laughter and rejoined the wedding party.

I was left standing in a sea of empty white and peach chairs, thinking out loud:

"*That bitch lost weight for Rasta, but wouldn't lose it for me . . .*"

CHAPTER 36

The Wedding Reception
5:15 p.m.

That damn Diana, hehe! I knew she wasn't going to let it go, but that's my wife. She could hold a grudge against a dead man fifteen years after death. The entire reception was abuzz about how beautiful Kayla looked in her gown, and how Timothy was hired to take the pictures. The mystery was quickly rising as to who hired him, so Biyell made a public statement and claimed responsibility, but we all knew it was Diana. She whispered to me a few minutes ago that it was her special gift to the happy couple, and from their laughter I can tell they enjoyed it to the fullest. She's on the dance floor right now doing the bus stop to Grover Washington's "Mr. Magic;" you should see her swinging and shaking her ass out there—proud as a peacock.

I'm not saying it was right, but I can understand why she did it; that little fucker had it coming. But enough about Timothy, let's talk about Fate—I mean Mrs. Kayla Ross. Kayla is tall and stunning; she looks just like a supermodel.

Hollywood couldn't write the love story of Rasta and Kayla; you had to be here to witness it for yourself. The whole thing is no short of what I consider a miracle. Kayla met Rasta in that McDonald's at a shallow point in his life, and then they reconnected again in the same McDonald's. The best screenwriters could not pull that one off. Somehow, on the day I found Rasta stretched out across his bed in that dark blue suit with that suicide letter on the side of his head, I knew a happy ending was still in God's plan.

I was right.

At a table to my right, Tyra, baby Brennan, Julian, and Tyra's mother are mingling while the two flower girls, Bylisha and Braylyn, run around the reception with the other kids, doing all the things kids do at family gatherings. Rasta was right about one thing; we are becoming a family, minus the drama.

Even Telly told me he made up with Erica.

Of course, I asked him whether he ended it with Heather.

"As soon as her plane lands tomorrow from her trip to Miami, I will end it." But you know Telly; he's full of shit.

The good news is, Telly was able to work a deal with Tamera's attorney regarding Bylisha. They met in the judge's chambers to reinstate Biyell's parental rights; their official court date is in two weeks. Telly said it's going to be an uphill fight because judges never like to issue reversal in cases where a parent has waived their rights, but the word on the street is that division may get a new judge in November—Telly's frat brother. So, even if things are put on hold in two weeks, there will be a chance to appeal.

Oh yeah, did I mention that Biyell purchased the vacant lot next to my house? He will start to build on it after they get a few more real estate flips under their belts. I love the idea, and that is just one more reason Tiffany is perfect for him; they work together harmoniously. I think he's making plans to wife Tiffany. It's still early, but I'll keep you posted.

At the next table over, holding one child in her arms while carrying another in her belly, sits Briana. I had the pleasure of chatting with her a few minutes ago. When we met at our house-warming, she went on and on about the wonderful things she's heard about me and how she always wanted to meet me one day. I'm glad that day finally happened; she is an angel inside and out. Good tidings continue to flow in their direction: the book Jarvis wrote based on the crazy shit that went on in our hub is on its way to becoming a bestseller.

However, I was saddened to learn that Monica is losing her cancer battle, and that Briana's mother is facing the same battle. Just a few moments ago, I saw the sadness in Briana's eyes when she talked about the finality of it all and the possibility of the same cancer knocking on her door one day. I shifted her mind back to now.

"You and that husband of yours robbed us out of a wedding. We wanted to see you walk down the aisle, too."

Briana blushed until her eyes were watery. The more she blushed, the more I hounded her about planning a wedding after the baby is born.

"It's time to come out of the shadows, Briana. I can think of no better way than a wedding, even if it's just our side."

"You really think people will come?"

"Do you see all of these people?"

Briana looked around. "Yes, it's quite a bit."

"Well, the majority of them are our family and friends on Diana and Rasta's side. Don't ever concern yourself with how many. Whenever there's food and an open bar, they're coming."

Briana hugged me again. It felt like I was welcoming her into a new family. I know we can never replace the family that turned their backs, but we can hug her until she feels better.

It was time for that point in the wedding where the bride tosses the bouquet, and the dance floor was jam-packed with single ladies. Damn, sixty percent of the women in attendance look like they're single, and Jarvis, Biyell, and Rasta couldn't care less. I can't speak for Telly; a dog gonna hump, but so far that dog is on a short leash.

Now back to Kayla.

There's a touch of the bittersweet in this day for Kayla, because her dad recently passed. Before he died, his lifelong friend promised him he would walk Kayla down the aisle, and today, he completed that promise. Rasta could not have picked a better wife. Not only are they perfect for each other, Kayla is a mortgage broker who writes for twenty-eight banks, and her best friend Tiffany is a real estate broker who finds the customers. Now tie in Rasta and Biyell, who now have their Louisiana Construction Licenses, and the sky is the limit. I also plan to invest in this new entity they've formed, 68 Day Investment Group, which will buy the homes Tiffany acquires from auctions. Telly will secure deeds, Rasta and Biyell will rehab the homes, Tiffany will find buyers, and Kayla will write the mortgages. Everything stays in our family—we all eat as a family.

Would you look at that—Tiffany caught the bouquet.

Here comes Rasta with a couple familiar faces, and a few I'm not familiar with.

"Uncle Glenn, I would like for you to meet some people who are very much a part of me. You've met DeShonta and Dr. Morton, and this is Marcel, Ashanti, Amanda, and Levi."

I hugged around a circle. "Well, it's so nice to finally meet all of you. Roderick talks about you every day."

Dr. Morton threw an arm around Rasta. "He was transported to us for help, but he helped us just as much."

"DeeDee and Dr. Morton, thank you so much for pulling this off and getting as many people as you could to my wedding. I'm honored." Rasta's eyes beamed in gratitude.

DeShonta smiled. "Since you gave that amazing presentation, our angel in Congress, LaDeisha Barthelemy, and her mother's charity have created a pipeline of grants and donations for mental health services. We're planning to open a second facility in

New Orleans East. It was important for us to be here to say thank you and celebrate."

"It's almost time for the show, I'm ready."

"Marcel, I'm ready too, let's take the stage."

Suddenly, the DJ lowered the volume on Michael Jackson's "PYT" and directly next to the booth, a band fired up. Rasta led Marcel to the stage, where the DJ handed him two microphones. Marcel was dressed in a black tuxedo with a hot pink shirt and tie. Even his shoes were hot pink.

At that moment, Rasta transformed into the hype-man of James Brown.

"Ladies and gentlemen, I have the pleasure of introducing tonight, the often imitated, but never duplicated, girls love him and their mothers do too, he put the Grand in Master Flash and the *P* in your Funk, please give me all you got tonight for Marcel Jackson and the Boogie Fat All-Stars!"

The band dropped it on the one!

"Doom, doom, Sometimes I want to leave, *doom, doom,* but then I say, *doom, doom,* it wouldn't make sense at all, anyway. *Doom, doom,* Forgive me baby, *doom, doom,* if I do wrong, *doom, doom,* I haven't been a true man for so long, *doom, doom.* But let me say before I forget, *doom, doom,* lovin' you baby, it's where it's at, yeah."*

The audience sang back to Marcel, and next to Kayla, his performance was the star of the evening.

I was done; I didn't see how we could top the next best thing to having Al Green on stage. Marcel sung his ass completely off and left the stage to jumping applause.

Next, it was time for a toast from the best man. We all sat together at a long table where a gleaming champagne glass waited at each plate. Kayla made her second appearance of the night wearing an all-white evening gown which allowed her to move about the room with effortless grace and charm. Once the wedding party was seated, Telly led off the toast.

"As best man of this amazing wedding, I would first like to start off by asking you to give Mr. and Mrs. Ross a round of applause for pulling off the perfect wedding. Isn't this lovely?"

The entire reception hall gave a standing ovation.

"I stand here as the best man, but I actually represent four other men who share this honor. If you don't mind standing, I would like us to lift our glasses to one of our own. Repeat after me, brothers . . . here's to Madden Night."

The Madden Night crew lifted our glasses.

"I, along with the other brothers, have been through a lot together in that apartment on Manhattan Boulevard. During the day it was the home of Lady Diana and Uncle Glenn, but on Thursday nights, it became a place where we went to get support and encouragement. Like so many men, my father wasn't able to equip and prepare me to face the many issues I would battle as a man, but I know I speak for all of us when I say I'm glad I had that little apartment every Thursday night. It was there that Uncle Glenn challenged all of us to grow up, straighten up our backs, and demonstrate the ability to commit to one woman."

It was then that I became emotional. Diana squeezed my hand.

"The couple you see tonight wouldn't have been possible if not for Uncle Glenn getting in our faces and demanding that we do the right thing, live right, and honor the women in our lives as blessings from God. Well I . . . I didn't . . . I . . ." Rasta stood to help Telly, who fought back his emotions.

"I didn't accept that challenge. I wasn't willing to give up the life that Uncle Glenn wanted us to give up. In trying to hold onto things I should have released, I almost lost my gift from God."

Telly turned and spoke directly to me. "Uncle Glenn, I invited someone here tonight who you've wanted to meet for some time. You told me several times that the cake test is undefeated, and you're right—she won the cake test. Erica, please come to the front. Erica, wherever you are, can you please make your way to the front?"

The wedding guests parted to make a pathway for a very puzzled Erica as she meandered up the middle.

"Ladies and gentlemen, I promise we will get back to our party, but I must do something first."

Telly gave the microphone to Rasta and requested that all of us meet in front of the table. Once I hopped my ass over there and stood shoulder to shoulder with the other brothers, the entire room, including us, gasped for air when Telly dropped down to one knee in front of Erica. Rasta finally figured out what was going on and ran around the table with the microphone.

"Erica, I know I have tested every patient bone in your body, and I'm sorry for that because you deserve better. You deserve what you want most of all."

For some strange reason, Erica's body tilted slightly forward. Her legs wanted to run in the reverse direction, but her heart wanted to feel every word. Her eyes could not believe she was looking at a diamond ring in a little black box.

"You deserve a good man, a committed man, an honest man. I believe I can be that man; I want to spend the rest of my life proving I am that man. God blessed me with you and my little princesses. Erica, I'm down on one knee asking and begging—will you please marry me?"

We think she said yes. Her head did nod.

And I cried.

And Biyell cried.

And Jarvis cried.

And Rasta cried.

And Diana stood with me because it was hard to wipe my eyes and balance on those crutches. And the guests let out a roar as Telly and his Erica shared a long kiss while Kayla cheered at the top of her lungs. After releasing Erica from his embrace, Telly reached for the mic again to finish his toast.

"I want to thank all of you for allowing me the opportunity to join my brothers as an honest man. Lift your glasses so we can toast the bride of the year and a dude who got lucky in McDonald's. I formally introduce, one more time, Roderick and Kayla Ross. Lift it up and drink it down."

It was the most fabulous toast I have ever witnessed. Telly proposed to Erica, and surprisingly enough, she said yes. We all lined up to hug her.

"Finally, I get to meet you. This is my wife, Diana."

"I have asked to meet you for well over a year," Erica said as she hugged Diana.

"You have no idea how much I have spoken to Telly on your behalf," I told Erica. "Though we'd never met, I was in your corner day and night. I told Telly you are the perfect woman; there isn't anything left to see, marry her."

"Uncle Glenn . . . *can I call you Uncle Glenn?*"

"They all do . . . and you're family now."

"Uncle Glenn, we have had a rough year," Erica yelled in my ear over "Back That Thang Up." "But I kept believing God was going to work it out, and just when I was about to give up, tonight happened."

"And I'm so happy it did. Congratulations and glory to God we have another wedding. Now that leaves one, but Biyell will be right behind you two."

We shared a laugh.

"Hello, can we get a hug in?" Biyell and Tiffany pouted behind us as a line formed behind them. Briana was also in that line. After about thirty minutes of warm embraces, Erica found my table again.

"Uncle Glenn, my daughters and their grandmother are also here, but we're seated in the far back corner. I would love for you to meet them, so do you mind if we relocate to your table?"

"Please bring them over; we have room at this table for ten more people," Diana called.

Erica disappeared into a herd of dancing suits and gowns, which the DJ worked into a frenzy with one classic New Orleans bounce song after the other. It feels good; even though I know it's still going to take some work with Telly, tonight was a good start, and I didn't have to break the code and tell Erica he was fucking her over with Heather.

Well, technically he's still involved with Heather until tomorrow when her plane lands from Miami, but I plan to be in the car with him to make sure he follows through. Now that I have met Erica, *how could any man not give his all to her*? She's beautiful. And I see why he feels that she wouldn't be into sexual acts like girl on girl and threesomes; she has a reserved air of innocence in her face. However, I can speak from firsthand experience—my wife is freakier than I am but looking at her you would never know it. I tried to explain to that knucklehead that within the sanctity of a marriage, anything is possible and probable if you're committed, comfortable, and willing to compromise.

My goal now that all my brothers are in committed relationships is for all of us to focus on building strong bonds and marriages. It's time for our conversations to change, and it's time to start doing things that include our queens. Maybe I will introduce spades night or date night or both. And yes, we will still keep our Madden Night, because we do need that time to work on ourselves. Thursday nights taught me that men need men. I'm not perfect; I need my brothers.

A puff of red hair moved in my direction as Erica navigated her way through the crowd again. At the end of each hand she held a little girl, and their grandmother followed a few paces to the rear. Telly also made his way over to our table and lifted the youngest of Erica's daughters in his arms. From their features and hair texture, it was no secret that Erica's daughters were biracial, and Telly had described her accurately: she did resemble Diana Ross's daughter Tracee Ellis Ross, only with rust-red hair.

"And what is your name, little princess?" my wife asked the

oldest daughter.

"My name is Rosa."

"And what is your name?" she asked the shy daughter elevated in Telly's arms.

"Extend your hand and introduce yourself." I could tell Erica had been working on their etiquette. "Remove your thumb."

"My name is Parks," the little girl said.

That's when Erica turned to introduce the girls' grandmother.

"Uncle Glenn, this is my mother—"

"*Derinda Edwards.*"

Erica chuckled. "Mother, so you've had a prior acquaintance with Uncle Glenn and I haven't?"

"Erica, that's not your uncle—that's your daddy," Derinda murmured.

In that circle I found thirty-four years I thought I would never redeem. I often saw my child in my dreams and always wondered how she looked. What name did Derinda settle on? Did she resemble her mom or me? Would she hug me if she saw me? If I died before holding her again, would she recognize me in heaven? Everything I ever wondered about the little girl I held only once before I was escorted out of the hospital came to light. All my questions were answered in that small circle.

The air left my lungs.

I forgot to breathe.

Time has been kind to Derinda. I'm in my fifties; we're the same age. She doesn't look a day past forty. How is that possible? Her body is the perfect silhouette of how well-kept beauty should look. While I look like Morgan Freeman, the skin on her face never aged past the eighties, and her rust-colored hair doesn't show even a strand of gray. Discreetly, I've wondered about her so many nights, and the person standing in front of me far exceeds any time-progressed image I constructed in my mind.

It was Derinda, and I tried my best to conceal what was happening inside of me; my heart skipped and never regained rhythm.

Erica is my only child, and Rosa and Parks are my grandkids. Derinda is the one who kicked me out of her life, and my wife is the one who delivered her into the world.

"Mother, what are you saying?" A vortex of clouds slowly funneled across Erica's face.

"Erica, I'm sorry I have to tell you this on a night like tonight, but I'm left with no other choice. I wasn't honest; your father didn't die in the Gulf War. Please find it in your heart to forgive me, but Glenn Braxton is your father. Now if you would excuse me . . ."

With that, Derinda bolted through the dancing crowd, leaving me alone with the truth. When I looked for Diana, I saw her dashing away in the opposite direction. My eyes found Telly, and it was then that the circle turntabled around me. Telly is dating my daughter. Lord help me. Telly proposed to my daughter. All that shit he talked about Erica was about my daughter. Telly's not marrying my daughter. Not now, not ever.

Fuck that!

Fuck that!

Fuck that fuck that fuck that!

FUCK!

I must have Erica call this off tonight.

I started to hyperventilate just as Erica moved nearer to me with the reverence of a princess approaching her father, the king.

"I have a daddy, and it's you," Erica said softly.

"I have a daughter, and it's you." I stood.

Erica collapsed in my arms and Rasta, who approached just in time, prevented me from falling.

Erica is Erica Braxton.

TO BE CONTINUED IN VOL 4 . . .

www.tjnovels.com

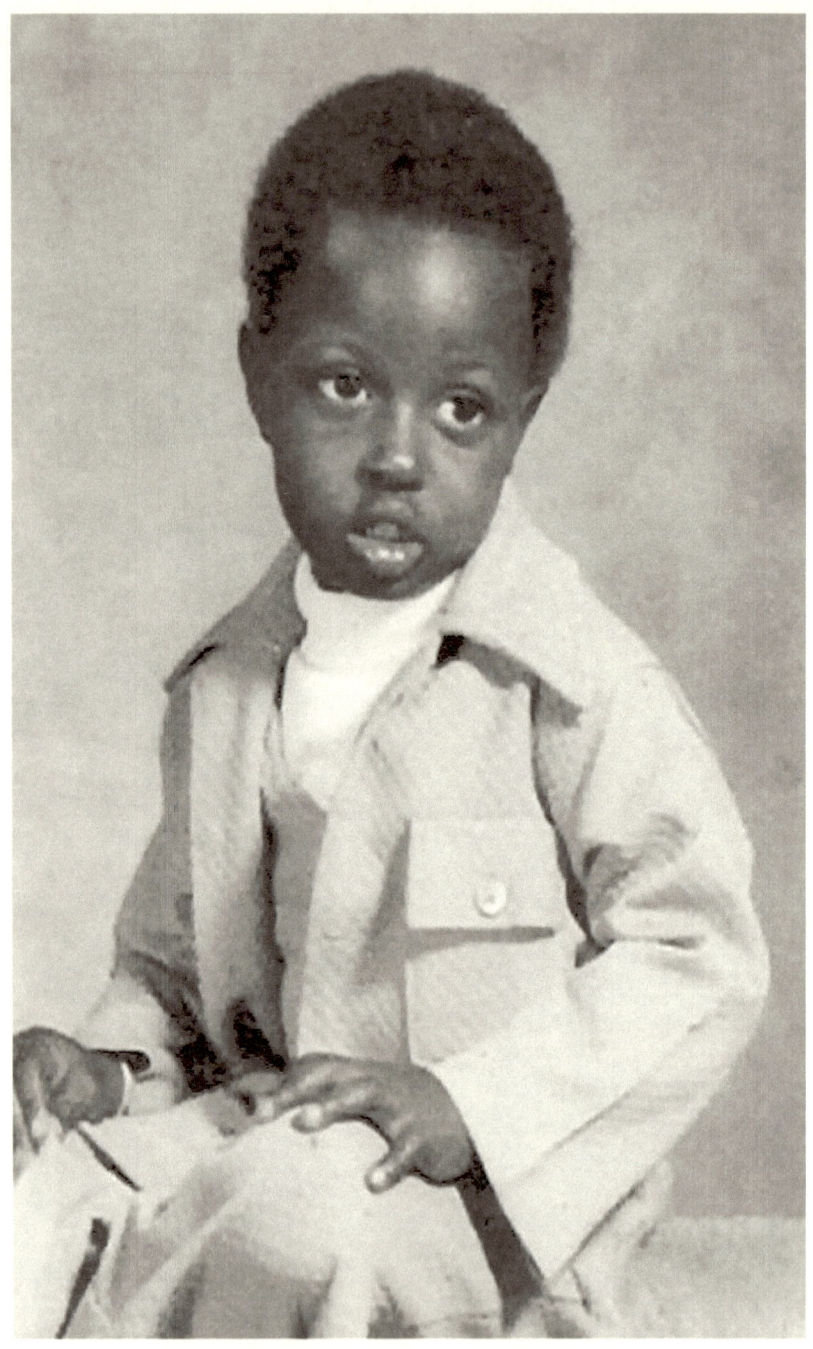

TJ Spencer Jacques - Age 3 (1974)

I'm author TJ Spencer Jacques and I have a Doctorate Degree in how to fuck up a good relationship.

Nice to meet you.

Thank you for reading the Infallible Series, your continued support of my novels motivates me every day. This project is a collection of my mistakes as well as the errors of my Madden Brothers: packaged in fiction – but tangible. I make no apologies for the rawness of this content. There are numerous books on the market about men who cheat, but I wanted to explain why we cheat from our point of view, and all the many ways we mentally justify our actions.

I would have you to know that I am the father of five young daughters, and with them in mind I wrote this series as a warning. I am also the father of three sons, as a preventative resource, I wrote Infallible to teach them the consequences of unfaithfulness. I also wrote Infallible for you.

Hope you enjoyed.

TJ SPENCER JACQUES
www.tjnovels.com

www.ingramcontent.com/pod-product-compliance
Lightning Source LLC
Chambersburg PA
CBHW021953170626
46808CB00001B/130